## USA Today Bestselling Author
# KRISTEN PAINTER

**EMBRACE THE SUCK:**
**A Paranormal Women's Fiction Novel**
First Fangs Club, Book Five

Copyright © 2022 Kristen Painter

All rights reserved. No part of this book may be reproduced in any form or by any electronic or mechanical means, including information storage and retrieval systems—except in the case of brief quotations embodied in critical articles or reviews—without permission in writing from the author.

This book is a work of fiction. The characters, events, and places portrayed in this book are products of the author's imagination and are either fictitious or are used fictitiously. Any similarity to real person, living or dead, is purely coincidental and not intended by the author.

Published in the United States of America

Vampire governor Belladonna Barrone is facing the challenge of her life. Literally. Can she outwit and outlast the vampire council? She has no idea, but she has no plans to go down without a fight.

If she manages to survive, another challenge awaits her. Can she handle the responsibility that comes with accepting the crown? Being governor is one thing. Being queen? That's a whole different set of problems.

And there's a whole new set of enemies out to make sure she doesn't succeed.

All Donna knows for sure is that it's time to embrace the suck.

*For all those that said they weren't reading another book after that cliffhanger - This one's for you!*

# Chapter 1

Belladonna Barrone came to almost as soon as she hit the floor of the great hall. Receiving the death sentence from the Immortus Concilio had been such a shock to her system that she'd blacked out, but white-hot anger had brought her back to her senses a few moments later.

Anger that was right now coursing through her veins like lava about to engulf an unsuspecting town.

Pierce Harrison, her personal assistant and newly turned grim reaper, was already at her side, helping her up. "Are you all right?"

"About as fine as anyone could be after a gut-punch like that." She glared at the blank screen in front of her where the image of the council had just been, wishing she could jump through it and strangle each and every one of them. How cowardly to pronounce such an unfair judgement, then disappear without answering any questions or explaining how that verdict was reached.

Because it had been unfair. Grossly so. They'd had no real proof that she'd had anything to do with Queen

Artemis's death during the fae battle because she hadn't.

Donna wasn't the only one who felt the injustice of the council's ruling, either.

Except for Governor Fitzhugh, who had yet to react, the people in the crowd who'd remained to watch the hearings all wore expressions that ranged from utter shock to downright horror.

She understood that maybe some of them felt that way on her behalf, but she also knew that seeing the council convict her, the newly appointed queen of the North American vampire nation, on such flimsy evidence meant they understood it could happen to any of them, regardless of what power or position they held.

And while they might be dealing with their own emotions, she was seething. This could not stand. Especially not now that she was queen. She could not be seen as a pushover. "Marcus, get them back."

"I will reach out to them immediately, Your Highness, but with the council there are no guarantees," he answered as he took out his phone. He was the late Queen Artemis's deputy, a position Donna didn't fully grasp, but she knew he was extraordinarily helpful.

She needed helpful right now. And not just because she'd agreed to take Artemis's place on the throne. Thankfully, Marcus was technically Donna's deputy now. "There has to be a way to contact them. They gave me twenty-four hours to tell them how I want to die. How am I supposed to give them my answer? Unless they just plan on reappearing when the twenty-four hours is up."

"I'm sure that's it." Marcus looked as unhappy as she felt. "And I don't think they'll respond until we tell them you are ready to answer them."

"Well, don't do that." She needed time. As much of it as she could get. Figuring this out wasn't going to be easy.

"I won't, Your Highness," Marcus said.

Fitzhugh pushed his way through the crowd to approach Donna. *"Your Highness,"* he scoffed. "What a joke."

She ignored Fitzhugh and continued to speak to Marcus. "Thank you. But anything you can do to get me an audience with them will be appreciated."

Fitzhugh put his hands on his hips and sneered at her. "Enjoy the crown while you have it. Seeing as how you're only going to be queen for a day." Apparently, he hadn't been paying attention when the council had put him under censure. He went on. "Sad, really. And by sad, I mean hilarious. I told you you'd get what was coming to—Ow!"

A small Valentino cross-body bag beaned him in the head.

The remaining crowd let out a mix of gasps and laughter as Francine Werther dropped her throwing arm to her side. "Shut up, you moron. You're the last person anyone wants to hear from right now."

"Yeah," Bunni said, snapping her gum for emphasis.

Pierce glared at Fitzhugh with the kind of penetrating stare only a reaper could muster. "Not to mention that is your *queen* you're speaking to in such a disrespectful manner."

Queen Francesca stepped forward with imperial grace and skewered Fitzhugh with her gaze. "Gloating over another person's misfortune definitely qualifies as conduct unbecoming. How much greater is that offense when that person is your ruler? Perhaps we should let the council know you've already violated your six-month censure?"

"Agreed." Pierce nodded. "Go home, Hawke. No one wants you here."

Fitzhugh's eyes narrowed. "As it happens, I'm not leaving for another twenty-four hours." He smiled. "Can't miss the *next* funeral, now can I?"

Temo started to lunge forward, but Neo's grip on his arm kept him back. Just in front of them, Donna's sister, Cammie, had a look in her eyes like she was mentally ramming a stake through Fitzhugh's heart. Maybe other parts of him, too.

Donna could easily imagine doing that herself.

Fitzhugh kept his irritating smile in place as he turned to stride out of the room. He snapped his fingers, calling out, "Quinton, Amanda."

His admin and blood servant followed behind as he

left. A few others in the crowd went with him. Not many, though.

The upside of that exodus was the crowd that remained looked sympathetic to Donna's plight. But they might have also been sticking around to see what happened next. Or perhaps some of them realized the point Fitzhugh had failed to grasp. She *was* their new queen. At least for those who resided in North America.

Although, right now, ruling was the last thing on Donna's mind. She exhaled, still angry, but a bone-deep sickness had settled over her. Like every cell of her being was suddenly nauseous. She leaned against Pierce. Twenty-four hours to live. How was that possible? How was she going to survive this? She tried to focus on the immediate. "Any luck, Marcus?"

He shook his head and looked utterly apologetic as he continued to madly text away on his phone. "I've let them know we need to speak to them again, but so far there's no response, Your Highness. I'm sorry."

"You don't have to call me that, you know. There hasn't been any formal swearing-in or whatever."

A half-smile flashed across his face. "It's what Queen Artemis would have wanted. And regardless of what the next twenty-four hours bring, you are our new queen. You deserve the respect due to the crown. Even if the coronation hasn't happened yet."

"You're very kind, Marcus." Donna turned as she felt a hand on her shoulder.

Queen Francesca was at her side. "I will do everything in my power to help you overturn this injustice."

Donna smiled. "Thank you. But I'm not sure what any of us can do just yet. Especially if I can't even speak to the council."

Pierce leaned in, his words so quiet they were barely a whisper. "You need to reach out to the emissary. His boss should be able to help."

"Agreed." After all, she partially blamed the Prime for putting her in this mess. He was the one who'd wanted her to be queen.

Three low chimes sounded throughout the house.

Marcus looked up from his phone, frowning. "My apologies. I thought that was set to silent. It just means someone's crossed the property line. Perhaps some very late guests to Queen Artemis's funeral. There were some who said they were coming but never showed up." He seemed genuinely upset. "I'll need to deal with this, if you'll excuse me, but I promise I'll be back to help as soon as I can."

"Of course." Donna couldn't imagine why late arrivals would bother him so much, but what did she know. Those were his fish to fry. She glanced at her team. "We should go back to the guest house and discuss what I'm going to do."

Cammie crossed her arms. "You realize this entire house is yours."

"True." Donna shook her head. "But I want privacy." There were too many funeral guests milling about. Her own fault for inviting them all to attend the council hearing.

"Dismiss everyone," Charlie said. "You're the queen. They have to listen."

Donna gave that a second to process. Her admin was right. If the attendees had listened to her before about showing up, they should listen to her now. Even more so with her new title. "Worth a shot."

She turned her attention to the lingering crowd. "Unless you're part of my staff or my immediate circle, I kindly request that you vacate the great hall. If you stay, I'll take that as you volunteering to be put to work in some capacity."

Then she immediately made eye contact with Francesca. "Except for you, Queen Francesca. I want you to stay. I value your counsel."

The vampire queen of Mexico nodded. "I am happy to help in whatever way I can."

The crowd dispersed slowly, but at least they were doing as she asked. It didn't seem anyone was lingering with the intent of volunteering, either. While the guests filtered out, Marcus came back into the room moving with more speed than usual. "Your Highness?"

She turned toward him. "Yes?"

But even as he began to speak, a man walked into the room behind him. Richard D'Angelo. "The Prime's emissary has arrived."

Donna nodded at the man she'd once known as her

human father. Those days were long gone, however. "Emissary."

He smiled at her. "Queen Belladonna. I come bearing the Prime's thanks for accepting the crown."

She didn't smile back. "I wasn't given a lot of choice. And it doesn't look like I'll have it for very long, so I'm not sure what he's so thankful for."

The emissary's smile disappeared. "Yes, about that. I am sorry."

"I'm not sure why. You didn't help me before. I'm not expecting you to do anything now. I'm not opposed to being surprised on that point."

He at least had the good manners to look unhappy. "Unfortunately, the council's ruling is rather ironclad."

Cammie stepped up to stand beside Donna. "What happens if Donna just refuses to acknowledge their sentence?"

He glanced at Cammie. "They would send their own forces to deal with her. It isn't much, I assure you, but they do have a small, effective team that does their bidding."

"By bidding, you mean they'd carry out the council's sentence?"

He nodded, looking none too pleased about it.

Donna couldn't believe this was happening. "So my choices are to tell them how I'd like to die, or they'll come up with their own method." She shook her head. "Does being queen mean anything?"

Francesca cleared her throat softly. "Not as much as

it should. But I suppose some would argue that a system of checks and balances does need to exist. However, without the possibility of appeal, that only works in one direction."

"You're right," Donna said. "The fact that the Prime can't even do anything—"

"I would like to reassure both of Your Highnesses that the Prime is petitioning the council on Queen Belladonna's behalf," Richard said. "He is doing everything he can, I assure you."

"Let me know when he accomplishes something." Donna was done talking to the emissary. She was wasting time. She turned to face her team. "We need to come up with an answer to this. I am not ready to leave this life."

Neo looked like she was fighting tears. "That ain't gonna happen."

"No," Pierce agreed. "It's not."

Charlie rubbed her chin. "Maybe this isn't the crisis we think it is."

"Explain," Donna said as Marcus rejoined them.

"Well, you're technically alive. You could die once without actually dying. You'd lose your soul, but you'd remain essentially the same otherwise. That's the beauty of a good turning, which you had."

Marcus shook his head. "Unfortunately, I can assure you the council doesn't just want her mortal soul. They mean to end her completely. I've witnessed enough sentencings to know that's the case in all of them."

"Based on Fitzhugh's glee over the sentence, I'd have to agree." Donna exhaled. "So much for that." She sank down onto one of the couches, the weight of the council's pronouncement hitting her hard. "I don't want to die," she whispered. "My kids need me. I have a grandbaby on the way. Too much to live for."

Cammie sat next to her and slipped her arm around her sister's shoulders. "We're going to figure a way through this." She lowered her voice. "Maybe I could track down the council and kill—"

"No." Donna cut her eyes at Cammie. "I know you mean well, but that's not going to solve anything." Outside of making her feel better.

Her team gathered around her, Pierce on the other side of her, Francesca on the couch across from her, the rest of them filling in the spaces. The emissary stayed in the room but kept his distance.

Charlie was the first to speak. "Gover—I mean, Your Highness, unless you want me to do something else, I'd like to begin a thorough search of the records of past council hearings, see if there's any kind of precedent we can use, any loophole that might benefit us, anything."

Donna took a breath as she lifted her head. "Sounds good. And I don't want any of you calling me Your Highness or Your Majesty or any of that. For the sake of appearances, ma'am will do. Unless we're in hostile company, then keep to protocol." She looked around at them all. "Understood?"

Nods answered her. Marcus raised his finger. "That's going to be hard for me to do. Years of habit, I'm afraid."

"That's fine. Do what makes you most comfortable."

"Thank you, Your Highness."

She went back to Charlie. "Take as many as you think you'll need to help with that, because it sounds like our best possibility so far."

Charlie nodded. "I don't know how many I'll need yet." She glanced at Marcus. "What do your archives look like?"

Marcus took a step forward to answer. "Ma'am, the library has extensive records on past council hearings."

That was good, Donna thought. "Is any of it computerized?"

"I'm afraid not."

That was not so good. "Sounds like a lot of work."

Bunni stood up. "We got this, Don—ma'am, you'll see."

Francine got up. "She's right. We're all going to pitch in and help, and we're going to find something. Don't you worry, honey."

"Thanks." But worry was about all Donna could do. "Remember, Charlie's in charge. Anyone willing to help, go with her and Marcus to the library. Marcus, you'll see that Charlie has everything she needs?"

"I will," he answered.

Neo raised her hand. "If you don't mind, I'm going to get my laptop and see what I can uncover on my own first. My sires are pretty well connected. Can't hurt to reach out to them. As soon as I do that, I'll join the group in the library."

Donna nodded, inwardly reeling from the need for all of this, but full of appreciation for friends who were so ready to support her. "That sounds great, Neo."

Francesca touched Donna's arm. "I'll have my staff join yours in the library to help. There are only three of them, but they have nothing else to do. In the meantime, I'm going to petition the council on your behalf and strongly request they revisit this verdict. Whatever power I have might as well be added to the effort."

"Thank you." As her team began to head off to fight this new battle, Donna dropped into deep thought, trying to come up with some possible solution.

Pierce and Cammie stayed seated while most of the others left. Will and his daughter, Harper, lingered. Donna glanced at them.

Harper cleared her throat. "I was thinking there might be something I could do from a craft standpoint. Maybe there's a spell or an incantation or something that could help? Even a curse. If you don't mind, I'd like to dig through my grimoires and see what I can find."

Donna narrowed her eyes. "Grimoires?"

"My magic and craft books."

"Oh." Donna thought about that. "You brought those with you on the trip?"

Harper smiled a little. "My sisters and I scan all of our most important books and make digital copies.

Easier to travel with and it ensures we don't lose anything."

"Good thinking. Sure, see what you can come up with."

"Okay," Harper said. She took off for the guest house.

Will hooked his thumb toward the library as he backed toward the door. "I'll help Charlie."

"I appreciate it," Donna answered.

Pierce sighed. "I'm happy to go to the library as well, but I keep thinking there's something else I should be doing. I wish my legal expertise mattered right now, but human law seems useless in this situation."

"It is," the emissary answered.

Donna had forgotten Richard was in the room. "Then what would work? You've been around a long time and been in these kinds of politics a long time. What's the answer when there's no system in place for me to appeal this unreasonable and unjust ruling?"

He took the seat Francesca had vacated. "I don't know." He hesitated. "There is one thing I can think of but I doubt it's something you'd like."

"I don't care about liking it." She'd confront Big Tony again if that's what it took. In fact, she'd take on the entire Villachi crime family. "Will it keep me alive?"

"It could. Depending on how things play out."

She stared at him, tired of waiting. "Well? What is it?"

"You are still friends with the fae king, correct?"

She sat back, unclear where this was going. "I am." While that friendship was pretty new, it felt solid to her. They'd made a treaty, after all. "What of it?"

Richard nodded like that was good news. "Do you think he'd grant you asylum?"

Her mouth opened as she considered his question. "He might."

"Then I suggest you ask him and find out."

# CHAPTER 2

Asylum with the fae. Donna wasn't sure how she felt about spending the rest of her eternity in that medieval stronghold the fae considered home. "What about the werewolves? There are at least two packs that would take me in. I know that for sure."

She didn't really, but she felt pretty positive neither the Medinas nor the Millers, her daughter's future in-laws, would want her put to death. That had to be worth something. Like a safe place where she could escape the council.

Richard shook his head. "That wouldn't be the same kind of safety the fae could offer you. The wolves don't have a home base the way the fae do. No magic that shields them from the outside world like the fae. Not to mention, most vampires' aversion to the fae is a fairly strong deterrent on its own. The council would have a much harder time raising a force to storm fae headquarters in search of you. If they could even find it, and then get in."

"Okay, but if I've been given asylum by one of the wolf packs and the council knocks me off while under the wolves' care, won't that be bad for vampire-wolf relations?"

"The council won't care about that. Those kinds of things don't affect them."

"Right," Donna said. "They affect the little people. Like me. And all those living under my rule." This was the Mob mentality all over again. She sighed in understanding. "How would me living with the fae work? Would I still be queen? Would I go back to being governor of New Jersey? Or would I just be a regular citizen?" She shook her head before he could say anything. "Doesn't matter right now, I suppose."

Richard started talking anyway. "I'm happy to answer those questions if you—"

"I won't be anything if I'm dead." She glanced at Cammie and Pierce. "You two might as well go help in the library. Will one of you let Charlie know I'm going back to the guest house to make a call in case if she needs me?"

Cammie nodded. "Sure."

"Do you want me to walk with you?" Pierce asked.

She smiled at him. He was so dear. Always looking out for her. "No. I'll be fine. And a little alone time would do me good."

"I understand." He got up with Cammie and they headed in the direction everyone else had gone in.

Which left her alone with the emissary. She stood, smoothing down her dress. "Here's a question you can answer. Why doesn't the Prime have better control over the council? If he's the boss of all of us, shouldn't he be the boss of them, too?"

Richard got to his feet as well. His expression darkened. "The vampire world is not much different from the human one in some regards. The Prime and the Immortus Concilio are supposed to act in harmony with one another, but they're also meant to balance each other in times of discord."

"Checks and balances, like Francesca said. Which makes good sense. But then why can't the Prime appeal this decision? At the very least he could demand they explain their reasoning for such a harsh sentence in light of how little evidence there is against me. We're talking none, really. You know that, right?"

"I understand," Richard said. "But you must also understand that vampire politics are just as dark and dishonest as human politics."

She squinted at him, trying to discern the real meaning of his words. Politics wasn't a subject she knew much about, nor did she care to, but she understood very well how the human Mafia got things done.

Extortion, coercion, and blackmail were all big parts of how they operated.

Was that what she was up against? A new kind of Mafia? It was starting to sound more like it with every passing conversation. "Are you saying someone on the council has dirt on the Prime? What could they possibly know that would make him so controllable?"

Richard continued to frown. "I'm not saying anything of the sort."

She noticed he hadn't denied it, either. "Listen, if you can help me, great. If you can't, I don't have time for small talk. My life is hanging in the balance here. Literally."

He nodded, letting out a sigh. "I am aware of that. If I hear anything from the Prime, I'll let you know."

"You do that." She strode away, leaving the great hall, the massive house and headed for the guest house she shared with her people. Her emotions veered from clawing desperation to gnawing anger to uncontrollable sorrow.

She slipped into the guest house, shut the door behind her, and let out a sob before she realized Neo was sitting on one of the couches.

She looked up at Donna. "You okay?"

Desperate not to dissolve into a sobbing mess, Donna just shook her head. There was no point in lying. Neo had eyes. Donna was sure her imminent breakdown was written all over her. She swallowed and tried to pull herself together. "I've never faced anything like this, you know?"

Neo set her laptop aside and rushed to Donna. "None of us has. But I swear, Donna, they are not going to take you away from us. I won't let them."

Donna couldn't help but smile at Neo's protectiveness. She hugged the younger woman. "Thanks. I appreciate that. Where's Harper? Upstairs?"

Neo nodded as she broke out of the hug. "Yeah, she's up there working. Is the emissary going to help?"

Donna snorted. "I don't think he can. It seems someone on the council has something on the Prime, enough to keep him from overruling them."

"For real?" Neo grimaced. "So not only is someone on the council in Fitzhugh's pocket, but one of them is also pulling the Prime's strings? This whole thing is like one of those crazy telenovelas that Bunni watches. Except with vampires."

Donna laughed. It was a nice feeling. "I don't know if I'd go so far as to say there's a council member pulling his strings, but Richard implied there is something going on behind the scenes that's preventing the Prime from stopping this sentence from being carried out." She shrugged. "Whatever that something is, the bottom line is he's not going to be much help."

"He was so desperate for you to be queen and now that he's got what he wanted, he just abandons you?" Neo's fangs were on full display as her eyes began to glow with anger. "Please, Donna, give me free reign. Let me do what I do best."

"I know what you do best, but what exactly are you thinking about doing?"

"I say this in the nicest way possible: Don't worry about what I'm doing. Don't ask me, either, because I won't tell you. I don't want you implicated."

Donna appreciated Neo trying to protect her, but she had a pretty good idea of what the young woman was about to do. Neo was going to hack something or someone in an effort to help. "Neo..."

She backed up, shaking her head. "I said don't ask. If you want me to leave, to get off the property, so that you really don't know what I'm up to, then I'll do that. I'm sure I can find a hotel nearby. But you're not going to stop me from doing everything I'm capable of to turn things in your favor."

Donna understood. She would do the same thing if their places were reversed. "I don't want you to leave. And I'm not going to ask about anything. But I also *really* don't want you to get into trouble on my behalf. Okay?"

Neo went back to the couch and picked up her laptop. "No promises. I'll be upstairs if anything changes, or you need me."

Donna knew Neo well enough to know there was no stopping her. Once she was alone, Donna got her phone out. Then she put it away. She wasn't quite ready to make this call to Ishalan. For one thing, she wasn't sure she could take more bad news if the fae king turned down her request for asylum.

For another, she felt weak and shaky and very much like she just wanted to lie down. Not exactly the most take-charge of attitudes, but the weight of everything on her shoulders pressed hard.

The best way to counteract how she was feeling was to feed.

She went into the kitchen, turned the faucet all the

way to hot, then went to the fridge, took out a bag of blood, and stuck it in a big bowl. When the tap water was hot, she filled the bowl to take the chill off the blood.

She leaned against the counter while she waited. The question she'd most been avoiding reared its ugly head.

*How would she want to die?*

A stake through the heart would be quickest, she imagined. If it worked. Or would she have to die twice? There would be some pretty intense pain, no doubt. Then nothing but ash. Facing the sun was out, since that would have no effect on a daywalker like her. What else was there? Firing squad? Would that even work? Drowning? She would never choose that. Besides, it probably would only take her mortal soul. Poison? Beheading? That sounded awful. They all did.

She straightened. Could Jerabeth come up with some kind of magic potion that would make it appear like Donna had been poisoned to death, only to revive her later?

Probably. But the green witch was back in New Jersey. And what were the chances that she could come up with such a potion and get it to the queen's mansion in Kansas before Donna's deadline was up? Probably not good.

Donna wondered again if she could reason with the council, but she already knew that wasn't possible. Was there something they wanted more than her life? What if she could offer them another treaty of some kind? Or find a solution to a problem that had been plaguing the vampire nation?

Like the fae.

She straightened, spurred by the energy of new ideas. What if Ishalan could help her create more treaties? What if she could bring about universal peace between all vampires and the fae, not just the North American vampire nation and Ishalan's people? If the council said no to that, they would prove they were only out to destroy her and not at all doing what was best for the vampire nations of the world.

Was universal peace between the two races possible? Hope filled her. For a moment. Then another thought came into her head. One about the five stages of grief and how quickly she'd moved to bargaining, the third stage. That just left depression and acceptance, after which it was game over.

She exhaled, poured herself a large glass of blood, and powered it down, hoping it would help her think more clearly. Or at least be able to get through a conversation with Ishalan without sounding as desperate as she really was.

She didn't think he'd hold that against her. He'd been pretty desperate when they'd met. Since then, she'd done a lot for him. Saved him from being an outcast. Given him a throne. Brought his only living family member back to him.

Was it arrogant to think that he owed her? Maybe.

She didn't feel arrogant. She felt lost. Like she was grasping for a lifeline that might not even be there.

She poured another glass and finished it, too. If nothing else, the sustenance would get her through the long hours ahead.

She pulled out her phone and dialed as she walked back to her bedroom, fully prepared to get his voicemail like usual.

She blinked in shock when he picked up after the first ring and said, "Governor. What a pleasant surprise."

"Ishalan. I didn't expect you to answer."

He laughed. "You caught me at a good moment. How are you?"

"I've been better." She sighed and closed the bedroom door behind her before going to sprawl on the bed. "It seems like lately I only call you because I need something. This time is no exception."

"That is what friends in high places are for, are they not? To help? What can I do for you? You sound unlike yourself."

"That's a fair description. I am definitely not myself. What you can do for me is…" She searched for the right words. "I can't believe it's come to this, but would you be willing to offer me asylum?"

The line went so quiet she thought she'd lost him. "Hello?"

"I'm still here. Just trying to absorb what you have asked of me."

"I didn't realize it was that large of a request. I understand if you're not able to—"

"I never said I was not able. I am just curious as to why you of all people would need such a thing."

"I should start from the beginning. If you have the time."

"For you? Of course. What has happened?"

So much. But he needed to know the important bits first. "Mostly the outcome of the hearing wasn't what I expected."

"Then my testimony did not help?"

"Nothing did. Despite all the evidence we had, the council found me guilty. And they have sentenced me to death."

More silence. Then a low, guttural string of words in Ishalan's native tongue that she imagined to be a curse. Whatever they meant, they didn't sound happy. "How dare they. You are a good woman, Belladonna. And a great governor."

"About that. I'm actually queen now. Hard to believe, right? Sort of another long story, but—"

"Queen? Of the North American vampire nation?"

She nodded, even though he couldn't see her. "Yes. Artemis left a letter naming me as her successor." The whole scavenger hunt for treasure was a story for another time. "I've inherited her entire estate, too."

"And they would still put you to death? Is there no respect for the crown? Not to mention our treaty? How can they not see what an asset you are?

Do they not fear an uprising? A revolt of your people?"

"Apparently not." That was the best answer she could come up with for most of his questions. She stared up at the ceiling.

"Tell them…tell them the treaty ends with your death. Tell them I will avenge you. Tell them—"

"Ishalan." A weak smile bent her mouth. "Your anger on my behalf is touching, but I don't think anything is going to change their minds. That's why I need asylum. I need to be somewhere they can't get to me. Or at least won't want to."

"I see. Would they ever stop hunting you?"

"I don't know. They might not."

"Then you would live the rest of your long life in my domain. You would be all right with that?"

Another thing she really didn't know. "I guess I won't know until I try."

He sighed. "If asylum is what you want, I will give it to you without hesitation. But you must know what a hard life it will be. You will have to be guarded constantly. Our treaty is one thing, but to have a vampire living in our world, the scent of your blood a constant temptation… Not to mention, there are those here who still hold a grudge about the fire you set."

She hadn't thought about all the possible complications. "Maybe it wouldn't be for that long. Maybe just until a compromise could be worked out with the council."

"The vampire council is known for its compromises?"

The sense of helplessness was fast returning, filling her with a dark dread that no solution was going to be found. "Not really."

Another long silence stretched between them, but Donna found a strange comfort in sharing it with Ishalan. It was like he was suffering with her.

When he spoke again, Donna could tell he was trying to be upbeat. "My niece will be thrilled to have you around."

That made Donna smile. "It would be wonderful to see Rixaline again."

"May I ask a delicate question?"

"Sure. You can ask me anything."

"How…that is, by what method have they said you are to die? If you would rather not discuss such a thing, I understand."

She shook her head, touched that he cared so much about offending her. "No, it's okay. Believe it or not, it's up to me."

"Up to you?"

She could hear the confusion in his voice, so she explained further. "Because I'm queen they made a special allowance for me. Such as it is. They're letting me decide how I'd like to die. Isn't that gracious of them?"

Ishalan began to laugh. Softly at first, then louder and with more gusto. After some time, he got hold of himself enough to speak. "Forgive me, Your Majesty, but this is the best news I have heard all day."

Now she was the confused one. She sat up and swung her feet over the side of the bed. "It is?"

"By all means. You are not going to die after all."

Still confused. "I'm not?"

"No. And I will tell you why."

Head full of thoughts, Donna raced back to the main house, went straight into the great hall, and found Marcus tapping away at his phone. "Where's the library? I need to talk to my people right now."

She realized instantly that Marcus was one of her people now, but he was smart enough to understand what she meant.

"Right this way." He headed through a set of double doors that led into a hallway.

She followed, mentally urging him to walk faster.

"Has something happened?" he asked.

"You might say that."

He brought her into the library. It was a massive space, two stories tall, and reminded her more of a college library than one for home use. Bless Artemis for whatever drive had caused her to amass such a collection. Donna's team was scattered about. Some at tables, books spread out before them. Some digging through the shelves, collecting more books.

They all looked up when she came in. She went straight to the table where Charlie was working. "Has there ever been a case like this before? Where the council allowed someone to choose how they were going to die?"

Charlie slipped a leather thong between the pages of the book she was reading to mark her place. "I've found two cases so far, which makes me think there will be more."

Marcus turned to leave. Donna put her hand on his

arm. "Please, stay. At least a minute longer. I want you in the loop on all of this. I didn't mean to imply earlier that you weren't one of my team."

"I know, Your Highness." He stayed put. "I am here for as long as you need me."

"Thank you." Donna looked to Charlie. "In either of those cases, did the council attempt to deny the accused's request? In other words, were they allowed to die in the manner they chose?"

Charlie nodded. "Yes, in both cases, the council abided by the accused's wishes."

Two cases wasn't much to go on. Donna looked at Marcus. "Please help them search. I'd like to find at least one more case that follows this precedent. The council sentences someone to die but allows them to pick the method and then follows through. I guess maybe you should look for cases where they didn't follow through and find out why. Or at least how the accused in those cases requested to die."

"I would be happy to." He shifted his attention to Charlie. "Where can I help?"

As she got him started with one of the many books they'd already pulled from the shelves, Pierce came over to Donna. "What's going on?"

"Ishalan gave me an idea." He'd given her more than that. "But I need the assurance that the council isn't suddenly going to change their minds and take away my right to choose my own death."

He shook his head. "I don't think they'd do that. Not after announcing it in front of so many people."

She frowned. "Pierce. If the council cared what anyone thought, they wouldn't have sentenced me to death in the first place. They do what they want."

"Perhaps you're right about the council. But I still believe there is every possibility Fitzhugh had something to do with this. That he somehow influenced one of the council members to make this verdict happen. You know what he's capable of." The anger was plain on Pierce's face. "Once this is behind you, he must be dealt with."

She gave him a quick half-smile. "I hope this does end up behind me. Having Fitzhugh as my number one problem would seem like a freakin' picnic at this point."

"You'll get through this. You'll see. As for Fitzhugh, he'll continue to do whatever he can to take you down."

"Maybe not if I really do survive the council's sentence. Maybe that'll be enough to shut him up. But either way, he'll leave. As soon as this comes to an end, he's going to want to get out of here as quickly as possible, regardless of whether I live or die."

Pierce's expression darkened further. "I'm sure he's already packing. He'll want to go home and gloat. Or think up his next grand scheme."

Her mind was going a thousand miles an hour. "Maybe we shouldn't give him that chance. In fact, I'm sure we shouldn't. He needs to be here. Where I can deal with him." She put her hand on Pierce's arm. "Actually, I need to talk to you and Marcus. You for your legal expertise." She looked at Marcus, who was about to sit down with a book. "You for your knowledge of the queen's reach."

He nodded. "At your service."

Pierce gestured over his shoulder. "I noticed a sitting room across the hall. I'm sure we can use that."

"I'm sure you're right, seeing as how this is my house." She smiled. Having a plan, even if she wasn't yet sure it would work, was starting to make her feel like her old self again. "I'll meet you two in there in ten minutes. I have another call to make."

She stepped out into the hall and walked deeper into the house, seeking some privacy as she dialed. She knew there might be others around. Privacy wouldn't be truly hers until the house was empty of guests.

With that in mind, she went back to the sitting room Pierce had told her about and out onto the terrace beyond its French doors. The terrace was much smaller than the one off the great hall, but she didn't need space as much as she needed separation.

Ishalan answered on the second ring this time. "Did it work?"

"I haven't spoken to the council yet. They respond in their own time. I'm calling for a different reason."

"They didn't respond to you? They should show greater respect for their queen."

"I agree with you, but I may not be their queen if

they're overseas, as I suspect, and since they're completely anonymous, I have no way of knowing. Probably for the best, because if I did know who they were..." Finishing that sentence would only get her into trouble.

"I understand completely. What is your reason for calling?"

"I need more help. Again, I'm not sure it's something you can do, but if you can, I would greatly appreciate it."

"I am at your disposal."

"All right, here's what I need."

A few minutes later, she finished the call and went back into the sitting room. Marcus and Pierce were there, waiting. Both stood as she came in. "Sit, please."

She took the nearest chair, a comfortable, overstuffed leather wingback that looked worn enough to make her think it had been someone's favorite. She glanced at the closed door. "Is this room secure?"

Marcus nodded. "As much as it can be with a houseful of guests. Which reminds me. Some of the guests, particularly those from overseas, have asked permission to leave."

"Get me a list of names and where they're from and I'll approve it."

"Right away."

"Now, on to what I called you in here for." She crossed her legs at the ankles. "What power does the queen have to deal with the governors who report to her?"

"Almost absolute," Marcus answered.

"So if I survive the council, I can deal with Fitzhugh in whatever way I deem fit?"

His nod came a little more slowly this time. "To a certain extent. Unfortunately, you'll still have to present your case to the council."

She barked out a sharp, short laugh. "The same one that sentenced me to death? The same one that's probably working on Fitzhugh's behalf? That would be a waste of time. You can't mean to tell me that the Immortus Concilio controls what I do as queen? You said the queen's power was almost absolute."

"It is. Depending on what you want to do. May I ask your plans for Fitzhugh?"

"At minimum, I want to replace him."

Marcus sighed with the kind of reluctance that told her that wasn't going to be easy. "A queen can easily appoint a new governor, should the existing one give up the position of their own choice or pass away while in office. To unseat an existing governor, you'd have to either have a valid reason or the support of the council. But that valid reason would have to be approved by the council."

Her anger was rising again. "So my hands would be tied."

Pierce raised a finger. "Let's say you defeat the council's death sentence. Which you will." He looked at

Marcus. "Is there any precedence for a queen declaring her monarchy independently ruled?"

Marcus's brows pulled together. "You mean revolt against the council?" His gaze shifted to Donna. "Would you build your own council?"

She liked where Pierce was going. New ideas began to grow in her brain like weeds. She could see all kinds of possibilities before her. "I wouldn't be opposed to that. And if I could get Queen Francesca to go with me on this, we could create a new vampire nation. Ruled with a much more even hand."

Marcus shook his head. "The Prime won't like this."

Her eyes narrowed but her excitement expanded. "The Prime might like it more than you think." She had so much work to do in a very small amount of time. Her phone vibrated. She checked it and found a text from Ishalan.

*No turning back now. Give them an hour at least.*

She typed back a quick response. *Thank you. I owe you.*

*Stay safe, Your Highness.*

*I will, Your Majesty.* With a smile, she tucked her phone away. "Pierce, I need to meet with Francesca next. Will you ask her to join me in here?"

"Of course."

"Marcus, ask the emissary to come in as well. I need to talk to him, too."

"I'll get him immediately."

"No, I want to speak to Francesca first. Then the emissary."

Marcus nodded. "As you wish."

"I assume Artemis had a pretty substantial security team here on the estate?"

"Yes, we have a team of twelve."

"Great. Get them on standby. I have a feeling I'm going to need them after I speak to the council. I'll give you further instructions soon. Temo needs to meet them all, as well."

"I'll make it happen," Marcus answered.

As he and Pierce got up to take care of her requests, a knock at the door interrupted them.

"Come in," Donna called out.

Charlie opened the door, a legal pad in one hand, the pages covered with writing. She wasn't quite smiling, but she looked hopeful. "We found three more cases. The council abided by the wishes of the accused in each one. There are no instances in which they did otherwise. I see no reason why they won't stay the course with you."

Donna wanted to believe that. There was so much resting on that hope. "Outstanding news. You and I need to draft a release for the governors' loop. I have a few things I'd like to make known in case the next sixty minutes don't go my way. And then I'll need another one to send in case things do go my way."

Charlie nodded as she took a seat and pulled a pen out from behind her ear. "I'm ready when you are."

"Thanks." Donna took a deep breath and glanced at Marcus. "After I speak to Queen Francesca, you bring the emissary in." She looked at her watch. "Wait forty-five minutes, then let the council know I'm ready to give them my answer. That should get them to respond, don't you think?"

"Yes, Your Majesty." But he didn't look happy.

Donna wasn't happy, either, but she was hopeful. Her hand went to where her crucifix hung beneath the neckline of her dress, a prayer filtering through her thoughts. She was only going to get one shot at this.

Ishalan's words had better do the trick.

4

Donna could have hugged Francesca, but she didn't know if that would be a violation of royal protocol. She had so much to learn. If she survived this. "You're sure? Because once we go down this path…"

"I understand. And I am with you." Francesca nodded, a twinkle in her eye. "Do you know how I became queen of Mexico?"

Donna shook her head. "I'm sure I should know, but I don't. I must confess, I wondered why you were able to rule your own country when Canada and the U.S. both have to answer to me."

"Perhaps then you've also wondered why King Lucho Vega rules the South American vampire nation, but doesn't oversee Mexico, as well."

Donna hadn't actually known that, but it was a

question worth asking. "I'll bite, no pun intended. Why is that?"

Francesca smiled. "Because I would not allow anyone else to rule my country or to tell me what my people should and should not do. Especially not a man." She laughed softly. "My father always said I was a headstrong child. I guess I never softened as I grew up."

Donna smiled but wasn't convinced it was that simple. "How did you accomplish that? Better yet, how did you get the council to agree to all of that?"

Her laugh was louder this time, bolder. "Simple. I didn't ask the council. Lucho and I made our arrangements, then we *told* them how things would be going forward. They had no choice but to agree or lose South America and Mexico."

Donna's respect for Francesca reached a whole new level. "That's amazing. You are a complete and total boss. Now I need to know how you got Lucho to turn over the rule of Mexico to you."

She shrugged one shoulder. "Just like the council, he did not want a war. You will find most people don't when the odds are uncertain. Wars waste time and resources, make messes that both the winners and losers have to clean up, and rarely solve anything."

Donna prayed that was true. That this attempt at independence could be that easy. And that they would have enough strength to make the council think twice. "You think that will be the case again? That the council won't want war?"

The glow in Francesca's eyes was utterly mercenary and slightly mischievous. "There is only one way to find out."

That's what scared Donna. "Do you think Lucho would stand with us as well? I feel like a third ruler would give us more weight."

"I agree, and I will speak to him. I think he will side with us. He has no love for the council. Very few of us do."

The thought of being free of the Immortus Concilio sent a shockwave of joy through Donna that almost made her yelp out loud with the pleasure of it. "Please do. There is so much strength in numbers."

"Indeed, there is." She looked at her assistant, Benito. "Get King Lucho on the phone for me."

Benito took out his phone. "Yes, Your Majesty."

Within moments, Francesca had it handled. Donna wished she understood Spanish so she could have made sense of Francesca's short conversation with the King of South America. She'd understood enough, though, and ultimately, his agreement to join them was all that mattered.

"I owe you a great deal," Donna said.

Francesca stood. "We are in this together. I wish you well with the Prime."

"You're welcome to stay."

"Thank you, but I must feed, and you should have your privacy for this. I promise, I won't be long. I want to be with you when you speak to the council again."

"I appreciate that."

As Francesca left, Donna gave Marcus the nod. Now it was time for her to do her part. She hadn't told Francesca exactly what she was going to talk to the emissary about, because Donna knew what a long shot this was.

Marcus quickly returned with the emissary.

Arms crossed and standing straight, Donna stared down the emissary as he entered the sitting room. "Good of you to join me."

Still a trip to think that the man across from her had once been her human father. That he was fifty percent responsible for her being here.

His brow creased at her tone. "Marcus said you needed to speak with me."

"That's right." She glanced at her deputy. "Marcus? Shut the door and join us."

He did as she asked, taking a seat on the couch with Charlie. Pierce stood by the windows, looking out into the night.

"What can I do for you, Your Highness?"

"I want to speak to the Prime. Now."

Richard shook his head. "I can't do tha—"

"You can and you will. Right now."

He frowned. "The Prime is not at your beck and call."

"Things are going to unfold in the next few hours. Things he can either know about in advance or be completely in the dark about. I'm guessing he'd rather know. Especially because they are *significant* things."

"You can tell me, and I'll relay the message."

"Not going to happen. This is an in-person conversation. Phone. Now." She leaned in slightly. "Trust me when I tell you this is information he's going to want. When everything blows up and he finds out he could have known beforehand, but you stopped that from happening..." She made an it's-going-to-suck-to-be-you face.

Richard looked steamed. She didn't care. Things had to happen the way she needed them to.

"This is highly unusual."

"You have no idea how true that is."

The stare-down continued for another two or three seconds, at the end of which, Richard made the right decision and took out his phone.

He shook it at her. "If I end up regretting this—"

"You'll what? Ground me?" She had too many other things to worry about than the Prime's errand boy being mad at her. "Just dial."

With a dour scowl, he did just that. A few moments later, he began to speak. "Your Eminence, Queen Belladonna would like to speak with you." He glared at Donna. "I told her that, sir, but she wouldn't listen." He nodded a few times. "Yes, of course. Yes. Perhaps. I understand. She says she has information you're going to want."

At last, he held the phone out to Donna. "The Prime will speak to you. Make it brief."

She had no intention of doing that. The conversation was going to be as long as it needed to be. She would not, however, be flip or disrespectful. She very much wanted the Prime on her side. "Hello."

"What is so important that you must speak to me directly?"

The voice was nothing like she'd expected. While gruff, it held the timbre of youth. So much so that it was difficult to get a sense if the speaker was male or female. A boy young enough for his voice not to have changed yet? It was possible.

And so bizarre that she got lost in thought longer than she intended. "I, uh, that is, there's something you need to be aware of."

"I gathered that. Hence the call."

"Right." *Get it together, Donna.* "You know about the council's verdict, and them sentencing me to death?"

"I do." His voice softened, making him sound even more youthful. "I am very sorry for that."

She took a breath. She knew what she needed to say. "Well, I'm done being sorry. I'm going to act. Effective in about twenty-five minutes, I am declaring my monarchy independent. The queen of Mexico and the king of South America are joining me in forming a new vampire nation. We will no longer acknowledge the Immortus Concilio as a ruling body with any say over us or our citizens."

Silence answered her, so she continued. "You can either join us in the Allied Vampire Nation and remain our Prime, or side with the council. If you don't join us, we will no longer recognize you, either."

"This is...a revolt."

Across from her, Richard's mouth had fallen open in shock.

She wasn't swayed from her course. "This is self-preservation. The council does what they want to whomever they want. And you are obviously powerless to bring them to heel. The time has come for a revolution. I'm sure other nations will join us as word spreads." Which it would, just as soon as Charlie got the press release sent to the governors' loop with permission to share. "What say you?"

"I don't know. I need to think."

"You don't have time to think. There's nothing to think about anyway. You either want things to remain as they are, or you don't."

Richard reached for the phone. "You can't speak to him that way."

She swatted his hand away, covering the mouthpiece. "Sit still or I will turn my reaper on you."

Pierce appeared at her side, glowering at the emissary. So help her, but that was hot.

Richard sat down.

On the other end of the line, the Prime found his voice. "It's not that simple."

"No? Why isn't it? What would happen if you told

the council to sit down and shut up? Would there be some kind of repercussion? You're supposed to be our supreme leader. The father of us all. And yet you cower like a child, refusing to act to save my life." She narrowed her eyes as the fire within her built. "Or is it the truth that you are merely a figurehead, powerless to do anything other than pretend that you're in charge? You have twenty minutes to give me an answer. If I don't hear from you, I'll assume you're against us."

She hung up and tossed the phone back to the emissary, her gaze going to Marcus. "I'm ready to speak to the council now. I want everything recorded for my purposes, and I want security in the room."

"I'm on it, Your Highness."

"Oh, and after that? Let's get this coronation ceremony set up as soon as possible. I have a lot of work to get done."

He smiled, a rare thing. "Right away, Your Highness."

Pierce looked at her. He was smiling, too. "Are you going to tell me what you plan to say to the council? Or is it just going to be a big surprise?"

She grinned at him, reveling in the moment. With or without the Prime's support, she felt good about all that was about to happen. "I'm not telling you. I figure if Artemis could be an enigma, so can I."

He laughed softly. "As you wish, Your Majesty."

## 5

The screen flickered to life and the council appeared. They remained cloaked in shadow, so it was impossible to figure out where they were or if they were even the same people she'd faced before or a totally new group.

Didn't matter. It wouldn't change anything.

The council member in charge leaned forward. His silhouette looked the same. "You are prepared to give us your answer, Queen Belladonna?"

She nodded. "I am." The cameras and mics Marcus had set up were on and recording everything, mostly because Donna didn't want the council to come back later and say she'd misspoken. Or hadn't told them everything.

She was done being played.

Perhaps that resolute sense of purpose was why she felt surprisingly calm. Being surrounded by friends helped. Cammie was at her right, then Charlie. Queen Francesca on her left. Pierce and Marcus just behind her. The rest of them formed a semi-circle around her: Temo, Neo, Harper, Will, Bunni, Francine, Kace, and even Hector, the sandman who drove the tour bus for Francine's rock-star partner and vampire sire, Lionel.

Francesca's small staff had joined them, too, adding a second layer of support.

Around them, in a third layer with some of the household staff, were the guests who had yet to leave. Not many had, other than the few Marcus had said wanted permission. She'd granted that quickly, figuring it was better to get them on their way than have them underfoot.

Fitzhugh was in that third layer, positioned halfway between Donna and the door. He looked so sure he knew how things were going to go she was surprised he wasn't eating popcorn.

She half hoped he tried to run when this was all over. *Go on,* she thought. *Test the queen's security. Or better yet, see what's waiting for you beyond the borders of this iron-bound estate.*

The councilman banged the gavel. "This session of the council is now called to order. The floor is yours, Your Highness. Please tell us how you'd like your sentence of death to be carried out."

She lifted her chin and stared at the council, visualizing Ishalan's words clearly in her head. He'd told her exactly what to say and how to say it. She trusted his wording. The fae were devious creatures known for taking advantage of any slight misunderstandings or slips of the tongue or language loopholes.

If anyone understood what she needed to say, it was Ishalan. "I choose to die of ordinary old age brought about by the progression of time and the natural order of things."

A few gasps could be heard from the guests. Then a few soft chuckles. Someone whispered, "Well done."

Loud and clear, Fitzhugh said, "Nice try."

Cammie squeezed Donna's hand as a smile crept across her face. "Perfect."

Charlie looked downright smug.

Donna glanced back. Pierce was grinning like he'd just won a prize. He winked at her as he caught her eye.

While the crowd around Donna murmured, the council members all bent their heads together. A weird hum purred through the sound system, announcing they'd muted themselves. Finally, the lead councilman banged the gavel again. "The council does not recognize that as a valid answer, Your Highness."

"Hah," Fitzhugh barked out. He was positively gleeful.

"I don't care." Donna glanced at Cammie and gave her a nod. Cammie nodded back, pulling out her phone to hit Send on the message they'd prepared. There was no turning back now.

Donna smiled and stepped closer to the camera projecting her image to the council. "Effective immediately, I, Queen Belladonna Barrone of North America, no longer recognize the Immortus Concilio as having any authority over the North American vampire nation."

The council fell silent, but the conversation in the crowd around them began to buzz louder. Fitzhugh seemed to be choking on his own saliva.

Queen Francesca joined Donna. "And I, Queen Francesca of Mexico, no longer recognize the Immortus Concilio as having any authority over the Mexican vampire nation. Also effective immediately. King Lucho Vega of South America stands with us, as well."

Vision filled Donna like never before. It inspired her to think what the future might be like with an honest council. "As rulers of the Allied Vampire Nation, we will appoint our own council. We find the Immortus Concilio to be a corrupt and capricious organization. Any attempts on the council's behalf to impede, discredit, or antagonize the three of us, any rulers who join the Allied Vampire Nation, or any of our citizens will be deemed an act of war and be responded to as such."

The councilman sputtered. "You can't do this."

"He's right," Fitzhugh snarled. "You can't. This is just a ploy to shift things in your favor and it's not going to—"

Donna snapped her fingers. "Security, silence Governor Fitzhugh."

The black uniformed team jumped at her command, restraining Hawke and shutting him up with a taser under the chin.

It was good to be the queen.

She turned back to the council. "I *can* do this. In fact, the secession has already been enacted. I would like to remind you that I have treaties in place with the fae and two wolf packs. When I say that I will respond to any act of aggression, you can be sure I mean to respond with every resource available to me. Are we clear, Councilman?"

The other council members put their heads together again and muted the sound while they spoke. The discussion took less time than the first one had.

The councilman returned to them shortly. "The council has decided your request to die by natural old age is acceptable."

"Great, but that changes nothing on this end. The Allied Vampire Nation goes forward. Have a nice life." Donna looked back at Marcus. "Cut the feed."

"Done, Your Majesty."

Next, she found Temo in the cluster behind her. "Temo, make sure Fitzhugh is secured. I don't want him getting—"

Before she could finish, Fitzhugh exploded in a whirlwind of strikes and speed, breaking free of the team that had hold of him. A moment later, he was gone.

"On him," Temo announced as he ran after the vampire.

"Go," Donna said to his back. "I don't think he'll leave the estate, however. Not with the number of fae he'll find out there."

Pierce raised a brow as he looked at her. "Ishalan?"

She nodded. "I called in a favor. According to Ishalan, the local fae clan is waiting at the property lines. Which reminds me, I need to fill him in on what just happened here. His words did right by me." But first, she turned to Francesca. "Well, we did it. How are you feeling?"

Francesca smiled. "Liberated. And more alive than I've felt in some time. Your admin sent your announcement out?"

"Yes. I'm sure the news will spread fast."

"It already has," Charlie said. She held up her cell. "My phone is blowing up."

Donna took a breath. "In a good way or a bad way?"

Charlie scrolled her screen. "Most look good. Excited. Some are asking what help you need." She glanced up at her boss. "Those that aren't happy probably just need some time to think it over. Or they have an in with the council that you just destroyed."

Donna shrugged. "Not my problem."

Francesca touched Donna's arm lightly. "I need to inform my people as well. And Lucho, too. If you need me, you have only to call. I'll be in my rooms for a while."

"Very good. Let me know if you need anything from me."

"I will." Francesca looked at her assistant. "Benito, gather everyone. We have work to do."

So did Donna. She just needed to absorb what had happened, some peace and quiet to consider the undertaking that was about to begin. She'd made more work for herself. But she'd survived the council.

That was all that mattered. She would live. For that, she owed Ishalan a debt. Although he would probably say they were even, in her book, he was free to call in a favor anytime he liked.

She exhaled. Finding the time for peace and quiet in this place wasn't going to be easy. Her friends swarmed around her, happy and full of questions. She got it. They wanted to know all the details. But some of those details she didn't have yet. This was a work in progress and would be for some time to come.

Richard stood a few feet away, eying her with a look she couldn't quite read. Was he upset? Did he think she was foolish? A hero? A loose cannon? All of the above? She really couldn't tell.

She held his gaze. "What is it? You seem like you have something on your mind."

As he stared, she got the sense that he was less than happy about whatever he had to tell her. Finally, he spoke. "The Prime wants you to know that you have his full support."

Dumbstruck, she just blinked. Then she pulled

herself together. "Good to know. Tell him I said thanks and I'll be in touch. Make sure I have his number."

Richard shook his head. "I can't do that. But you have mine. You can always reach out to me."

"I guess that will have to do. Are you leaving?"

He laughed once. "And miss the coronation? Not hardly."

"Then I'll make sure Marcus finds you a room."

"Thank you."

She closed her eyes. Things felt like they were spinning out of control. There was so much she needed to deal with. So much she needed to do. She opened them again, about to call for Marcus when he appeared before her.

"What can I do to help, Your Highness?"

"The emissary needs a room. Once Temo catches Fitzhugh, he'll need to be restrained in a secure location. And we're all going to need some sleep very soon. The sun will be up in less than an hour. I know there are other things that need my attention, too."

He nodded. "I will find the emissary our best available quarters. I've also had some of the staff working on transitioning Artemis's personal space so that you might take it over. As for Governor Fitzhugh, we have cells in the basement that will suit your requirements. I'll see that he's placed there with a twenty-four-hour guard. If it's all right with you, I'd like to sit down with Ms. Rollins and work out how best we might coordinate our efforts."

Donna looked at Charlie. "Do you have time? Because it would be great if you and Marcus could get on the same page."

Charlie nodded. "I agree." She smiled at Marcus. "I'm available whenever you're ready."

"Thank you," Donna said. This was all going to work out. "And I appreciate that you're making room for me in the house, Marcus, but I'm happy in the guest house for the time being."

"As you wish." He glanced at Charlie. "If you could give me a few moments to get the emissary settled, I'd be happy to meet with you in the sitting room across from the library. I can even show you your new office space."

Charlie grinned. "Sounds great. See you shortly."

Marcus took off. Most of the remaining guests, likely sensing that the sun was on the rise, had started to head back to their rooms. Donna addressed the friends of hers who remained. "I know you all have questions. And there's a lot to talk about. But I'm beat. And the sun's about to rise. How about we adjourn until tomorrow around four thirty or so?"

Francine just smiled. "Honey, you take all the time you need. You're the queen. You can do that, you know."

Donna laughed. "I suppose that's true. But there's so much to be done."

"Sleep sounds like a great idea," Pierce said.

A few others nodded, Neo included. "You just tell us

what needs doing and we'll do it." She winked at Donna. "Right after I get some Zs, though, you hear me?"

"I hear you. All right. Let's get back to the guest house, then." Donna turned and saw a woman standing in the far doorway. A woman she'd thought was long gone. She went still, her gaze locked on the figure. "Claudette?"

Her vampire sire stepped forward. "Surprised to see me?"

Donna nodded. "I think we all are. We thought you were gone."

She shook her head. "No. Just sulking in my room. After I found out what Hawke said…" She glanced at Neo, who'd sent her the audio files of Fitzhugh confessing he'd never loved Claudette. "Anyway, Your Majesty, I just wanted to say that if you are ever interested in replacing him, I can probably help you out with that."

Donna's brows lifted. "Charlie?"

"Yes, ma'am?"

"Make Claudette my first appointment in the evening."

# 6

Donna had just finished brushing her teeth when she heard the door open and close.

Temo's voice called out. "Boss?"

She went out to see what news he had. "Did you catch Fitzhugh?"

He nodded, smiling. "We did. He's locked up in a cell in the basement." His brows shot up. "Which is huge, by the way. You should see it."

"I'm sure I'll get the tour tomorrow. Thank you for taking care of him. That's a weight off my mind."

Temo's grin expanded. "Happy to do it. And I mean that."

She laughed. "I'm sure you do. Sleep well, Temo."

"You, too, boss."

Donna went back to the room she was sharing with Cammie, who was already in bed. "Did you hear that?"

Cammie looked up from the book she was reading. "Temo caught Fitzhugh?"

"Yes."

"Outstanding news."

"Agreed." Donna was exhausted, but even the thought of sinking into the plush mattress couldn't take the edge off how wound up she was. She got into bed beside her sister and lay there, trying to sleep, and failing miserably. "My head won't stop."

"I'm sure," Cammie said as she put her book aside. "Maybe you should write it down. All the stuff you need to get done, I mean."

"I should, you're right. That will help. I also really want to talk to Christina and Joe Jr. but I don't want to wake them."

"Text them. They'll respond when they can. And at least you can let them know what's going on."

"Good idea. I need to text Ishalan, too. He's the reason I'm still alive, you know. He told me what to say and precisely how to say it. The fae are known for that sort of thing."

"He did well." Cammie grinned. "You should send him a gift basket. In fact, I might even send him one myself. Know any place that delivers to magical fortresses?"

"No," Donna said. "But Marcus probably does. Or Charlie. Between those two, I don't think anything's impossible."

"Probably not," Cammie said. "You're lucky to have them."

Donna sighed. "I'm lucky to have all of you. Being queen is not going to be easy."

"Might be easier once you get rid of Fitzhugh." Cammie rolled her head back and forth on the pillow. "I can't believe Claudette is still around. I really thought she bailed."

"Same. I'm glad she didn't, though. I guess she must have been holed up in the house, licking her wounds. I have a feeling she's going to be the lynchpin I need to ditch him once and for all."

"A woman scorned…"

"Exactly." Donna stared up at the ceiling. Her hand went to her crucifix. "I really hope I don't screw this up. A new vampire nation isn't a small undertaking."

"You've got an incredible team around you. And the support of Queen Francesca, King Lucho, and the Prime. More will come, too, I'm sure." Cammie turned onto her side. "Could I give you a little advice?"

"Sure. Anytime." Donna rolled to her side as well, so she was facing her sister.

"One thing I learned being Venari that might help you is don't let anyone pressure you into a quick decision."

Donna tucked her hand under her cheek. "How does that work, exactly, when you're facing down a drooling demon that's trying to kill you?"

Cammie laughed softly. "It's really not meant for in-field decision-making. More like when you have the time, you should take it. Unless you know exactly what to do, it's okay to think about a problem. You're the queen. No one has the power to push you to act. You act when you're ready."

Donna nodded. "That's a good point. I feel so often like if I don't get things done immediately, then I'm somehow shirking my duty."

"Isn't that just how women normally feel?" Cammie narrowed her eyes. "That's what I hear anyway. I haven't lived a normal life, so I can't comment on what normal is."

"You will never be normal no matter how long you live." Donna smirked at the former warrior nun. "But you're right again. Most of us definitely think other people's priorities somehow take precedence over our own needs. No more. Not for me anyway. People are going to have to learn to wait. Especially now that I'm queen. The only people who will get priority are my family and closest friends."

Cammie smiled in a way that made Donna think it had nothing to do with the subject at hand.

"What?" Donna asked.

"Nothing." Cammie yawned. "We should get to sleep."

Donna didn't buy that the smile meant nothing, but she let it go. "I need to text the kids."

"Start a group text. A family one. Include me. Then I can be in on it."

"Okay." Donna picked up her phone off the nightstand.

"Turn the light off when you're done." Cammie rolled over to face the wall. "'Night."

"Will do. 'Night." Donna sent a quick note to the new family chat, but there was no way she was going to tell them everything on text. *Missing you both. Glad to have Aunt Cammie here with me. Things are crazy but I'm dealing. Talk soon, okay? Love you.*

She put her phone down, turned off the light, and continued to lay there while her brain worked overtime. Cammie's breathing became deep and even and she sounded very asleep. Donna was jealous. Sleep wouldn't come. That seemed to be a new thing with her. It sucked. She couldn't afford to get rundown when she was supposed to be in charge.

After a while, she got up, grabbed her phone, and tiptoed out to the kitchen. No one else was up, thankfully. The lights were off and all of the curtains pulled. Since the guest house had been designed with vampires in mind, it was sufficiently dark for almost eight a.m., although here and there light peeked through where the window coverings weren't quite flat against the wall.

Donna lay down on the couch, pulled the throw off the back of it and covered herself, then scrolled through some of her social media in an effort to make herself nod off. It was incredibly boring to look at what people had eaten, the endless pictures of their grandchildren, and the posts about their aches and pains.

Wasn't like she could join in the conversation. What was she going to do, show off the glass of blood she'd had earlier? Post about how she was about to welcome a half-werewolf grandbaby? Comment that she'd never felt better?

Social media wasn't meant for vampires.

For fun, Donna looked up an old college boyfriend. Jack Weber. He was still cute. Still reasonably in shape. Divorced, with one daughter just starting college and another about to graduate high school.

She stared at his picture. He looked happy. What would her life be like if she'd married him instead of Joe?

Very different.

She put her phone down and stretched out on the couch. It was pretty comfortable but sleep eluded her. She picked her phone back up and texted Ishalan.

*Your words worked. I survived the council. Thank you. I owe you.*

His answer came back quickly. *I am very pleased, but now we are just about even.*

She laughed softly. Just as she'd predicted. *I never thought I'd consider you a friend, but I do. And I'm glad of it. Thank you for your help.*

*You are welcome. Did my brethren get Fitzhugh?*

*No, but they may have kept him from leaving the prop-*

*erty. He's safely secured until I can deal with him. I'll keep you posted on how that goes.*

*Until then, be safe.*

*You, too. My love to Rixaline.* She put her phone aside again. Maybe she'd turn on the TV, find an old movie and see if that would put her to sleep.

Or she could find Hector. He was a sandman. He'd helped her sleep once before. But he was probably sacked out in Lionel's rig. Hector had driven Lionel's tour bus as part of their road trip out here. All thanks to Francine, who Lionel had turned into a vampire and then fallen for.

Thinking about those two made Donna smile. Lionel, the ancient vampire-turned-rockstar, and Francine, the octogenarian firecracker. They made quite a couple.

Which brought her thoughts around to Pierce. Her feelings for him had begun to deepen, right about the time that Will had turned Pierce into a reaper to avoid the council's wrath. The turning had worked remarkably well.

The council had dismissed the charges against Pierce. He was no longer human, and since a reaper's scythe was deadly for vampires, they hadn't apparently wanted to open that can of worms.

For that, she was immensely grateful. But the changes in him meant he could no longer serve as her human blood supply, either. Which was fine. She'd much rather have him safe.

She saw him differently now, anyway. He'd been transformed into a much darker version of himself. He was incredibly smart, deeply caring, and as charming as ever, except he was also *more*.

Becoming a reaper had taken the polish off him. Not in a bad way, either. There was something dangerous about him that hadn't been there before. And not just because she could see the shadow of death that hovered around him like a dark cloud. He'd gone from Cary Grant to Steve McQueen.

Maybe she could go climb into bed with him and see if that helped her sleep. She almost gasped at the bold idea, rolling her lips in to keep from laughing at herself. Wasn't like he'd say no to her, would he? She was the queen.

Not *his* queen, technically. He wasn't a vampire. And now that he wasn't her blood donor, he was only here because he wanted to be. Well, that much had been true since day one, she supposed. But when they'd met, being her blood servant had been enough for him.

Would being around her without that connection be enough?

She got up, wrapped the throw around her and walked to the window, pushing the curtains back to peek outside. The skies were gray. Maybe with more snow. She peered closer. Actually, it *was* snowing. Tiny flakes, but snow all the same.

Wouldn't it be glorious to lay on the couch and read

a good book while a fire crackled in the hearth and the snow drifted down outside?

But those days were gone for her. At least for a while. Maybe someday she'd get the chance to live that sort of carefree life. But not anytime soon. Not while so much rested on her shoulders. She sighed and turned away.

And saw Pierce standing in the kitchen, the navy silk of his pajamas reflecting the soft light of the appliances.

"What are you doing up?" she said softly.

He rolled his shoulders. "I wish I knew. Too much on my mind, I guess. What's your excuse?"

"Same. I'm exhausted but my mind won't shut down."

He nodded. "I guess we're on the same page there." He paused. "Hey, you want to go for a walk? Have a look at your new property?"

She thought about that. "I'm in my pajamas."

"So am I." He grinned and shrugged. "Throw on your coat and some boots. That's what I'm going to do. No one will know. Besides, you're the queen. You're allowed to be eccentric."

She nodded. "I can basically do anything I want, can't I?"

His eyes narrowed, the look in them pure amusement. "Anything with anyone."

7

She did exactly what he suggested: Put on her long winter coat, the tan one with the detachable fur collar, and her new winter boots. Quite a look with her pajamas. She stuck a beanie hat and gloves in her pocket in case the cold got to her. She didn't care what she looked like. If someone had a problem with the way she was dressed, then that was their issue to deal with, not hers.

Besides, most everyone here was a vampire, and as far as she knew, she was the only one of them who could daywalk.

She met Pierce at the front door. He'd done exactly as he said he would. He'd put on his coat and boots right over his pajamas. She liked that. Better to be eccentric with someone than alone.

He'd put on a beanie hat, too, so she pulled hers from her pocket and tugged it on.

He smiled. "Ready?"

She nodded. "Absolutely."

He opened the door for her and out they went. It was bitter cold but refreshing at the same time.

He closed the door softly and offered her his arm. "Which direction?"

She took his arm, looking around. "Isn't there supposed to be a lake behind the stables?"

He nodded. "I believe so. Let's go over and check it out." He started forward, then stopped. "Do you have your phone?"

She felt her pockets. Nothing. "No. I must have left it on the coffee table. But you know what? Being without it for a couple of minutes is fine. Do you have yours?"

He shook his head. "We probably both shouldn't be unreachable."

She frowned and let out a long sigh. "Fine."

He smirked. "Okay, forget it. We won't be gone long, right? Half an hour?"

"Right. They're all asleep anyway."

"True. All right, onward." He started walking again.

She kept pace with him easily, despite his long legs. They went down the driveway and followed the road past the main house. The stables were easy to see, even though they were set back from the house quite a bit.

A narrow paved road, wide enough for a single vehicle, connected most parts of the estate. They stayed on that, especially because the snow had started coming down more heavily.

"This is nice, isn't it?" She looked up at him. "It's so quiet here. Very different from Wellman Towers. Very different from every place I've ever lived, actually."

"Does that mean you've made your decision about moving here?"

"I have. It makes sense to be here, centrally located. What do you think?" His firm was in New York. Though he'd essentially taken an undetermined leave of absence, that didn't mean he'd want to put his career behind him permanently.

"A change of scenery might be nice."

"Yeah?" She smiled up at him. Having him around would make everything perfect.

"Sure. Especially for you. Let's be honest, there aren't many places in New York or New Jersey where you aren't still known as the Mob boss's wife. And when your divorce finally comes through, it'll be news again. Just like it will be when Joe eventually goes to trial. Being out here would insulate you from a lot of that."

"Good point. That reminds me, I should reach out to Rico and see if they have a trial date set yet. Things will really ramp up then."

"Again, being here would solve that."

She slanted her eyes at him. "But how would it work out for you?"

"Are you asking me if I would miss you? Or if I want to move out here with you?"

There was no hesitation for her. "With me. But I mean, if that's not what you want, then I completely understand and—"

He stopped and pulled her into his arms. They were about halfway between the stables and the main house. "What I want is to be with you. Wherever that is. You never have to wonder about where my head's at on that. Ever. And if I haven't made it clear already, I love you, Donna."

She smiled up at him. "I love you, too. Maybe not exactly the way you want me to, but I do."

"I know you do. And I'm fine with whatever that form of love is. If things stayed exactly the way they are right now between us for the rest of our days, I'd be fine with that."

She tipped her head. "You really mean that?"

"I do. But if that ever changes, I promise you'll be the first to know."

"Okay." She stared at him a moment longer, willing him to kiss her.

And because he always seemed to know just what she needed, he did.

The kiss made her want to stay in his arms for a long, long time. In fact, it soothed her enough to think she might finally be able to sleep when they returned to the guest house.

He held her after the kiss ended. "Do you want to

go back? Or go on to the lake?"

The snow drifted down in fat flakes and enough had accumulated to coat the ground in white. "I just want to stay right here."

He laughed softly. "Whatever you want."

The sound of an approaching vehicle pulled her out of the moment. "What's that?"

"Must be someone arriving." He took her hand. "Come on, let's go around the side and have a look."

Together, they jogged to the far corner of the mansion and peered around. They were a long ways from the main entrance, but it was a decent vantage point.

"That's a cool vehicle." She pressed close to him to see better. "What is that? I can see the Mercedes logo, but I've never seen one that looks like that."

The big black vehicle had come to a stop beneath the wide shade of the covered drive. The Mercedes was boxy in a kind of military way. Made Donna think of a Hummer, but this thing looked a whole lot more serious. The dark windows made it impossible to see inside, which was no doubt the purpose.

"Mercedes AMG G63. Usually called a G-Wagon. And that one looks like it's been customized." Pierce pointed toward the bottom of the utility vehicle. "See how low it rides? Probably because it's been armored. And judging from the darkness of that window tint, the interior is UV safe."

She looked at him. "Vampires?"

"That would be my guess. A dignitary who is late to the funeral?"

"Marcus said there were some he hadn't heard from. This must be one of them. Too bad Charlie's not here. She'd probably recognize whoever it is."

Pierce frowned. "I should have let you get your phone. You could have snapped a picture for her to ID."

She shrugged. "I'm sure we'll meet whoever it is soon enough. But it would be nice to know who it is ahead of time."

"Agreed." He sank back against the wall. "Door's opening."

The driver hopped out, as did a passenger from the seat beside him. Both men were dressed in black pants and black sweaters, and looked very special ops. Both carried large, black umbrellas. They opened the doors right behind the ones they'd gotten out of, opening the umbrellas at the same time.

"Definitely vampires," Pierce said.

From the driver's side, the side farthest from Donna and Pierce, stepped a handsome man in black jeans, a charcoal crew-neck sweater, black leather jacket, and black leather gloves. He had bronze skin and dark brown hair. His eyes were hidden behind sunglasses.

From the opposite side came a beautiful woman in head-to-toe ivory cashmere. Sweater, pants, coat, although as the wind blew her coat out, it revealed a leopard-print silk lining. Her gloves were ivory leather, as were her boots, which sported familiar red soles.

She shared much of the man's coloring, but her hair was a deep reddish-brown streaked with caramel and fell around her face in a mass of waves. She pulled her sunglasses off as the man who'd opened her door held the umbrella over her, despite the fact there was no real sun to speak of and they were well under cover.

Her eyes were as black as obsidian.

"Wow, she's pretty. Who are they?" Donna whispered.

"I have no idea," Pierce whispered back. "But if you're still not tired, we could go find out."

She glanced down at her outfit. "Not in my pajamas. And maybe not now. They're probably going to get a room and go to sleep, don't you think?"

"Maybe. Probably. Unless they're also daywalkers, which is unlikely, since they seem to be taking precautions against the sun."

"Then let's let them be. I'm not in the mood to meet anyone. And if it's anything urgent, Marcus will message me, don't you think?"

"I'm sure he will." Pierce tipped his head in the direction of the guest house. "Speaking of bed, we should get back. You have a long night ahead of you and it's pretty cold out here."

They started walking.

"I could go for a hot chocolate."

He smiled. "With a little something extra in it to help you sleep?"

"Like what?"

"A shot of whiskey?"

She laughed. "I think I'll stick to just the hot chocolate. If I'm not asleep ten minutes after I get back into bed, I'm going to find Hector."

"I'll help you."

She was thinking about the two new arrivals when they got back to the guest house. While Pierce quietly made them hot chocolate, she checked her phone. Nothing from Marcus. There was a text from Joe Jr., telling her that he loved her, too, and couldn't wait to catch up. He also told her to "embrace the suck," which made her laugh.

He said it was his new work motto.

He was in the Air Force, and an early riser, so it was no surprise that he'd been the first to respond. Christina was probably sleeping in. And when she did get up, she'd probably find an enormous breakfast waiting on her.

Donna had no doubt that the Millers would spoil their soon-to-be daughter-in-law rotten. Christina was about to marry their only son and give them their first grandchild. Not only that, but according to the Millers, births had been down in their pack, meaning that this child represented a lot of hope for all of them.

Hope was a good thing. Donna stared through the wall in the direction of the main house. Just like she hoped those new arrivals hadn't brought trouble with them.

8

Donna woke up and checked the time on her phone. She laid the phone on her chest, reluctant to get out of bed. Four p.m., which seemed like enough sleep. Maybe not a full eight hours, but she'd take what she could get. At least the walk, or maybe Pierce's hot chocolate, had done the trick.

Cammie was already out of bed. No surprise there. So was everyone else, judging by the muted conversations she could hear beyond her bedroom door.

All Donna could think about were those two mystery visitors . Maybe she'd get some kind of cosmic bonus and find out they hadn't stayed. She smiled. Sure, that *might* happen.

She picked up her phone again to look at her messages. One from Christina, telling her how great everything was and how she and Jeanne Miller were going out shopping for baby clothes.

Donna's smile was wistful. She wanted to be the one doing that with her daughter, but she also knew that Jeanne was a good woman who'd do right by Christina. Donna just couldn't help but feel like she was missing out.

The good news was there was nothing from Marcus, so maybe those two new vampires were just very late funeral guests. She wanted to believe that as she pulled back the covers and put her feet on the floor.

Her loud exhale was followed by a yawn. She was desperate for a hot shower and some hot coffee. Maybe both at the same time. She laughed. Anything went now that she was queen.

She pulled on her robe and headed for the kitchen. The gang was all there. Temo, Neo, Kace, and Bunni sat around the table, finishing up breakfast. Francine, Harper, and Will were watching the news. Everyone was dressed and ready for the day.

Charlie, busy on her laptop, was in the living room in one of the single chairs. She looked up as Donna came in. "Morning, ma'am."

"Morning, Charlie. And everyone. Where's Cammie?"

"Out for a run. Pierce is in the shower. How'd you sleep?"

Donna shrugged one shoulder. "Well enough. Anything pressing?"

"You have a meeting with Claudette whenever

you're ready, but I have some other news. The king of Russia would like to meet with you. He's very interested in joining the Allied Vampire Nation."

"Oh?" Donna went straight to the coffee pot. She got a mug out and filled it. "That would be great if he did. Although having to deal with more Russians gives me pause."

Charlie snorted. "I understand. But I promise, Konstantin Novikoff is nothing like the Mob you dealt with before. He's quite a character. He was turned when he was nineteen. He's almost four hundred years old now, and he's been a vocal opponent of the Immortus Concilio for a long time."

"And they haven't done anything about him?"

Charlie just smiled. "Russia is a big place. The Russian vampire nation is huge. And Konnie is well-liked. I'm sure they would have done something about him if they could have, but I guarantee there would have been an uprising."

Donna liked the sound of that. Another powerful ally. "Then by all means, set up the meeting. Will I have to go to him?" She'd never been to Russia. She'd never wanted to go, either. But now? Maybe it wouldn't be so bad.

"Probably not," Charlie said. "I'll let you know."

Donna added sugar and creamer to her coffee, then slowly sipped the hot brew. She let that first sip get into her bloodstream before speaking again. "Anything else on the agenda?"

Charlie nodded. "Marcus wants to meet with you today."

Donna held her cup a little tighter. "Did he say about what?"

"No, but my guess is the coronation. After speaking with him yesterday, I have a better understanding of what's involved. *All* the governors are expected to be here."

Donna blinked. "All fifty of them."

"Yep. The ceremony will be live-streamed as well, but yes, we're about to get a whole new slew of guests. Some of them are already here, obviously, so they will probably stay, but any guests who aren't invited to the coronation need to go home to make room for those who are."

"All right, that's issue number one. But can the main house really put up that many people?"

Charlie shook her head. "No, but that's one more reason why we need to get moved out of here and into the main house. Anyone who can't fit into the main house or the guest house will have to seek lodging in town or make other arrangements."

"Does lodging in town even exist?"

"Yes, there are a few places. But I suspect those who drive will come in RVs like we did. And there are hookups on the estate, remember."

"Right." Donna sighed. Her hopes for a quiet evening seemed to be moving even further into the distant future.

Charlie closed her laptop and stood. "This isn't anything for you to worry about. It's up to Marcus and me to assign rooms, and anyone who doesn't get one will have to figure things out for themselves. That's a job for their staff, not us."

Donna drank some more of her coffee. "So how do you figure out who gets a room?"

"Seniority plays a big part." Charlie's brows went up in obvious amusement. "So will openness to the new Allied Vampire Nation."

Donna nodded in understanding. "Then any good or bad responses you've gotten will be weighed."

"Exactly." Charlie tapped her fingers on her laptop lid. "There were a couple of cranky responses to the announcement. They'll be looking for a place to stay elsewhere."

Donna snorted. "Well, like you said, that's up to their staff to figure out."

"Yes, ma'am. Nothing for you to worry about."

"All right. I'm going to shower and get ready, then head over to see Claudette and Marcus."

"Can I make you some breakfast while you shower?"

Donna looked around the kitchen. "I should eat. And drink."

"What would you like? I'll have it ready."

Donna made a face. "That's not your job. I can fix my own breakfast."

"When you move into the main house, the cook will take care of that. But for now, I'm happy to help."

Donna acquiesced. "Any kind of blood is fine. And a couple of scrambled eggs would be great. Or whatever's easiest. Thank you."

"You're very welcome."

Donna took her coffee with her to the shower. No matter how good the hot water felt, she didn't linger. She was eager to get as much done today as possible. Including talking with Claudette.

With that in mind, she dressed to impress. An elegant black dress with a black and white plaid blazer, red stiletto pumps, and a few simple but expensive pieces of jewelry. She completed the look with moderate makeup and blown-out hair made sleek with a drop of serum to keep it smooth.

She took her empty coffee cup and walked back out to the living room.

Kace whistled as she entered the room.

Francine elbowed him in the ribs. "That's your queen you're whistling at. Show some respect."

Kace rubbed the spot where she'd made contact. "She's not my queen. I'm a gargoyle, remember?"

Francine put her hand to her mouth. "Sorry, honey. You're right."

Donna just shook her head as she picked up the glass of blood waiting for her on the counter. "Mine, right?" She asked Charlie, who was emptying a small pan of scrambled eggs onto a plate that had two sausage links and a couple of orange slices on it.

"Yes, that's yours." She handed Donna the plate. "And so is this."

"Thank you." She took it to the table, which was now empty, and sat down.

Pierce came in as she began eating. His damp hair was combed into place and he was in sweatpants and a T-shirt. "Morning. You want some company for your meeting with Claudette?"

"I do, actually. You, Charlie, and Temo." She looked at Temo, who was on the couch with Neo. "If none of you have anything else going on?"

"I wouldn't miss it," Temo said.

"We'll be there," Charlie said.

Pierce nodded. "I'll go change right now. Five minutes."

"Ten," Donna countered. "I need to eat and brush my teeth."

They arrived at the main house twenty minutes later. The snow was still coming down and had begun to accumulate in earnest.

As soon as they walked into the house, Charlie texted Claudette, then glanced at Donna. "I told her fifteen minutes in the sitting room."

"Perfect."

Marcus approached. "Good afternoon, Your Highness. I trust you are well?"

"I am. How are you?"

"I am fine, thank you for asking." His brow bent. "I do have a matter to discuss with you as soon as you're free."

"I heard. Can you give me some idea of what it's about?"

He sighed and glanced over his shoulder. "It's a complicated matter but suffice it to say that we might have a small hiccup to deal with."

There was no such thing as a small hiccup in Donna's world. She knew that from experience. "Does this have anything to do with the two visitors who arrived earlier?"

He blinked in surprise. "You saw them?"

"Pierce and I were out for a walk."

"Ah. I forget the daylight has no effect on you. Yes, it is about them."

"Who are they? What do they want?"

He went still, as if weighing his words. At last, he spoke. "Artemis's children. As for what they want, there's no pretending otherwise. They want the throne."

## 9

This wasn't a complication Donna wanted or needed. She stared at Marcus. "And you think this is a small hiccup?"

He made a face. "I'm not sure, really. There's some paperwork to be looked at. A claim of primogeniture is being made."

Donna squinted. "Primogeniture is basically the rule of inheriting a throne from a parent, right? I'm obviously behind on my royal protocol, but interestingly enough, the Mob works the same way a lot of the time."

"Correct," Pierce said.

Marcus frowned and nodded in agreement. "Lillis, Artemis's daughter, claims that the throne is hers by birthright. That Artemis had promised it to her all her life. Her brother, Yavi, backs her up. As one might expect."

Donna shook her head. "But that's not how vampire thrones work, right?"

Marcus rubbed his left temple. "Sometimes they can. Or rather they used to, centuries ago. Your Highness, I did not have a long discussion with them when they arrived. It was daylight and they were exhausted from travel. Barely coherent, if I'm being honest. All they wanted to do was sleep."

"I'm sure. Where are they from?"

"I believe they currently reside in Paris. I expected them to arrive, but sooner. They will take Artemis's ashes back with them to be interred in the family crypt."

Donna remembered Marcus mentioning that during the funeral. "I need to meet with Claudette, but then I will speak to those two. And whatever else you need me to do. I would like to see the rest of the house, as well."

He nodded. "I don't imagine they'll be up until after dark. Once you've spoken to Claudette, it would be my honor to show you the house and your new personal quarters."

"That would be great."

He clasped his hands behind his back. "Is there anything else I can do for you?"

"Not that I can think of."

"Very good. Just let me know."

"I will." She looked at Charlie and Pierce. "I suppose we should go to the sitting room."

"Yes, ma'am," Charlie answered.

Donna led the way. She wasn't sure what to expect out of this meeting. She had no illusions that Claudette's help would be free. It didn't matter. Taking Fitzhugh down once and for all was worth a pretty hefty price.

Pierce muttered something under his breath that Donna didn't quite catch. As they went into the sitting room, she glanced at him. "What did you say?"

"Only that Artemis's daughter can't be allowed the throne. Think about it. What kind of ruler would she be when she hasn't even been living in North America? I guarantee she and her brother want the throne only because they want everything that comes with it."

"Power, you mean?" Charlie asked.

He nodded. "And this estate and all the other homes and wealth."

Donna took a seat in the leather wingback. "I'm sure you're right, but we'll figure a way through that." She hoped. "Right now, let's focus on our New York problem."

"Absolutely," Pierce said.

Claudette showed up a few minutes late, but Donna was in a forgiving mood. "Claudette."

She bowed her head as she came in. "Good evening, Your Highness."

Donna smiled. "Good evening. Must be odd to address me that way after all we've been through."

Claudette raised her head. "I think you'll make an

excellent queen. And I know that I owe you an apology." She looked away. "I never should have gotten involved with Hawke. I knew that. But..."

"You were angry."

She nodded. "I thought I'd find a way to get my dignity back if I could just absorb a little of his power for myself. And then I began to believe the things he said. How wrong I was." A morose glaze came over her eyes. "How very wrong."

"We all make mistakes."

"I made a fool of myself." Anger seemed to take over her face. "He doesn't deserve to rule. He's an egotistical despot who wields his power like a whip to keep those around him under his control. He treats the role of governor like a blank check."

"He's not the only governor who abuses his power." Charlie had given her a list of the worst offenders. Donna continued. "Things are going to be very different in the Allied Vampire Nation. Governors will be held accountable. Complaints will be taken seriously. A new, *fair* council will be put in place."

Claudette lifted her chin. "That's wonderful. And as it should be. As it should have been. I wish you great success."

"You say that as if you won't be around to experience it for yourself."

"I was thinking I'd go back to France. Start over." She sighed. "A simple life might be best for me for a while. I need to regroup. Do some thinking. Stay out of the light for a while, as it were."

Donna nodded. "I understand." She gestured at the seating close to her wingback. "Why don't we have our chat? I'm sure you're anxious to leave."

"I am, but if it's all right with you, I'd like to stay for the coronation."

"That would be fine." Donna preferred that, actually. That would give her team a few days to begin the process of unseating Fitzhugh. And Claudette would be around to help if they needed more from her. Donna waited while Claudette took a seat.

Charlie, and Pierce did the same, making Donna realize they must have been waiting for her cue. She really needed a lesson in royal protocol.

"So, Claudette. What can you tell me about Fitzhugh that will give me sufficient grounds to remove him from office?"

Claudette's eyes narrowed. "You realize that being queen means you can just remove him, no questions asked? Especially now that you've declared the Immortus Concilio no longer has any say."

"You're right, I could. But unseating him without the appropriate evidence would make me as bad as Fitzhugh. I'd be abusing my power just like he does." She shook her head. "That's not who I am. You should know that."

Claudette glanced at her lap. "I do know that." She looked up again. "I can't tell you much, but I can show you quite a lot." For the first time, Claudette smiled. "Fitzhugh has been siphoning funds from the governorship's account for years, using them for personal use. Homes, vehicles, lavish parties. Even a boat. And I can give you his books to prove it."

That was far more than Donna had anticipated. "That would be everything I needed."

Claudette's smile widened. "Good. I have them all on a thumb drive."

Donna looked at Pierce. "Can you handle this? Charlie's got enough on her plate. I want the information vetted."

"Yes. I'll have it done as soon as possible."

"Thank you. Ask Neo to help if you need it." She faced Claudette. "Where is this thumb drive?"

"I have it with me. In my quarters."

"Pierce will go with you and collect it." Donna stood. "Thank you for meeting with me, Claudette. Now, if you'll excuse me, I have other matters to attend to."

Without waiting for a response, she strode out of the room.

Charlie followed. "Would you like me to get Marcus for you?"

"Yes. I want to see these quarters I'm going to move into, then maybe we can get some of the household staff working on that. I want to see the rooms for the rest of you, too. And any other rooms I need to know about."

"I'll let him know." She whipped out her phone and started texting.

There was only one way to deal with Artemis's children, and that was to take a firm stand. The best way Donna knew to do that was to embrace her new position.

She had to steep herself in being the queen until royalty seeped from her pores. Moving herself and her staff into the house she now owned seemed like a pretty good first step.

"Marcus will meet us in the great hall in about ten minutes."

"Thanks." As they walked, a realization hit her and she sighed.

"Something wrong?" Charlie asked.

"We're about to get a tour of this enormous house and I'm in stilettos. Granted, they don't bother me like they used to, but these aren't exactly walking shoes."

Charlie smiled. "I will run back to the guest house and grab a pair of flats for you."

Donna tipped her head. "Charlie, you don't need to be fetching my shoes."

"Ma'am, with all due respect, that's what I'm here for. To do whatever you need me to do. Nothing is beneath me, I promise."

Donna could have hugged her. "I know that about you, Charlie. And I appreciate how you take care of me more than you know. I just meant someone back at the guest house could bring them over. Someone who isn't already doing something important."

Charlie laughed. "Ah, good point. Shall I ask Bunni?"

"No. She'll just bring me more heels. I'll text Cammie and ask her. She might like to see the tour of the house, too." Donna got out her phone and sent her sister a quick text with the request.

She looked at Charlie again. "Is there any kind of handbook that comes with being queen? There's a lot I don't know. Like in the sitting room, none of you sat when I did. You were waiting on me to ask you to sit or something, weren't you?"

Charlie nodded. "Yes. That's pretty standard. The king or queen goes first or gives permission for something to be done. They walk ahead, they eat first, sit first, leave first. As for a handbook, I don't think there's anything like that. I'll see what I can find."

"Thanks. Also, I was thinking about giving Pierce a new position. Personal bodyguard, maybe? Or something. Now that he's a reaper, he can't continue to be my donor, but I want to make sure he's still on the payroll. Do you think making him my bodyguard would upset Temo?"

"Not at all. Temo heads up your whole security team. They'd pretty much just work together to protect you. Which they are already doing. It would just be in a more coordinated way."

"Okay, good."

Charlie tapped something into her tablet. "You are going to need another donor. Would you like me to find some candidates?"

Donna sighed. "That's such a personal thing."

"I understand. As you're the queen, it wouldn't be uncommon for you to have more than one. Would that make you feel better? If you had a few? That could help the process be less personal. You wouldn't be relying on the same person every time."

"Maybe." Being that intimate with someone, even though they were volunteering to feed her, didn't feel like a relationship Donna wanted to get into right now. "Let me think about it."

"Whenever you're ready. In the meantime, we need to make sure you keep your strength up. Bagged isn't the same."

"I know."

Marcus walked in. "Ready for the tour, ma'am?"

"Can't wait," Donna said. "Except that I am waiting for my sister to bring me a change of shoes."

Three low chimes echoed through the house.

Marcus frowned. "More visitors? I can't imagine who that could be. I'm sorry, but if you'll pardon me, I'll see who it is."

"Go right ahead." Donna took a seat on the leather couch. "Charlie and I will be right here."

Charlie sat beside her as Marcus backed out of the room. "I'll return as soon as possible. Thank you."

"No problem." Donna looked at Charlie. "Teach me more about royal protocol."

For the next few minutes, Charlie did just that. Donna was amazed at how much deference the queen commanded. When Donna was in a room, everything was supposed to orbit around her.

That was going to take some getting used to. Especially because it all felt very much like how the Villachi family – and all those who'd worked for them – had treated Big Tony.

Marcus came back, a bothered look on his face. "Your Majesty, there's a man at the door who says he needs to speak with you. I tried to tell him that you're very busy—"

"Donna? Donna, where are you?"

At the sound of that familiar voice, Donna got to her feet. "Rico?"

10

Rico Medina strode into the great hall like he owned the place. "There you are. I guess I should be calling you Queen Donna now." He grinned. "Congratulations on that. If Big Tony could see you now, huh?"

Donna just stared at him. The FBI agent looked as good as he always had. No, that was a lie. He looked better. Whatever he'd done to recover from being captured and tortured by the fae had worked. Big time. He wasn't Pierce, though. "What on earth are you doing here? I mean, it's great to see you, but I never expected to see you here."

"I'm sure you didn't. And I don't mean to intrude. All the transitional stuff must be a little overwhelming, but if there was ever a woman capable of taking control, it's you."

"Thanks. But I still don't know why you're here."

He glanced at Marcus and Charlie. "About that. Could we talk in private?"

"Sure." She looked at Charlie. "Maybe you and Marcus could work on the coronation details for a couple minutes?"

Charlie smiled. "Text me when you're ready."

"I will." Donna sat back down as Charlie and Marcus left. She patted the cushion next to her.

Rico sat.

"I know you mentioned that we needed to talk at the pack funeral. What's so important that you drove all the way out here from New York?"

"Drove?" He made a face, then laughed. "I flew. Werewolves don't have the same kinds of restrictions vampires do. Although I understand you don't exactly have those restrictions, either. Daywalker, huh? Explains how you managed the fallen werewolf's funeral so easily."

She nodded. "I have been very fortunate to end up with such an extraordinary second power."

Which was as far as anyone outside of her inner circle needed to know, Rico included, although he'd once been about as inner circle as a person could be.

"That's for sure. I heard about the treaty with the Indiana pack, too. To say you've been busy is an understatement."

"Did you also hear that Christina is marrying the Millers' son, Noah?"

He shook his head, clearly surprised. "I did not. Congratulations. That practically makes you family."

"Thanks." She leaned in. "She's also expecting my first grandchild."

"More congratulations are in order then." He smiled in sudden understanding. "Let me guess—the treaty was Tom Miller's idea, wasn't it? To smooth the marriage path?"

"It was. You know your werewolf politics very well. Not a surprise. If anyone should, it's you." His grandmother was the alpha of the New Jersey pack, and his mother was the alpha-elect.

His expression became serious. "About that. Pack business is why I'm here."

Donna liked LV and Maria. She hoped very much nothing was wrong with either of them. "Oh? Everything all right?"

"Everything is great. But my grandmother would like to step down as alpha and enjoy her retirement. She's bought a beach house in South Carolina. Says she doesn't want to spend another winter in this kind of weather."

Donna laughed. "I can totally understand. I always said I was going to get myself a place on the beach in Florida. No wonder I like LV so much. But what does that have to do with you needing to talk to me?"

"With my grandmother stepping down, my mother will become alpha. And I will become alpha-elect."

"Hey, congratulations to you, too, then. That's great." She still didn't grasp why he was here.

"Thanks. Unfortunately, none of that can happen while I have unpaid debts."

Now she was really lost. "Again, what does this have to do with me?"

"You saved my life, Donna. I owe you."

She shook her head. "No, you don't. You would have done the same for me." He almost had when she'd been about to become a witness for the FBI against her husband. Rico had been her lifeline.

"Except I do. It's a pack rule. I cannot take a leadership position until I have a clean slate. Which means my grandmother can't retire, because my mother can't take over for her until I am capable of becoming alpha-elect."

"What am I missing here?"

He looked reluctant to explain. "I realize what needs to happen will probably complicate your already complicated life, but there's nothing I can do about it. I really hope you understand that."

"I'm trying."

"Good. Because I owe you a year of my life."

Donna squinted at him, trying to understand. "And that means what exactly?"

"For a year, I am yours." He spread his arms out. "In whatever capacity you want me."

Donna looked around to make sure she wasn't on some kind of hidden-camera vampire reality show.

This had to be a joke. "You're kidding, right? This is some kind of new queen initiation prank or something."

"No prank. Not kidding. I'm yours for the next three hundred and sixty-five days. Please say that you accept."

She stared at him, trying to find words. He was right that this was going to complicate her life. And possibly her feelings for Pierce. It was impossible to forget what kissing Rico had felt like. "I guess I have no choice."

She didn't. She couldn't keep LV from retiring.

He smiled. "Thank you." He leaned in, threaded his fingers through her hair, and did something completely unexpected.

He was absolutely as good of a kisser as she remembered. As a breath shuddered out of her, he pulled away. "Sorry. Shouldn't have done that. You're the queen now. I need to remember that."

She nodded, hoping her ability to speak returned soon. She cleared her throat. "Right. Royal protocol and all that. And the fact that you and I cannot be a thing."

"Right. Won't happen again." He looked around. "Is all of this yours now?"

"It is." She'd never been happier for a change of subject. Although if she needed to bring it up again, she would. She didn't want Rico believing there was a chance of something happening between them. "Pretty impressive, huh?"

"I'll say. Makes your house in Jersey look like a converted garage."

"Will you stay in the FBI?"

He looked at her again. "You mean when I become alpha-elect?"

She nodded. "Yes."

"I will. Until I become alpha, and by then, I'll hopefully be able to retire and do that full-time."

"What about being here for a year?"

"I've put in for a leave of absence."

"That's not going to be so great for your career, is it?"

"Thanks to you helping me bring down the Villachi crime family, I'm a bit of a golden boy. As long as I show up for all my court dates, I'll be fine." He grinned. "So do you have any staff openings?"

"Not really." Except for blood donor. Donna wasn't sure that was the smartest place to put Rico. Not when werewolves were reported to be so…tasty. She smiled, hoping to keep the hunger out of her eyes. "But we'll find a place for you in some capacity when you're here permanently."

He made a face. "I'm here. Starting now."

"You mean you brought all your stuff with you?"

He shrugged. "What's to bring? I've got a couple of bags, but I'm a light packer."

She took a deep breath and exhaled. "What were you going to do if I said no?"

He laughed softly. "You weren't going to say no. You'd never stand in the way of my grandmother's retirement."

Donna frowned at him. He knew her too well. Maybe biting him on a regular basis was exactly what he deserved. "Until we get you settled, stay out of the way."

"Yes, Your Majesty."

She stood up, slanting her eyes at him as she smoothed down her dress and adjusted her jacket. "I can't believe I have a whole year of this to look forward to."

He let out a noise that was halfway between a bark and whoof. "Queen looks good on you."

She frowned at him.

He instantly held up his hands. "No comments like that in front of anyone else, I swear it. Nothing but the utmost respect."

"Remember that." She let her eyes glow and her fangs descend just a bit to remind him who he was dealing with. "Or I will call this off and send you home, regardless of what LV hopes to do with the rest of her life. I'm already being challenged for the crown. I don't need any additional aggravation, understood?"

"Perfectly. As far as anyone else knows, I'm just your lapdog." He winked.

"Good. Because I'd hate to have you neutered."

After Donna briefly explained the Rico situation to Marcus, Pierce, Charlie, and Cammie, who'd finally shown up with Donna's flats, the tour of the house began.

Marcus led them straight to the elevator. "We'll begin with your private quarters, Your Majesty. That way if anything isn't to your liking, I can have the staff fix it immediately."

"Good," Donna said. "I want to move in today if possible. I'd like as many of my people in the main house as can be arranged."

Marcus nodded. "There are quite a few guests here, but I'm working on sending them home as politely as I can. I believe most of them are hoping to be invited to stay for the coronation."

"Only governors," Donna replied. "And Queen Francesca, of course." She glanced at Charlie. "Unless there's anyone else you think I should invite?"

Charlie glanced down at her tablet as the elevator stopped. "I'll go through the guest list Marcus gave me again, but your plan is sound."

Marcus led them off the elevator into a large foyer, beyond which were a set of large double doors. Both were open, giving a view down a wide hall with more doors along its length. He gestured at it. "The queen's apartment."

"All of it?" Donna asked.

"Yes." He smiled brightly. "Shall we?"

"Lead the way."

He took them in, pointing out the rooms as they went past, stopping briefly at each open door to give them a peek inside. There was a small reading room, a suite of three offices, one larger than the two ancillary ones, then an exercise room, and a space that Marcus simply referred to as the meditation room.

At that point, they'd reached another set of double doors.

"The inner sanctum," he said as he pushed them wide.

"Wow," Cammie said.

Donna nodded. The space beyond was done in clean lines and simple colors. Sandstone tile floors, antique cream walls, brushed bronze fixtures, touches of gold, pale blue, and soft coral throughout. "It's like a modern version of an ancient temple."

"It looks very Artemis," Pierce said.

"It does," Donna agreed. It felt a lot warmer than the governor's penthouse, which definitely seemed cool at times with all the white.

"Too much Artemis?" Marcus asked.

Donna looked around and considered the question. The ceiling of the hall was painted to look like a blue summer sky, scattered with clouds and a few random magpies in flight. She smiled at those. "No. I like it."

"Then let's look at the rest," Marcus said.

Beautiful, interesting art and gorgeous but simple furnishings decorated the spacious living room. The kitchen, while small, was as gourmet as could be. The theater room was dark and cozy, with seating for twelve.

Maybe there was hope for a movie night with friends and family after all.

Additionally, the apartment had a well-appointed guest room, and finally, a master bedroom. The bed sat in the center of the room, a mammoth four-poster of pale wood, each corner a fluted column as wide as a person. The columns supported an iron canopy awash in sheer silk panels that made the bed seem as if it floated in the clouds.

Donna nodded. "This will do."

The rest of the apartment followed similar lines. Everything about the place seemed designed for peace, tranquility, and relaxation.

This had been Artemis's escape, Donna realized. She'd spared no expense making it that, either.

The bathroom would have made any spa aficionado weep. The tub was a deep, fat oval that could have easily held three.

Donna didn't want to think about how many it had held, and how often. Not now that this was her space.

Marcus gestured to a set of mirrored double doors. "The closet. I apologize that it hasn't been cleaned out yet, but I thought you might want to have a look at her things. See if anything suited you. Otherwise, we'd be happy to take care of it."

Charlie started for the doors, looking over her shoulder at Donna. "Do you mind?"

"Go ahead." Donna was as eager to see the late queen's wardrobe as her admin was.

The interior was two rooms deep, all white with mirrors and glass everywhere. Thick white carpet went wall to wall and sumptuous crystal chandeliers illuminated the space. In the very center of the first room was a large island dresser.

In the center of the second room was a platform, two steps high.

Across from the platform was the largest mirror in the room, trimmed in gold and covering almost the entire wall.

No surprise that Artemis had enjoyed looking at herself. She was a beautiful woman.

"I'll go through all of her things," Donna said. "While I don't think our styles were all that similar, it might be nice to keep a few pieces as tributes to her."

"If I might make a suggestion?" Marcus waited for her response.

"Of course."

"You'll need a gown for the coronation. And with us trying to accomplish that in a short amount of time, I thought perhaps you might find something in here that would work. We can have it altered, obviously, although you two weren't that different in size. Unless you'd prefer something of your very own. I realize I'm suggesting a glorified hand-me-down, but considering the circumstances—"

Donna smiled. "I love that idea. I think it's brilliant." She really did. There was something bold about Donna wearing one of the late queen's gowns for her own coronation. It would certainly make a statement that Donna wasn't shying away from her new position. "Artemis was my grandsire, after all. It would be fitting that I wear something of hers. Thank you for suggesting that."

"You're welcome." With a smile, Marcus nodded toward the second adjoining room. "Her personal vault can be accessed through there. That's where you'll find all of her personal jewelry and everything that's in the royal collection. Along with anything else she felt was valuable."

Donna glanced in that direction. "How will I open it? I don't have the combination."

"I do," Marcus said. "As a fail-safe."

"Smart," Donna said. But sad. She'd have to do that as well. Being a vampire definitely meant living a life that held some danger.

Being a vampire nation's queen only exacerbated that risk.

"We'll change it for you, of course."

She nodded, somewhat lost in thought. *Silly.* There was no going back, so dwelling on what might have been was a waste of time. "Where are the rooms for my staff and friends?"

"This wing has two smaller apartments for those you wish closest to you. There is also a larger apartment and more smaller ones on the floor above this one."

"Aren't most of those already taken?"

"Some," Marcus answered. "But as with Artemis, the queen's staff serves at her pleasure. You may choose who you wish to keep of the existing staff and who you wish to dismiss."

Donna hated the idea of firing anyone. "Do you think some of them will want to go?

Marcus looked a touch uncomfortable. "I'm afraid they will. Please don't take it personally. Some of them were with Artemis for decades. They've taken her death very hard. It's only natural that they'd want to move on."

"Sure, I understand that. And I don't take it personally." It made her life easier if they went of their own free will. "Anyone who wants to leave will be given the appropriate severance package and wished well. I only want people around me who want to be here."

He smiled. "Very good."

That was one hurdle down. "Let's see the two smaller apartments that are part of this wing."

Donna soon learned that Marcus's idea of small was very different from her idea of small. The first apartment had three bedrooms with their own bathrooms, a large living room, a dining room, and a kitchen.

The second was a two-bedroom with all the same amenities.

Donna looked at Pierce, Charlie, and Cammie. "What do you think? We can make these work, right?"

When Cammie didn't say anything right away, Donna said, "Cammie, I was thinking you could just take the guest room in my apartment."

She shook her head. "That wouldn't be fair to you. What if Christina or Joe Jr. come to visit? I'd be fine with something upstairs."

Once again, Donna could tell that Cammie was feeling like she didn't fit in. "I don't need a meditation room. That can easily become another guest room. I want you with me. I like having you close."

"You're going to have a houseful without me."

Charlie nodded. "She's not entirely wrong. Are you sure you want all of us underfoot? It might be too much."

Donna frowned. "You won't be underfoot. We all live together now. Why would continuing that here suddenly be too much?"

"But we're on three different floors in the guest house," Charlie countered.

"You don't have to decide now," Marcus said.

"Except we do," Donna said. "I want everyone moved over here as soon as possible. For now, Cammie, you take the guest room in my apartment. Charlie and Pierce, the three-bedroom. Neo and Temo can be in the two-bedroom. Everyone else can take a room upstairs."

They all nodded in agreement.

On a roll, she continued. "How soon can the staff move our things over?"

"I can have them start immediately," Marcus answered.

"Perfect. Let's do that. And then I want to focus on the coronation." The sooner the better, as far as she was concerned. Especially now that Artemis's daughter seemed like she was going to challenge her for the throne. "How soon can that happen?"

He narrowed his eyes slightly. "We should allow a week for those traveling."

"How about five days," she countered. "Anyone who can't make it by then can watch via live-stream. I think that's reasonable. And I want to move forward."

He nodded. "A wise decision, in light of the arrival of Lillis and her brother. Five days it is." He looked at Charlie. "We should begin planning as soon as I notify the staff about moving you all over here."

"I can help," Pierce said.

Marcus nodded. "Excellent. There will be invites to extend, a banquet to organize, the ceremony itself, guest arrangements in the house—which reminds me, there's the issue of the lingering guests from the funeral to deal with."

Donna looked at her admin. "Charlie, get Neo, Temo, and Kace over here and have them work with the security team to assist with the departure process."

Charlie pulled out her phone. "On it."

Donna thought about it. "You know what? Get Rico

to help with that, too. If he's going to be here, he's going to pitch in when we need him. He was FBI. He knows how to handle people."

"What do you want me to do?" Cammie asked.

"Would you mind organizing all the stuff as it's brought in? Not unpacking, just making sure it all goes in the right rooms. That kind of thing." That wasn't much of a job, Donna knew, but she didn't know what else to have her sister do.

"Sure." Cammie seemed slightly disappointed.

A new thought occurred to Donna. "Moving in here means we need to move out of Wellman Towers, too. And I need to appoint a new governor to take my place."

Charlie nodded. "Yes, all of that needs to happen, but it's nothing I can't handle. As for a new governor of New Jersey, I have a short-list of candidates if you'd like to look them over. I've prepared their bios as well, so you can get a sense of who they are and how well they might handle the job."

"You're worth your weight in gold. How about you give that list to Cammie first?"

"Me?" Cammie made a face.

"Yes. Who better to vet the potential vampire governor candidates than a former Venari?"

Cammie smiled. "Interesting idea. I'm happy to do it."

"Great, thank you." Donna rubbed her hands together, feeling like things were coming together, even if just in a small way. "Actually, Marcus, once you get the staff working on the move, I want you to tell our two visitors that I'm ready to meet with them now. Let's deal with them first, then move on to the coronation."

"I don't think they'll be awake yet, Your Majesty."

Donna smiled. "I'm the queen. They work on my schedule, not the other way around. Also? I don't really care."

# CHAPTER 12

A big, crackling fire roared in the fireplace as Donna sat in the great hall. She'd had a large wingback set just slightly at an angle to the first seating area, which put the fireplace behind her. The warmth was a welcome thing, but that wasn't why she'd moved the chair. The wingback was the nearest she could come to a throne.

Having the fire behind her was mere chance, but maybe her two visitors would read a deeper message into it. Like she could handle the heat. Or something like that.

Her stilettos were back on, and her team was positioned around the room in such a way that they would be able to hear everything and come to her assistance, should Artemis's children try anything stupid.

Donna had no idea what to expect but she was taking no chances.

Closest to her were Pierce on one side, Charlie on the other. Cammie and Rico sat by one of the big windows, nearest the fire.

Temo had opted to stand by the main entrance. Neo, naturally, had decided to bookend him by that doorway.

Harper, Will, Francine, and Kace were seated at the farthest end of the room. Bunni was still in the shower or primping. Donna considered that fortunate. There was no telling what the brash young woman might say or do.

Francine was crocheting, which amused Donna to no end. Kace was on his phone, Harper had brought her laptop. Will was sketching in a notebook. New leather designs, she imagined. She loved how laidback they all seemed.

Like this was no big deal. Donna hoped that was true.

She'd thought about inviting Queen Francesca, but she didn't want to put the monarch in the midst of this battle. If that's what it turned out to be. Francesca had done enough for Donna. If Donna was going to truly be queen of North America, she couldn't have another ruler working as her backup every time trouble arose.

Marcus entered. "They'll be here shortly. They were not happy to be woken up."

Donna smirked. "I'm fine with that."

He smiled faintly and moved to stand near the fireplace. "Is there anything I can get you?"

"I should probably have some water. I don't know how much talking we're going to do. Thank you. Will you offer them something to drink when they arrive?"

"Absolutely." He went to the bar to get her water.

"Good. Water, alcohol, coffee, blood, whatever they'd like." She was curious to see what they'd choose.

Blood, she guessed. Especially after traveling. Unless they'd fed after they'd gotten here. If so, maybe they wouldn't want blood again so soon.

They hadn't brought a donor with them that she'd seen. Unless the bodyguards were doing double duty. Could they actually not have a dedicated donor? She'd imagined Artemis's children lived a life of luxury and privilege, but maybe she'd been wrong.

She supposed she'd soon find out.

They walked in about ten minutes later, scowling and obviously perturbed.

Donna greeted them with a regal nod and a placating smile.

Marcus stepped forward to make the introductions. "Your Highness, this is Lillis and Yavi, Artemis's offspring, grandchildren of Zenos."

He shifted his attention to them. "Your queen, Belladonna Barrone, founder of the Allied Vampire Nation, friend to the fae, liberator of the werewolves, maker of treaties, breaker of codes, defender of the innocent, and destroyer of corruption."

Donna worked hard not to react, but she gave Marcus props for representing her like that. Even if he had been watching a few too many Game of Thrones reruns.

She remained seated, clearly a power-play on her behalf, but so be it. "Welcome to my home."

Lillis's eyes narrowed, but she raised her chin ever so slightly.

Next to her, her brother frowned. "About that—"

"Won't you take a seat," Donna interrupted. "Marcus, our visitors look thirsty."

He nodded. "Can I get you something to drink? Our menu is vast."

"Coffee," Lillis told Marcus. "Sweet and light." She sat on the couch but turned her entire body toward Donna.

Yavi sat opposite his sister, facing her. When he answered Marcus, he kept his eyes on Donna. "Blood. Fresh. Then whiskey, neat."

Instantly, she took a dislike to him. He reminded her of the vampire in her basement. And one Fitzhugh was more than enough. She imagined from his attitude that Yavi must be the driving force behind this quest for the throne. Lillis must be the oldest, giving her the stronger claim.

Marcus excused himself with a slight bow. "Right away."

Donna jumped in but kept her tone as pleasant as possible. "Marcus tells me you live in Paris and that you've come to take Artemis's ashes back to be interred there."

"That's right," Lillis answered. She wore a long ivory sweater dress with the same ivory boots she'd had on when Donna had first seen her. A short strand of polished amber chunks circled her neck, partially hidden by the ivory fur vest she wore over the dress.

"It's good of you to make such a long trip for such a

small errand. We certainly could have shipped them to you." Donna paused while Marcus crossed in front of her with their drinks. "I suppose you'll be leaving at nightfall, then?"

"No." Lillis sipped her coffee. "We've come for more than our mother's ashes. We've come because her throne is rightfully mine. I realize you weren't aware of that, and of course, we don't wish to create any ill will, but it's what she would have wanted."

And there it was, Donna thought. She kept her expression calm. "I imagine she would have wanted her children at her funeral as well."

Yavi glared at her. "Our mother left us everything. Her throne, her estate, her wealth, everything."

Donna cast a cool eye on him. "Her attorney, Walter St. Simons, will argue that, especially because her last will didn't mention either of you at all. But I am happy to have him look over any paperwork you might have in support of your claim."

She gestured toward Pierce. "This is my personal attorney, Pierce Harrison. I'll have him look over the paperwork as well. I assume you brought some kind of proof with you?"

Lillis glanced at her brother.

He reached into his jacket pocket and produced a folded piece of yellowed parchment. He tossed it onto the table between them, then picked up his glass of blood and downed it in a few swallows.

Donna liked him less and less with each passing moment.

Marcus retrieved the paper and handed it to her.

"Thank you." She unfolded it and read the thin scrawl covering the page. The message was simple and short.

*To whom it may concern,*

*I leave all my worldly possessions to my children, Lillis and Yavi, to be divided equally. To Lillis, my eldest, I leave my throne.*

*Artemis*

Not the most heartfelt thing she'd ever read. Not the most convincing. Donna peered more closely at the signature, her lip curling in distaste. "Is that signed in blood?"

"Yes," Yavi hissed. "Which makes it as binding and legal as can be."

She glanced at Pierce for some kind of reassurance, but knew he'd probably have to research this. Or they'd have to call St. Simons in.

He held out his hand.

She gave him the will.

He read it over, taking a long hard look at it before doing the same to Yavi. "This could have been written by anyone. Just as this could be anyone's blood. It will have to be authenticated, as I'm sure you know."

Yavi seemed frustrated by Pierce's assessment, but nodded. "Of course. But we'll be taking possession of the estate immediately. Clearly, there can be no argument that our mother has left that much to us. We are her only children. It's only natural her possessions would pass to us."

"There can and will be all kinds of arguments." Pierce shook his head as he tossed the letter back onto the table. "Possession will be staying with Queen Belladonna until proven otherwise. In fact, nothing will happen until the letter is authenticated. And even if it proves to be by Artemis's own hand, there is no date. This very well could have been written years ago, unlike the most recent will and letters, which bequeath everything to Queen Belladonna."

Lillis and Yavi looked downright perturbed if not stunned.

Pierce snorted. "Surely you see what a feeble case you've presented. A document such as this, with no real providence, is vulnerable to a multitude of challenges. You cannot expect us to simply hand everything over with a smile and best wishes based on such thin evidence."

Donna loved Pierce in lawyer-mode. It was a beautiful thing. Add in the whole reaper thing and he was something to behold.

Lillis finally spoke up. "It would be in your best interests not to make enemies of us."

Donna pinned her with a gaze. "Are you threatening me?"

Lillis got to her feet. "Take my words as you wish."

"Then I take them as a threat, which means you've

already made yourself my enemy." Donna stood, thankful her stilettos gave her a few more inches of height than Lillis. "You will leave my estate the moment the sun sets, or you will be escorted off the property by whatever means my security detail sees fit. Am I clear?"

Yavi's eyes glowed *red* as he jumped to his feet. "That's less than an hour from now. You will regret this."

Lillis nodded, her eyes glowing red, too. Mary and Joseph, what was that about? Lillis glared at Donna. "Nightfall will be your deadline as well. Turn over the estate and the throne, or we will be forced to destroy you."

Then she and her brother vanished in a burst of vampire speed.

Donna shook her head. "That went worse than expected." She glanced at Marcus. "Why the devil did their eyes glow red? What kind of vampires are they?"

Marcus stared after them, horror in his eyes. "Devil might be accurate. I didn't realize…I'm so sorry. Now I know why Artemis wanted nothing to do with them."

Donna's brows lifted. "She wanted nothing to do with them? You're just telling me this now?"

He finally looked at her. "I didn't want to prejudice you until you'd spoken to them. I thought perhaps they could be bought off with some money and one of the smaller properties. I honestly didn't think they'd come with a letter that can only be a forgery."

Pierce snorted. "That much seems obvious."

Cammie was at Donna's side as the rest of her crew gathered around.

Marcus still hadn't explained.

"What didn't you realize?" Donna asked.

With a resigned expression, he shook his head. "Artemis might have been their mother, but from what I just saw, there's only one explanation as to what their father was."

"*What* their father was?"

He flattened his hand against his chest as if to calm himself. "A demon."

# Chapter 13

Donna almost sat back down as her knees went weak. "I want them out of the house as soon as possible." She looked at her sister. "You know about these things. Is there any way to keep them out of the house once they're gone?"

Cammie shook her head. "Not unless you can find a priest willing to consecrate the place, and the chances you'll get a capable priest willing to perform that ritual on a vampire's estate are pretty slim."

"Can't you do it? You were a nun."

Cammie thought it over. "I can try, but that's all it would be—a try. There'd be no guarantee it would hold."

Donna groaned softly. "There's got to be another way."

"Salt," Cammie said. "But they're daemons, which is just another way of saying they're half vampire, half demon. That makes them a lot harder to deal with. Salt probably won't be enough."

Harper came forward. "I can work on something. A spell maybe. Something that mimics the feel of a sanctified building. It might at least slow them down."

"Okay," Donna said. "You and Cammie work together on this."

"I don't know anything about witchcraft," Cammie argued.

"But you know about demons. And daemons, apparently. Your knowledge alone makes you useful." Donna shot a look at Marcus. "Are there any resources in the library for this kind of thing?"

"There should be. I'll find everything I can."

Charlie clutched her laptop tighter. "I can help research."

"Me, too," Francine said as she gathered up her crochet work.

"Good," Donna said. "Let me know the minute you figure something out."

As they headed off, Marcus spoke. "I know you want them out of the house, but that may not be an easy task."

"Are you saying you're outgunned?"

"Possibly." He looked ashamed to admit that.

Kace gave Marcus a nod. "I'll help."

"So will I," Will offered.

"Same here," Pierce said. "In fact, my scythe might help to convince them." He looked at Will. "Assuming it's as lethal to a daemon as it is to a vampire?"

Will stroked his beard. "I've never had to test that one. Might be interesting to find out."

"I'd rather get them out of the house without killing them," Donna said. "That's not going to be a great headline. *New Queen Kills Predecessor's Children.* Let's try to avoid anything resembling that, shall we?"

Marcus nodded. "Very wise. I'll call security now and assemble the best team, but if you want to ensure the last rays of the sun don't get them, we can't put them out just yet."

"That's all right. Gives them one less thing to be mad about." Donna took some comfort in the fact that Artemis's security was on the job. After all, that team had kept Artemis safe for years. And there was no way those years had gone by without issues. They had to be good at what they did.

Rico walked over. "Can I make a suggestion?"

"Sure," Donna answered.

"Let me approach the local pack. See if I can get you a treaty with them as well. If this goes south, it wouldn't hurt to have the backup."

"You're right. I think that's wise. Marcus can get you a vehicle if you need to have a face-to-face meeting."

"I may." Rico took his phone out. "I'll make a few calls and get things moving." He went off to do that.

Donna sank into the wingback, doubt plaguing her. "Not that I wanted to, but maybe I should have offered them some money. Or one of Artemis's homes. I can't possibly use them all anyway."

"I'm not sure that would have worked," Pierce said. "They seemed pretty intent on all or nothing. And giving up the throne to them would be disastrous."

"I know, which is why that is absolutely not going to happen. I really hope they leave on their own." She stiffened. "I just realized I need to call Ishalan. See if he can get the local fae to back down."

"Back down from what?" Pierce asked.

"I called in a favor and had him recruit the locals to swarm the perimeter in case Fitzhugh made a break for it. I figured he'd retreat if he saw all those fae waiting for him. If they're still out there, I don't want to keep Lillis and Yavi in."

"Not even for one extra minute," Pierce agreed. "Call him right now. Where's your phone?"

"In my—" She patted her jacket pockets. "Well, I thought it was in one of my pockets." She looked around. "Did I set it down?" She rolled her eyes and groaned. "I did. I was taking a picture of that enormous tub to send to Christina, and I must have left it on the bathroom counter when we went into the closet."

"Come on," Pierce said. "I'll go upstairs with you to get it. I don't think you should go anywhere alone right now."

She stood again. "I know you're not trying to scare me, but do you really think they'd attack me?"

"Yes. I do. Look at how much wealth and power they'd stand to gain if you were no longer in their way."

"Right." She hooked her arm through his. "I was going to make you my personal bodyguard anyway. Might as well start now."

He smiled as they walked toward the elevator. "You were?"

She nodded. "I felt like you needed a new position since you can't be my donor anymore. And who better to protect me than a reaper?"

His grin widened. "I couldn't agree more."

They found her phone right where she thought she'd left it, on the bathroom counter. She dashed off a text to Ishalan, then tucked the phone into her pocket where it should have been. "This is some apartment, isn't it?"

"It is. And it should be. It's where a queen lives."

She smiled. "It doesn't seem real. Maybe after the coronation it will."

"Maybe," he said. "Might take longer."

She leaned against the countertop, which according to Marcus was a large slab of creamy onyx, sliced thin enough to allow light to shine through it. "I knew being queen was going to mean more trouble. I'm not even officially on the throne and I have the Daemon Twins to deal with." Not that they were actually twins, but it amused her to call the evil duo that.

"We'll handle it," Pierce reassured her. A soft buzzing sound came from his jacket pocket. He pulled his phone out and checked the screen. "Marcus says the security team is assembling in thirty minutes in the south wing."

She closed her eyes and said a prayer that it all went

well and they got Lillis and Yavi out without incident. When she opened her eyes, Pierce was smiling. "What?"

"It'll only take me ten minutes to get there. Which means we have twenty minutes to check out that closet."

"You do love to dress me, don't you?"

He laughed. "You wear clothes so well. And you look so beautiful in them."

She smiled at the compliments. "Are you trying to distract me from the attempted takeover?"

"Maybe." He tipped his head toward the closet. "What do you say? You do need to find a dress."

"All right." She relented, in part because she knew how happy it would make him, and in part because a distraction wasn't such a bad idea.

He flung the doors open and turned on the lights. "This closet might actually qualify as one of the Seven Wonders of the Manmade World."

Donna laughed. "It *is* pretty spectacular. I think it's bigger than the first apartment Joe and I had."

"It's definitely bigger than the one I was living in when the firm hired me."

There was so much to look at, she didn't know where to start.

"You should wear color," he said as he began to rifle through the racks. "No black. Black for a vampire queen seems too predictable. And you are definitely not predictable. Besides, black won't show up as well on the live feed. Something vibrant would be better."

"Then what color?" she asked.

"Not sure yet, but I think we'll know the dress when we see it. Or we see it on you." He stopped to look at a spangled cobalt blue number. "As you well know, the hanger rarely does a garment justice."

"You have definitely taught me that." She pulled out an ivory gown with thin gold and silver threads woven through the fabric. "What about this?"

He glanced over. "Channeling your inner Lillis?"

"Ew, you're right. Does she ever wear anything but ivory? I guess that's her look."

"It does show off her coloring well."

"Artemis liked it, too."

"That she did," Pierce confirmed.

After a few more minutes, they had a handful of dresses pulled, but Pierce had to go and wouldn't leave without her.

Not that she wanted to be left alone anywhere right now. Not until Artemis's children were out of the house. Thankfully, the sky was darkening.

She went back downstairs with him. He walked her to the library so she could help with the search to find a way to protect the house and not be alone. "Thanks."

He nodded. "Of course."

"Be safe."

"I will."

She kissed him on the cheek before he left, then

went over to the table where Cammie and Harper were sitting. Harper was paging through an ancient leather-bound volume. Cammie had a smaller, similar version but hers looked to be in Latin. "Find anything?"

They both looked up. Harper spoke first. "Salt still seems to be our best bet."

"But," Cammie said, "we're thinking there must be something we can add to it to fortify it for our particular use. Not a lot on daemons so far, though. They're pretty rare creatures."

"Just our luck." Donna took a seat across from them. "What about some kind of magic something?" She looked at Harper. "How would you keep a vampire out of your house? If that's what you wanted to do?"

"A ward," she answered right away. "But that's a spell put on the entire house. It's not a substance that can be mixed in with anything else."

"Is there any way to make it into a substance? Or why not just ward this house and surround it with salt?"

Harper shook her head. "I can't ward a house filled with vampires against vampires. You'd all be miserable. Trust me. You know how the fae hate iron? Same thing, I'm guessing. Probably would feel like something's trying to eat your skin off."

"Oh. Yeah, let's not do that." So much for that, Donna thought.

"Wait a second," Cammie said. "You just gave me an idea."

"I did?" Donna leaned in. "What was it?"

"There are some very rare kinds of demons that don't respond to the usual weapons. I only faced them twice in my time as a Venari, that's how rare they are. For those demons, we used ashes."

Harper made a face. "I can't see how that would work."

Cammie shook her head. "Not just any ashes. The ashes of their own kind. It's essentially fighting fire with fire."

Donna blinked as a weird feeling came over her. "Are you saying what I think you're saying?"

Cammie tilted her head to one side as if coming to terms with her own idea. "If you think what I'm suggesting is we use Artemis's ashes against her children, then yes."

# Chapter 14

Donna sat back. "That's a pretty wild idea."

What would Artemis think if she knew her cremains were being used to stop her children from attacking the queen she'd chosen to succeed her?

"Yeah," Cammie said. "I know. Maybe too wild."

Harper chewed her bottom lip. "That might actually work. It's so hardcore it almost has to. Let me research my craft library and see what I can find out about ashes and incorporating them into a spell or ward of some kind. That's death magic and it's pretty dark stuff. Not something I usually delve into, but in this case it might be exactly what we need."

Donna jumped up. "Hang on. We're not going to have Artemis's ashes if I don't stop Marcus from giving them to her kids."

She raced out of the room, dialing his number as she headed for the south wing.

He answered quickly. "Your Highness?"

"Have you turned over Artemis's cremains to her children yet?"

"No, I—"

"Good, don't. Bring the ashes to the great hall and I'll explain."

"On my way."

She got to the great hall well ahead of him and went straight to the fireplace. The fire was still crackling away, embers glowing bright. She really hoped this worked.

Marcus came in, the gilded box Donna recognized from the funeral in his hands. "I have the ashes."

"Great. We need them. We'll have to replace them with ashes from the fireplace. Then you can give those to her kids."

He nodded and began looking around. "All right, we can do that."

She smiled, amused and amazed at how ready he was to do as she asked. "Don't you want to know why?"

He went to the bar and took out a large brandy snifter, into which he carefully poured the ashes. "I assumed you would tell me what you wanted me to know."

"I appreciate that attitude. I really do. But you are allowed to question me, you know. I mean, it's fine with me."

A few stray particles of ash floated through the air as he finished emptying the box. "It might be fine with you, but it's not standard royal protocol."

"Ah, yes. The SRP. Well, I'm telling you it's all right to ask questions. And we need Arty's ashes because we think they might be the solution to keeping her children from reentering the house. Harper's looking into how to use them to protect us."

His brows lifted slightly. "That's interesting."

"Isn't it?"

He brought the emptied box to the fireplace, set it down on the hearth, then used the scoop tool to refill the box and showed it to her. "What do you think?"

She looked in. "Maybe a bit more."

He nodded and added half a scoop.

"Perfect." She glanced at Marcus. "You think they'll notice? They aren't quite the same color."

"I doubt they'll even look inside the box." He shrugged. "I wouldn't be able to tell anything was amiss. I don't think they will, either." He put the lid back on. "Let me know if there's anything else you need. Oh, the ashes in the glass. What would you like me to do with them?"

"I'll take care of those. You stay safe getting those two out of the house. I don't trust them."

"Neither do I and I promise we'll take every precaution. And I'll let you know the moment they're gone." With a practiced bow, he excused himself.

She went back behind the bar and dug around for something more secure than the brandy snifter. One wrong move and tiny flakes of Artemis would be everywhere.

She found a box of swizzle sticks that would be easy enough to empty out, but a box didn't seem like a great container for ashes. She searched until she found a jar of olives, about half full.

Good enough. She dumped the olives into a serving

dish, then rinsed and dried the jar. Finally, she carefully transferred the ashes to the jar and screwed the lid on tight. "Much better."

She took the jar to the library, setting it down triumphantly in front of Harper and Cammie. "There you go. Artemis."

Harper made a face.

"Wasn't much of her left, huh?" Cammie picked up the jar to have a closer look.

"Just what Ishalan could gather."

Cammie set it back down. "It'll have to do." She glanced at Harper. "You think it's enough?"

"Hard to tell, but like you said, it'll have to do." Harper stared at the jar. "Maybe I can add some amplifying ingredients to the mix. Use those to make a mountain out of our molehill, as it were."

"Keep at it, then," Donna said. "This is all we have so far. And it's about to be dark outside, so hopefully, those two are also about to be gone. I want the house protected as soon as—"

Her phone went off. She checked the screen. "Marcus needs me. Back shortly."

Cammie looked up. "You want me to go with you?"

"Probably not a bad idea. Come on."

They walked out together, headed for the south wing.

"I should have brought my sword. I might just start carrying it. Did he say what was up?" Cammie asked.

"Just that he thinks I should join them."

The walk took about ten minutes and showed them more parts of the house they'd yet to see.

"If this place was any bigger, it would have its own zip code," Cammie said.

"Right?" Donna marveled at how the rooms just went on and on. A lot of this was guest quarters, though. Which was good. They were about to host fifty governors.

As they turned down the hall toward the south wing, Marcus and the security team came into view. Pierce, Temo, Kace, and Will were all there as well.

In the midst of them were Lillis and Yavi. They looked oddly chill.

"Thank you for joining us, Your Highness." Marcus's expression seemed off. Like something had surprised him, and it wasn't seeing Cammie with Donna. "Lillis and Yavi wished to speak with you before they depart."

Donna nodded. "That's fine." She looked at them as she approached. Cammie hung back, which Donna understood. "What did you wish to discuss?"

Lillis stepped forward. "My brother and I have decided to leave. We apologize for the distress we caused you when we first spoke. Our only excuse is that the loss of our mother has left us in a fragile state, as you might imagine."

Behind her, Yavi clutched the box of ashes, his expression on the grim side. Was that his attempt at grief?

"I'm sure," Donna said. She remained unconvinced. If they'd really been that affected by her death, why hadn't they made it to the funeral? She couldn't wait to get Cammie's take on this performance.

"We only ask two things of you, if you would be so gracious. Please consider the letter we shared with you. We believe it is our mother's last wish that her children not be forgotten, so perhaps you might find a way to remember us?"

The nerve. Donna kept her cool. "We will take another look at the letter, I assure you."

"Thank you," Lillis said. "Regardless of that outcome, we would very much like to attend your coronation as a way of offering our support and putting any ill will behind us. A way of starting over."

"I will consider that." Did they really think that was going to happen? Donna almost laughed. "I assume you've given your contact information to Marcus so we can reach you?"

Lillis nodded. "We have. Thank you for your hospitality."

"You're welcome. Safe travels." Donna didn't trust either of them, but that didn't keep her from smiling and putting on a good face. If they could pretend, so could she.

Marcus walked them to the door, where their driver and other attendant met them to escort them to their Mercedes. Some of the security team walked out with them, others stayed at the door, and the rest headed upstairs with Pierce, Temo, Kace, and Will. To do what, Donna wasn't sure.

She shot Cammie a look and they both retreated down the hall a few paces, stopping where they could watch the G-Wagon from a window. She didn't believe the Daemon Twins were leaving of their own free will. Just like she didn't believe the sincerity of the apology or the new attitude or anything that had come out of Lillis's mouth.

"This is part of some greater plan," Donna muttered with great certainty.

"One hundred percent," Cammie answered.

The daemons got in their car. Donna kept her eyes on them, but was aware of Marcus's approach. She glanced at him. "I don't believe any of that."

"Neither do I, Your Majesty. Even so, I'm glad they left without incident."

"So am I." The G-Wagon pulled away and headed down the long drive. "Even if I feel like we're just waiting for the other shoe to drop. Where did my guys go? Looked like they were headed upstairs."

"They were," Marcus answered. "They went to sweep the rooms where Lillis and Yavi were staying."

She raised her brows. "Good idea."

"Thank you," he said. "Has your team made any progress on protecting the house?"

"Some," Cammie answered. "But I took a break to walk Donna here."

"Is there anything I can do to help?" Marcus asked.

The black vehicle was a shadow behind the trees that lined the far reaches of the estate's road. Donna looked at her sister. "Do you guys need anything?"

"Nothing I can think of, but Harper could tell you better than I could."

"Then let's go back and see her," Donna said. "Because now that the Daemon Twins are gone, this needs to happen quickly."

"Perhaps after that, Your Majesty, you might spare me for an hour?" Marcus asked.

"Of course."

"Thank you. I need to take a statement from Fitzhugh."

Donna sighed. "For a time there, I actually forgot about him. I suppose that statement is part of the process of removing him?"

Marcus nodded. "His side must be represented if you want this process to be without reproach."

"Of course. Pierce is working on vetting the evidence against Fitzhugh, but with Artemis's children here, I'm not sure what, if anything, he's gotten done."

"I'll ask him. Fitzhugh has to be allowed to answer to any charges against him."

"Right," Donna said. "And I do want this all done by the book. There can't be any smell of impropriety in this or he'll just whine and cry about corruption. It'll make me look bad."

Cammie snorted. "You think anyone would really buy that coming from him?"

Donna nodded. "For those who are on his side? It's all they would need as a rallying cry against me and the new nation. I don't want to give them any excuse."

"You're right." Cammie held her hands up. "Keep it as proper and transparent as possible. Give him no ground to stand on."

Donna's stomach grumbled. She put her hand against it. "I don't feel hungry, but I guess I am."

"Mid-evening meal will be served in the main dining hall in approximately forty-five minutes," Marcus said.

Donna laughed. "You realize I have yet to eat a meal in this house since I've been here? I'm assuming all remaining guests will be there?"

"If they want to eat, they will be."

Donna thought about that. "Might be the perfect time to ask some of them to leave."

# CHAPTER 15

Cammie returned to the library while Donna walked with Marcus to the great room. While they walked, she arranged with Marcus for another meal to be catered in the library for her team. While she was doing that, Rico showed up.

"Did I miss all the excitement? I don't see anything broken and no holes in the walls."

Donna shook her head. "They left like it was their idea. With a couple of caveats, of course. That we look more closely at the letter they brought and that I invite them to the coronation, which isn't going to happen. They even threw in an apology for good measure. Blamed it all on their grief. You know, the grief that I guess also kept them from attending their mother's funeral."

Rico frowned. "You didn't buy any of that, did you?"

She shot him a look. "You should know me better than that."

He grinned. "I do."

"Listen, we need a statement from Fitzhugh. His side of the story about why he shouldn't be removed from office. Also, his explanation of where all the misappropriated funds went, once Pierce confirms they're gone. Do you think you could handle that? You're used to interrogating people. I figure you might be able to get something more out of him."

Rico nodded. "Sure, I can do that. Just let me know when."

"Marcus will keep you in the loop." She glanced at her deputy. "Right?"

"Yes, ma'am."

"Now," Donna said. "Any luck with the local pack?"

"Lots of it. They're happy to form a treaty with you and will send soldiers if you need them. All I have to do is call."

"Excellent. You've earned your dinner."

He rolled his eyes. "You're enjoying this a little too much."

She laughed. "I've only begun to enjoy this. But I'm serious. I need a companion for the mid-evening meal and all the rest of my team is busy doing other things or working in the library to figure out how to protect the house against the Daemon Twins. So you're my date. I hope you're hungry."

"I'm a werewolf. We never turn down food."

"Great. And just on time, here's Pierce. I want to see him before we go into the dining room." She waved at the reaper as he approached. "Find anything?"

"In their rooms?" He shook his head. "No. But I'm thinking we should send Neo up there to do a more thorough electronic sweep, just to be completely certain."

She nodded. "Might not be a bad idea to do that sweep in any room they were in."

"I'll get her on it."

"Thanks. I hate to remind you about other work, but where are you on those financial files that Claudette gave you?"

He took a breath. "Only halfway through. I'll get back to work on them as soon as I talk to Neo."

"Okay. I'm having a meal sent to the library for all of you. Rico's going with me to the mid-evening meal, where I plan to uninvite all the guests who really need to go home. Do you think you can get through those records in an hour? Because I'd really like to get Fitzhugh's statement and that can't be done until we can show him what he's up against."

Pierce nodded. "I absolutely can. It's not like anything's hidden in his personal books. It's all there in black and white. Claudette did us a big favor."

"I know she did." Donna leaned in and kissed his cheek. "Thank you for all of your help."

He smiled. "You're welcome."

"When you're done, find Rico or Marcus and give them the files on Fitzhugh. I'm going to have Rico take the statement."

Pierce glanced at Rico. "Putting all those years in the FBI to work, eh?"

"Got to do something to earn my keep around here." Rico stuck his hands in his pockets. "I'm happy to help with whatever."

"Good to know," Pierce said.

Marcus cleared his throat softly. "Ma'am, if you can give me a few minutes, we can go over the list of guests who are still here."

"Sure." She glanced at Rico. "Did you bring a jacket with you?"

"You mean a sportscoat? Yeah, I have one."

"You should probably wear it to the meal."

"And shave?"

Her gaze dropped to his stubble-shadowed jaw. "Wouldn't hurt."

"I have my orders."

As he left, Pierce took his leave as well. "I'll be in the library if you need me."

Donna exhaled. "All right." She turned to Marcus. "Show me who needs to go home and let's discuss how we're going to handle getting these people out of here."

Harper came in as they finished reviewing the list and deciding on the best way to ask folks to leave. She was practically glowing. "I figured out how to create the ward line. I need some supplies, but I can do it."

"What supplies?"

"More ashes. Particularly those from hawthorn and yew trees."

"We have both of those on the property," Marcus said. "We can get you as much ash as you need."

"Great," Harper said. "I'll also need black pepper."

"I'm sure one of the cooks can supply that." He

looked at Donna. "If you'll excuse me, I'll see to those things immediately."

"Yes, go." Donna turned back to Harper. "Thank you."

"I'm really happy I could do this."

Donna smiled. "That makes two of us. Tell me what I can do to help."

"Don't worry about it. I've got plenty of help. Although maybe you could round them up for me? I could use the guys to cut some of that wood, then it'll have to be chopped up into small pieces and burned. The smaller the pieces, the faster it'll burn."

Donna nodded and took out her phone. "They'll get it done." She sent a group text, asking for everyone available to meet in the library to help with preparations for the house protection spell.

Then she looked at Harper again. "Now, I need to get myself ready to tell most of the current guests that they need to leave."

Harper grimaced. "Trying to make room for the governors who are coming in for the coronation, huh?"

"Yes. So not only will they be mad at me for kicking them out, but they'll be extra mad when they find out they don't get to attend the coronation in person."

Harper shrugged. "So let them. They need you more than you need them."

Donna stood as she thought about that. "Good point. It's sometimes hard to remember that my new position gives me much greater authority. Those who get to stay are the ones who matter the most. The rest would do well to focus on why they haven't been invited to stay."

The sound of slow clapping interrupted them as Queen Francesca walked into the great hall. "Very good, Donna. That is a smart thing to keep in mind. Your power and your position."

"Thanks, Francesca. Are you joining us for the meal?"

"I am."

Harper backed away. "I need to get to work. Thank you for your help."

Donna nodded. "I'll make sure Marcus brings you that pepper."

"Great." With a wave, Harper disappeared out the door.

"How are things going?" Francesca asked. "I understand Artemis's children were here?"

"Yes, but they're gone now."

"I assume one of them thought the throne belonged to them?"

"Very astute. That's exactly what happened. They presented a letter supposedly from Artemis, but it smelled fishy. Then, after making threats and promising trouble, they suddenly had a change of heart, apologized, and left. I'm pretty sure that means they're on to Plan B. Whatever that is."

Francesca frowned. "That's not good."

"No, I'm sure it isn't, but we're preparing for it.

Harper, who just left, is working on a spell of protection for the house specifically designed to keep them from reentering."

"Good." Francesca smiled. "You don't waste time, do you?"

"I try not to."

"How are the plans for the coronation coming?"

"Slowly." Donna blew out a breath. "There's so much else to do."

"Such as?"

Donna glanced at the floor. "Well, Fitzhugh is in a cell in the basement and he needs to be dealt with. We need to appoint a new council. There are other rulers who want to join the new nation, like the Russian king, who I'm supposed to talk to. Additionally, we should probably put some kind of mission statement together. I need to appoint a governor of New Jersey to replace me. Then there's—"

Francesca put her hands on Donna's shoulders. "My dear friend. King Lucho and I can handle the council and the mission statement. We'll draft a list of names for the council and come up with a preliminary statement and get them to you in a day or two for you to look over. Will that help?"

Donna smiled. "Yes. So much. Thank you."

"You are not in this alone."

"Something else I need to remember."

Francesca dropped her hands. "I can help with the coronation planning, as well."

"I'm sure Marcus would appreciate that. He's probably got more on his plate than I have on mine."

"When will it be?"

"Five days from now. Or five days from whenever the announcement is sent out."

Francesca made a face that clearly seemed to question that decision. "So soon?"

Donna nodded. "It needs to be. The sooner that's done with, the sooner everything else can move forward."

"And the more protected you'll be. I understand. Sooner is better. You may technically be queen, but once the ceremony takes place and that crown is put on your head, it becomes very real. To everyone."

"I certainly hope so."

Rico walked back in. Not only had he shaved, but he'd combed his hair and put on a suit. Charcoal, with a crisp white shirt open at the neck. He looked *very* nice.

Francesca apparently thought so, too, judging by the sparkle in her eyes and the width of her grin. "Hello, there."

Donna figured she'd better do the intros right away. "Queen Francesca, this is my friend, Rico Medina. Soon to be the alpha-elect of the New Jersey pack."

She extended her hand. "*El hombre lobo.*"

He took her hand and kissed her knuckles, the briefest gleam of wolf in his eyes. "At your service, Your Majesty."

Donna almost rolled her eyes. "Rico will be joining me for the meal, if you'd like to sit with us."

"Thank you, I would like that very much." Francesca continued to hold Rico's hand. Or maybe it was the other way around.

Either way, Donna didn't care. Rico might be here to serve at her pleasure for a year to pay off his life debt to her, but that didn't mean she was going to get romantically involved with him. If he wanted to pursue Francesca, and she was willing, more power to them.

The natural chemistry between vampires and werewolves was a well-known fact.

Donna had felt some of that chemistry in the early days of being turned. But lately, Pierce had captured her attention in a way he never had before.

He was exceptionally good to her. As handsome as a man could be. And loyal to the core.

Meanwhile, Rico might sniff around Donna and say the right things, but watching him with Francesca was a good reminder that he truly was a wolf at heart.

It made her realize that while she might find Rico attractive, she was actually in love with Pierce. And not just in a deeply platonic kind of way.

"Why don't you two go ahead and get seated?" Donna said. "I just remembered something I need to do. I'll join you shortly."

Rico offered Francesca his arm. "May I escort you to dinner, Your Highness?"

"By all means." She looked over her shoulder at Donna. "We'll see you in the dining hall."

Donna nodded, then made for the library.

The front table had been covered in white linen and a small buffet set up with covered chafing dishes. The meal she'd requested for her staff and friends. Except there wasn't anyone there. They must have left to work on the ingredients for the protection spell. But Pierce was supposed to be going over Fitzhugh's financials.

She was about to leave when she heard a sigh. She took two steps to the right and realized Pierce sat at a desk against the far wall, which had been blocked from view by an easel holding a framed piece of art. He had a laptop open in front of him, a pen and an open notebook covered in notes. He was adding more, his brow furrowed in thought.

She smiled and walked toward him.

He looked up instantly and smiled back. "I thought you were going to dinner to deliver the bad news to the guests who've overstayed their welcome."

She laughed. "I am. But there was something I needed to do first."

He pushed his chair back to face her better. "Oh? What's that?"

"This." She sat on his lap, took his face in her hands, and kissed him. Soundly. Until she was sure that he understood her feelings for him.

When she leaned back, he stared up at her without saying a word. He blinked twice.

She smiled. "I should go to dinner now."

He nodded. "Okay."

It amused her how he seemed slightly dazed. To wake him up, she kissed him again. "See you after?"

He nodded.

"I love you, you know."

"I love you, too."

"And I'm so glad." Still smiling, she got up and walked out. With a man like Pierce at her side, there was nothing she couldn't accomplish.

# CHAPTER 16

The meal went smoothly. Rico and Francesca kept each other happily engaged in conversation. Donna was glad for that. It gave her a chance to go over the statement she and Marcus had prepared—at least when guests weren't stopping by their table to congratulate her on ascending to the throne. Most of them seemed sincere. Some seemed like they were putting in a last bid to stay for the coronation.

Didn't matter. She wasn't budging. She needed space for the governors and a few other dignitaries, although the governors took priority. They had to. According to Marcus, they would be required to pledge their fealty to her.

A rather ancient tradition, but the vampire world was rife with old rituals. It would be a good test to see who meant it and who was going through the motions. A way of gauging their support.

Then there was the matter of Fitzhugh. Obviously, she was going to replace him. But with whom? She had one idea but nothing concrete. And what was she going to do with him once he was removed from office? Ban him from his state? Let him live elsewhere in infamy?

Maybe he'd retreat to Europe. Marcus said he had a

lot of connections there. But would that just cause a pocket of hate to form against her?

Because there was no doubt in her mind that Fitzhugh wasn't going to take being unseated lightly. He'd retaliate in some way. That was just his nature. She'd seen it time and time again.

She was sure he was right now foaming at the mouth in that cell, eager to get a crack at her.

Well, he wasn't going to get it. She never needed to see him again. Marcus had told her as much.

She pushed her plate away. The chicken Kiev, wild rice, and glazed carrots had been lovely, but nerves had dampened her appetite. Besides, dessert was being carried out. Lemon cake with fresh raspberries dusted in rosemary sugar. The last course. And the sign that it was time for her first official announcement as queen. She took a sip of water, then stood.

Almost instantly, the conversation at the rest of the tables went quiet. Amazing to think that they'd been watching her that closely. Cammie's words about royal protocol rang in Donna's ears. "Ladies and gentlemen, I hope you all enjoyed your meal."

Lots of nods and smiles. She watched the faces. Tried to memorize the ones who weren't so eager to please.

"As you know, this estate will be hosting my coronation very soon. And as much as we wish you could all attend in person, we simply don't have room with all of the governors due to arrive. If you are not a governor, or you have not yet received an invitation to stay, we ask that you please have a safe trip home. Anyone needing transportation help, please see Marcus. Have a good night."

She counted plenty of sour expressions. Some looked disappointed. Others like they didn't care. A few got up to leave immediately, ignoring dessert. Not her. She sat back down, and a plate of cake appeared before her. She picked up her fork, completely ready to reward herself for getting through that.

Francesca leaned over. "Well done."

"Thank you. That wasn't as hard as I thought it would be."

"Isn't the royal we a remarkable pronoun? Makes everything seem like a decision by committee." Francesca laughed.

Donna joined her, nodding. "Yes, I agree. It's a great thing." She dug into her cake and made short work of it, thankful for her vampire metabolism. If she had to worry about fitting into a coronation dress on top of everything else, she'd probably run screaming for the hills.

Not that Kansas had any hills.

Was this really about to be her life? In this enormous estate? With more staff and rooms than she could count? How bizarre. She felt like a stranger looking through a window at someone else.

But that someone else was her, and this really was her life.

She finished the last bite, laid her fork across her plate, and got up to leave. Rico got to his feet as well. She shook her head. "You can stay if you like. Doesn't matter to me. I have a lot of work to do."

Francesca patted his hand. "Sit. Keep me company while I have coffee."

Rico glanced at Donna. "You're sure?"

She nodded. "Positive."

She went directly to the library. Cammie had returned, as had Charlie and Neo. All three worked on laptops. Bunni was sprawled out on a chaise reading a magazine. Francine sat on one of the couches, crocheting. "Where are all the guys?"

"With Harper," Cammie answered. "Burning the wood she needs for the spell, turning it into ash. How did the announcement go over?"

"All right. Except for dirty looks, no one threw anything at me."

Francine smiled. "That's good. Although if they had, you could have yelled, 'Off with their heads!'" She laughed. "I've always wanted to yell that."

"Probably good you aren't the queen, then," Donna said as she laughed. She went to sit beside Francine. Whatever she was crocheting looked vaguely familiar. "I have a question for you."

Francine held up her work. "It's a bunny rabbit for your new grandbaby."

"Aw, that's very sweet. Thank you. But that wasn't my question."

"Well, ask away, honey. Anything."

Donna took a breath. "How are things with you and Lionel?"

"They're just fine. I miss him, though. We haven't been apart this long in a while. Even when he tours I see him as much as I can. I get the feeling he's about ready for a change."

"Oh? What happened with that movie deal he went to L.A. about?"

"It's just a cameo part, but he wants to do it. Probably going to take a week or so. But that might be his last big thing for a while." Her fingers worked the buttery yellow yarn with amazing speed. "He says when you get to be as ancient a vampire as he is, you need some fallow years. That's what he calls them. Years where you lay low and let people forget about you. Otherwise, the fact that you don't age and never die starts to stick in people's minds."

"Fallow years. I like that term. I guess I'm too young to have thought about that yet."

Francine smiled. "We both are."

"So you think he's ready for that change now? Even with how successful the band is?"

Francine shrugged. "Sure. The band would forgive him. Especially with the kind of publicity the movie will create, which will sell albums like nobody's business, and the money he'd give them to soften the blow. Why? You have something in mind?"

Donna nodded. "I do. How do you think Lionel would like to be the governor of New York?"

Francine's mouth fell open and she stared blankly at Donna for a couple of beats. Finally, she smiled. "Oh, honey, I think he'd just love that."

Donna grinned. "And that would make you the First Lady of New York."

"Boy, that suits me, don't you think?"

"With the kind of parties you throw? Absolutely."

Francine's expression went back to being serious. "Wait. Is this for real? Or are you just testing the water? Is he one of many possibilities?"

"Nope. He's my first choice. And my only choice. If you like, I'll call him right now and make the offer. Of course, it's not official until Fitzhugh is removed and I make the announcement, but that's just a matter of days."

Francine set down her crochet yarn and took out her phone. She tapped away at the screen. "There. I sent you his number."

"Thanks." Donna picked up her phone as it vibrated with the incoming text. "I'm going to call him." She hit dial, then put the phone to her ear.

"Hello?"

"Lionel, this is Belladonna Barrone."

"How are you, Governor? Although Frankie tells me I should be calling you something different."

Donna smiled. "It's true. I'm not the governor anymore. I guess you could say I've been promoted."

"Congratulations, Your Highness. I'm thrilled for you. And about all the changes Frankie's been telling me you're making."

"Thank you. I'm glad to hear you say that, because the reason I'm calling is about one of those changes."

"All right. I'm all ears."

"If you're interested, I'd like to appoint you as the new governor of New York."

A short moment of silence passed. "That's a huge honor, that you would think of me. Thank you for that."

"You're welcome." She smiled at Francine, who seemed to be hanging on every word. "But it's because I truly believe you're the right person for the job. You've got the age to give you experience, you clearly know how to work a crowd and make people happy, and from the way you are with Francine, I know that you're kind and thoughtful and concerned about the well-being of those around you. Also, Francine will make an exceptional First Lady."

"That she will. Does she know about this?"

"She does. In fact, she's sitting right next to me."

"Would you mind if I speak with her?"

"Not at all. I'll give her the phone." She held it out to Francine. "He wants to talk to you."

Francine took the phone. "Hi, sweetheart." She nodded. "Yes, she told me all about it." More nodding. "I do. You'd be great at it. And I would help you. Whatever you needed." A few more seconds passed. "All right, then. Love you, too."

She handed the phone back to Donna. "He wants to talk to you again."

Donna put the phone to her ear. "I'm here."

"I humbly accept."

"I'm so glad! Thank you!" She couldn't stop smiling. "Now, this won't happen until I deal with Fitzhugh, but as soon as I do, I'll let you know. Then I'll make the official announcement. In fact, if you'd like to come out for the coronation, that might be a great time for all of that to happen."

She winked at Francine. "Not to mention, I know a certain someone who'd love to see you."

"I'll *make* it happen. Thank you again."

"You're very welcome. See you soon." She hung up, exhaling in relief. "I'm so glad he said yes. He's going to be a fantastic governor."

Francine looked teary-eyed. "Oh, he is. He'll be the best, I promise. Thank you. And I'm so excited he's coming out here. Thank you for inviting him."

"I thought you'd like that." What Donna liked even more was that one of her To Dos was well on its way to being Done.

# CHAPTER 17

Harper came in a few minutes later, a smear of ash near her temple. The men all filed in behind her, a few of them smudged with ash as well. "The spell is ready. We could use everyone's help getting the ward line in place around the house." She looked at Donna. "Except for you. We all agreed you're the one with the most to lose. The one they'd want to hurt the most. You should stay inside. If it's okay for me to say that."

"It is, of course." Donna frowned as the women around her got up to join Harper's group. "You really think I'm in that much danger?"

"No," Pierce answered. He'd changed into jeans and a canvas jacket with a thick T-shirt underneath. She loved him in a suit, but it was nice to see him looking casual. "But we're not taking any chances."

She wanted to argue, but now that she was queen, she knew things had to change. The way she was protected was one of those things. "Okay. I'll stay inside. But I need to do something."

Bunni, who was moving about as slowly as possible to join the others, came to a complete stop. "I could stay behind. Help you organize your new apartment."

Francine frowned. "Bunni, we're all helping outside. Come on, now. You can do it."

With a put-upon sigh, Bunni dragged herself the rest of the way over to join the group.

Neo nodded at Donna. "I just finished proofing those financials Pierce gave me. You want to look at them while we're outside?"

"The stuff on Fitzhugh? Yes, absolutely."

Neo grabbed her laptop and put it on the coffee table in front of Donna. "There you go."

"Thanks," Donna said. "You realize most of this won't make that much sense to me, so I might need one of you to explain a few things when you get back."

"No problem," Pierce said.

"Good." She shifted to Rico. "Then you're ready to tell him what he's up against and get his statement?"

"I am."

She nodded. "I'll be happy to have this over and done with."

"We all will," Charlie said.

"When the spell is done, maybe you, me, and Marcus can get to work on some coronation stuff. I'd like to knock some of that out tonight, if we can."

"That would be great." Charlie closed her laptop and stood.

"Agreed," Marcus said. "We definitely need to get the invites out at the minimum."

"Then that's tonight's task." Donna gave them all a smile. "Thank you, Harper, for figuring out this spell.

And thank you all for helping. We'll sleep better once this is taken care of, don't you think?"

They all nodded.

Harper turned to her troops. "All right, men take the front of the house, women take the back. There are buckets of the salt and ash mix by the doors. Everyone grab one and spread it around the house. Surround it all. Make sure there's no break in the line or the ward will be breachable. Normally, the ward would go into a trench but the ground is frozen solid and covered with snow, so we're just going to do the best we can."

After they departed, Donna scrolled through the spreadsheets on the laptop's screen. She really didn't know what she was looking at. Just lots of figures. Some negative ones in red. Were those the amounts that Fitzhugh had siphoned off?

If so, it was a lot of money.

She paged down to the final totals, and let out a low whistle at the figure in red. Was that correct? Nearly fifty million dollars over the last twelve years? The amount was staggering. So was the idea that he'd been getting away with it.

If he had any personal assets, they would be forfeit to pay off that debt, but something told her he probably couldn't cover that amount.

Lionel was going to be taking over a mess. Good thing he had his own money and Francine's incredible townhouse. The New York governor's penthouse might need to sell a floor to stay solvent. Or all of it.

How had Fitzhugh even bought that place at the Montevetro? Not only was the building fairly new but it was on the Upper East Side in a very desirable part of town, making it prime real estate. Maybe it was mortgaged to the hilt.

Maybe Fitzhugh had been mortgaging it for his own use. She was going to have to get someone to look into that. Charlie, most likely.

Donna frowned and sat back. Had Artemis known what a mess Fitzhugh was making of things? Donna hoped not, because if the late queen had, that also meant she'd allowed him to stay in power despite his embezzling.

That didn't sit well with Donna. She wanted to have kind thoughts about the late queen. To never have to speak ill of the dead. Especially of the woman who was partially responsible for Donna being where she was today.

Donna felt like there was so much she didn't know about Artemis. Her children were a great example of that. Donna had no idea Arty even had kids. With a demon baby daddy, no less.

That was more than a little troubling.

Maybe Marcus could tell her more. Or maybe he wouldn't want to share. Hard to say.

It would be nice to know if there were any other skeletons in Artemis's closet.

She glanced at the ceiling, her thoughts shifting to the enormous closet she and Pierce had begun to go through. Maybe wearing one of Artemis's dresses *wasn't* the best statement to make at the coronation.

She sighed and got up, going to the windows. The house was well-illuminated and the reflection from the snow made it even brighter. From the angle of the library, she could see Kace and Temo working their way around the right side of the house, Pierce and Marcus on the left.

Then, at the very edge of where the light faded, something moved in the shadows. She shook her head, wondering if it was just a trick of the light. Maybe just some kind of nocturnal animal. Or her overworked mind imagining things.

She looked at Kace and Temo again, paying close attention to the line where the light met the dark. That line seemed to ebb and flow. Almost as if the darkness was alive.

Her gaze went back to Pierce and Marcus. The same thing happened near them.

A chill went through her that had nothing to do with the snow on the ground. She ran to the great hall and looked out the French doors, trying to find the women. Cammie was just coming across the terrace, sprinkling a line of ash and salt next to the house.

Donna opened the door, but kept her voice down. "Hey."

Cammie looked up. "Hey."

"Have you…seen anything in the dark out there?"

Cammie glanced over her shoulder. "Like bogeymen?"

"I'm serious."

Cammie went back to sprinkling. "I am, too. They're real you know. And no, I haven't seen anything."

A scream cut through the night air.

Cammie dropped her bucket and whipped out a blade from her boot. "Stay inside. And shut the door."

Before Donna could react, Cammie pushed the door closed, forcing her back inside. Then Cammie ran off toward the scream.

Donna pressed herself to the glass, trying to see. Even with her enhanced vision, there was no penetrating the darkness beyond the lights. There was no moon or stars to help, either. Not with the cloud cover.

She felt like she might hyperventilate. Her heart pounded. Not knowing what was going on was sheer torture.

She didn't have to wait long. Several people came running toward the terrace. Kace was front and center.

And he had Bunni in his arms.

Cammie ran ahead of him and opened the door. "Get back, Donna."

"What's going on?" She retreated deeper into the room.

Kace came in, Bunni draped over his arms. Her hot pink puffer coat was slashed across the chest and one arm, oozing white stuffing as if she was a giant rag doll that had split its seams. He went straight to the nearest couch.

"What happened?" Donna asked as Marcus came in behind Kace.

He shook his head. "She was attacked by something. So was one of the security team. He didn't make it. There was nothing left of him but ashes."

Donna's stomach fell. "Oh, no. That's terrible."

Cammie finally came in. She glanced at Donna and shook her head like there was bad news to be shared, but she didn't want to do it just yet.

Next in was Temo and Neo with Francine and Charlie. Francine had a trickle of blood on her cheek, but the wound that had caused it had already healed.

Donna sucked in a breath. "Francine, are you okay?"

She nodded, but looked shaken. "I'm all right. Need to sit down for a minute though. Catch my breath."

"You want a drink?" That seemed the least Donna could do.

"Bourbon," Francine answered as Temo helped her to a chair near the fire.

Donna went to the bar to get the drink.

Cammie met her there.

Donna looked at her sister. "What happened out there?"

Cammie's steely expression revealed nothing. She glanced toward the windows and the darkness beyond. "I'd say we're being scouted for weaknesses. We need to get that salt mixture in place and that spell finished."

"Scouted? By who?"

"Not a who," Cammie answered as she made eye contact with Donna again. "A what. And more than one. Demons. Lots of them. And I'd guess there's even more on the way."

# Chapter 18

Donna poured Francine's bourbon. "The Daemon Twins are behind this. They have to be."

"Seems like the most logical explanation," Cammie answered.

Marcus glared at the darkness outside. "Their hasty exit makes so much sense now."

"They'll pay, you can believe that." Donna took the drink and a damp cloth to Francine. "You have a little blood on your cheek."

Francine accepted the drink. "Did they get me?"

"Here," Charlie said. "Let me help." She took the cloth from Donna.

"Thanks." Donna went straight to Bunni. Kace held her hand and Marcus was tapping away at his phone, presumably getting help. Bunni seemed unresponsive. Donna felt gutted. "Is she going to be all right?"

Kace shook his head, more concern on his face than Donna would have expected, considering how Bunni had been getting on his nerves lately.

Marcus looked up from his phone. "I've asked Dr. Ogden to come as soon as he can. He was Artemis's physician, not that she ever really needed him. Hopefully, he'll be able to tell us something. He knows a great deal about supernaturals."

"So does my guy. Too bad he's not here." Dr. Fox had never let Donna down.

Marcus pressed his palm to Bunni's forehead. "She seems warm to me."

"Me, too," Kace said. He squeezed Bunni's hand.

"Like a fever?" Donna frowned. "You don't think she's sick, do you? I thought she was attacked. Look at her coat. Something obviously did that."

"She was definitely attacked." Marcus glanced at her. "And I don't think she's sick so much as…" He sighed. "I hesitate to say it."

"Out with it," Donna said. "We don't have time for hesitation."

Marcus nodded. "Of course you're right. I believe she might be infected."

Donna recoiled slightly. "With what?"

"Demons are nasty creatures," Cammie answered. "If they can't possess you, they'll infect you." She walked over, nodding at Kace. "Open her coat. See if they managed to break the skin."

Kace unzipped Bunni's partially exploded puffer coat. The white bedazzled tank top she had on underneath was just as destroyed. It and her hot pink bra were stippled with blood. Wounds were visible beneath the shredded fabric.

Donna's heart sank. "That's not good, is it?"

"No," Cammie said quietly. "She's not healing like she should because of the toxins. Demons carry their poison in their claws and teeth." She looked at Marcus. "How good is this Dr. Ogden?"

"Very good," Marcus answered. "The best. He was the queen's official physician, after all."

Cammie nodded. "He'd better be good. He's going to have to be to save her."

"I feel just awful," Francine said. "This is all my fault."

"I'm sure that's not true," Charlie said.

"But it is," Francine argued. "Something came at me out of the dark. Did this to me." She tapped a finger against her cheek. "But Bunni jumped in front of me before it could attack again. That's how it got her."

Donna froze. "So whatever attacked Bunni cut your cheek?"

Everyone turned to look at Francine.

Charlie put her hand on Francine's forehead, then nodded. "She's warm, too."

Nausea swept through Donna. She pointed at Marcus. "Tell that doctor to step on it. I'll pay his speeding tickets."

He nodded and took out his phone again.

She moved on to Cammie. "You must know something that will help them."

"Humans, yes. Vampires?" Cammie shook her head. "I've never had to save a vampire from a demon infection."

"Well, you do now. What do you need?"

Cammie made a face. "I don't think what works on humans will work on Bunni and Francine."

"Why not?"

"Well, for one thing, it involves a lot of holy water and crosses."

Donna swallowed. That wasn't going to work. "We have to do something."

"You're right," Cammie said. "We do. But we also need to get Harper's spell finished or nothing else is going to matter. The house will be overrun."

"I don't see how we can finish it." Donna glanced toward the windows, praying she saw nothing move out there.

"We can," Cammie countered. "We just can't send any vampires out to help. That's who the demons are targeting."

"You're sure?"

"No, but demons are pretty narrow-minded. If they've been summoned to take down vampires, that's what they're going to focus on."

"There are a few humans on staff," Marcus said. "I can get them."

"No." Cammie seemed adamant. "Humans are too easily possessed. The demons would only take control of them and use them to get inside. Any other non-human, non-vampires around?"

Marcus nodded. "A few, including two coyote shifters."

"Get them here," Cammie said. "With them, Temo, Harper, Kace, Pierce, Rico, and myself, we'll finish the border of salt and ash. Shouldn't take us more than forty-five minutes. Maybe an hour. Any extra lights you can turn on outside would help. Demons aren't especially fond of bright light, which means if we can last until morning, we should be all right. They'll retreat then."

That was something to cling to, Donna supposed.

Marcus sent the message on his phone before answering Cammie. "We'll turn on everything we have. There are lights around the stables as well." His phone buzzed. "Bianca and David are on their way here."

"What about Hector?" Pierce asked. "He's not human."

Donna frowned. She hadn't seen the sandman in a while, but he'd been keeping a fairly low profile, so it hadn't worried her. "Is he still on Lionel's tour bus?"

Pierce nodded. "As far as I know."

"We can't leave him out there. He should be in the house with us."

"I'll get him." Pierce started for the door.

"Thanks," Donna said. "Cammie. Do you think he could use his magic to put the demons to sleep?"

Cammie shook her head. "Demons don't sleep. Ever. They hibernate during daylight but it's not sleep the way we know it. Good thought, though."

Donna sighed. "I'm glad you're here. We'd be lost

without you. None of us know as much about demons as you do."

"I'll do whatever I can to help."

"Thank you," Charlie said. "Because we're going to need it."

"That's for sure." Donna looked at her sister again. "Think, Cammie. Is there anything we can do for Francine and Bunni before the doctor gets here?"

Cammie glanced at Bunni, then Francine, who was at least upright. "How do you feel?"

Francine tried to smile. "Not so great, but not as bad as Bunni. I guess I got less of the poison than she did."

"I think so." Cammie looked at Donna. "It would probably help if they could both feed. The fresher the source, the better."

Donna sighed. "We'd need a human donor for that."

"I'm sure the humans on staff would be willing," Marcus said. "They knew who they were coming to work for when they joined the queen's staff."

"All right," Donna said. "Get them here, too."

As he called the humans, two middle-aged people came in, a man and a woman. Both had dark hair, sharp brown eyes, and slim, wiry builds. They bowed to Donna.

"Thank you for coming," she said. "You must be David and Bianca."

"We are, Your Majesty," the man said. "Marcus said

you needed us to help with something outside. We are at your service."

"Thank you," Donna answered. "We're spreading a ward line around the house to protect it against daemons. And now apparently demons." She gestured at Harper. "This is Harper. She built the magic. Do as she instructs."

David and Bianca nodded. "Yes, Your Majesty."

"Come on," Cammie said. "Let's get this done."

Harper headed for the door. "And as quickly as possible."

As the rest of the team followed them, Donna went to Bunni's side and took the young woman's limp hand in her own. "She feels really warm."

"I imagine the fever will intensify as the infection spreads." Marcus lifted Bunni's head to slip a pillow underneath. "Dr. Ogden will be here in fifteen minutes."

"Good." She glanced at Francine, who remained sitting in the chair. Neo had taken Charlie's place and was kneeling in front of her, talking softly and keeping an eye on her. "And the human staff?"

"They're day shift but they're getting up and coming downstairs."

"Give them whatever bonus you think appropriate for their willingness to help."

"That's very kind. I'll see that they're properly compensated."

"What about our remaining vampire guests? A lot of them are packing right now and preparing to leave."

"We'll get them safely into their cars and they should be fine, but I'll make sure they all know what's going on. Once they've been warned, the decision to leave during the attack should be up to them."

"Agreed. We aren't going to put anyone out of the safety of the house against their will." Donna sighed. "It's always something, isn't it?"

"I promise, there are some calm moments."

"I'll believe you when I see them for myself." She shook her head as her attention returned to the young woman in front of her. "Bunni won't be able to drink."

"No," Marcus said. "But I imagine Dr. Ogden will be able to give her a transfusion or something."

Will got up and walked to the hearth. "Is there anything I can do? I feel useless."

"Put another log on that fire," Donna suggested.

He did that, sending a small shower of sparks up the chimney. "Now what?"

Francine lifted a shaky hand. "Maybe you could carry me over to the couch? I'm not feeling so good."

He rushed to her side as she started to slump forward. Neo caught her and helped her into Will's arms.

"We should get them both up to their rooms and into their beds where they can be comfortable," Donna said. If anything happened to either woman, she would have Lillis and Yavi hunted down and made to pay.

Actually, that was already going to happen. She couldn't allow an attack like this to go unanswered. Not when they'd caused the death of a member of the security team and injured her friends. "Have those room assignments been made?"

Marcus nodded. "They have. Follow me."

# Chapter 19

Neo helped Francine get changed and into bed while Donna saw to Bunni. Marcus had already arranged for their bags to be brought up, so Donna opened Bunni's suitcase and dug around until she found something for her to sleep in.

Turned out to be a Hello Kitty shortie pajama set. Not all that surprising.

Donna got Bunni out of her shredded clothing, washed the remaining blood off her, being careful of the wounds, then got her dressed in the pajamas and tucked under the covers.

Donna sat on the edge of the bed and watched the younger woman, wishing that her abilities extended to healing.

Bunni had to be all right. She just had to be. So did Francine. Guilt wracked Donna. They were here because of her. They'd been outside because of her. Yes, they'd chosen to come on this trip, but there was no way this wasn't her fault.

Lillis and Yavi would pay. She didn't know how yet, but they would.

A soft knock on the door pulled her concentration away.

She glanced at it. "Come in."

Marcus entered with a young man in a white lab coat. He had neatly combed red hair and a smattering of freckles that his glasses did nothing to hide. He didn't look old enough to be in college, let alone be a doctor. "Your Majesty, this is Dr. Ogden."

Donna frowned without meaning to. "Hello."

The young man smiled knowingly. "I realize I'm not what you expected. I'm not what anyone expects. I assure you, I know what I'm doing. I'm also far older than I look. Pixie blood. It's the fountain of youth. A blessing and a curse, you might say."

"Oh." Donna offered her hand. The doctor shook it. "Thank you for the explanation. And for coming on short notice. Did Marcus explain what is going on?"

"He did." Dr. Ogden looked past her at Bunni. "May I examine the patient?"

"Of course. Do you need anything?"

"Not at the moment, no." He went right to Bunni, taking her temperature first thing.

Marcus turned his back to Bunni while he spoke to Donna, presumably to give her privacy during the exam. "The human staff are here. I've sent Michael to Francine's room, as she's still lucid. I've let Dr. Ogden know that Anita is available for Bunni."

"Good. Thank you." She watched Ogden as he examined Bunni's wounds. After a few more minutes, he was done.

He covered Bunni up, then faced Donna. "The fresh

blood will help. There are a few medications we can try but this isn't a typical infection we're dealing with."

"I understand. Tell us what you want done and we'll see that it happens."

He nodded. "In Francine's case, regular feedings should do the trick. It might take as long as thirty-six hours, but I believe she'll make a full recovery."

"And Bunni?"

"Blood will help her as well, but obviously she can't intake fluids on her own right now. I would like to set up an IV and give her regular transfusions."

Donna shook her head. "That's fine, but I don't think any of us know how to do that."

Dr. Ogden smiled. "I don't plan on leaving until this crisis is over, Your Majesty."

Donna exhaled. "Thank you. Whatever you need, just let us know. How soon do you need the blood?"

"I can have the IV set up in a few minutes, so anytime would be fine. Is the donor ready?"

Marcus nodded. "She is."

"Then go ahead and send her in."

"I will," Marcus said. "Can we get you anything, Dr. Ogden? Something to eat or drink?"

"When I'm done here, a cup of coffee with lots of sugar would not be unwelcome."

Donna smiled. "I'll make sure there's a fresh pot at the bar in the great hall, but if you want it brought up, that's fine, too."

"I'll come down when I'm done. I can give you an update that way as well."

"That would be appreciated." She glanced at Marcus. "I'm going to check in on Francine, then I'm going downstairs. They should be nearly done laying that ward line."

"Very good, Your Majesty. I'll get Anita in here and see to anything else the doctor needs."

Donna went across the hall to Francine's room. She was tucked into bed, sitting up and looking reasonably well. Pale, maybe, but nothing like what Bunni was going through. A middle-aged man sat in a chair beside the bed, rolling his shirt sleeve down. Neo stood by the window, looking out.

The man got up and bowed to Donna. "Your Highness."

"Please, sit. You must be Michael."

He stayed standing. "I am."

"Thank you for helping Francine. I greatly appreciate it."

He smiled. "I'm happy to help."

"Good, because she's going to need you again before this is over." Donna looked at Francine. "How are you feeling?"

"Better. Michael helped a lot."

"Well, Dr. Ogden is coming in to check on you. It seems you have a ways to go before you're officially done with this. Let me know if you need anything."

"Honey, you have enough on your plate without having to worry about me."

"Nothing is going to stop me from worrying about you or Bunni."

Michael cleared his throat softly. "Your Highness, I would be happy to stay with Miss Francine if she'd like. I typically work in the kitchen, but I can take care of anything she needs."

"Oh, that would be fun," Francine said. "Maybe we could find a movie to watch. I love that Dwayne Johnson. He used to be a wrestler, you know."

Neo snorted. "Pretty sure everyone knows that, Francine. I can hang with you, too. Keep you company."

Donna smiled. Francine sure sounded like her old self, but she wondered how long that would last when the new blood in her system wore off. "If you're willing to stay, that would be wonderful, Michael. Thank you."

"You're welcome, Your Highness."

Dr. Ogden came to the door and Donna stepped out of the way. "I'll see you later, Francine. Do as the doctor says."

"We'll see," she countered with a wink and a grin. Her smile faltered when she saw Dr. Ogden. "My lands, how old are you? You don't look like you've lost the smell of your diapers."

Shaking her head, Donna ducked back out into the hall. Francine would be fine. Bunni, on the other hand... With a heavy heart, she glanced at the young woman's door before heading downstairs.

No one from the warding team was back yet. She walked to the great hall's bank of French doors and peered out. The snow was coming down again, making visibility hard. She stared into the darkness, looking for any signs of movement, but the drifting flakes made her see things that weren't there.

At least she didn't think they were.

She went back behind the bar and started a fresh pot of coffee. That probably broke some kind of royal protocol, but she didn't care.

As the brew began to percolate, she heard the front door open and close and the stomping of feet. She went to the foyer, her gaze instantly finding Cammie and Pierce in the group. The warding team was back. She was glad to see Hector with them. Snow dusted their hats and coats and clung to their boots. "All done? Everyone safe?"

Harper nodded. "Everyone's safe and the house is secure."

"I'm so happy to hear that. Did you...see anything?"

"Yes," Pierce said. "But they kept their distance, thankfully. How are Francine and Bunni?"

"Dr. Ogden is doing everything he can for them. Francine will be fine, I'm sure. Bunni's condition is more serious."

"I might go up and sit with her," Kace said. "If you think that would be all right."

Donna smiled. "I think there's nothing she'd like more."

As they talked, a handful of funeral guests walked into the foyer, trailed by household staff carrying their bags. Donna had more questions to ask Harper, but now was not the time. She looked at the guests.

The man in front, Governor Martindale of Connecticut, nodded at her.

"Governor Martindale." She'd seen him with Fitzhugh and thought they were friends, but didn't know if that friendship also implied allegiance. Either way, she would be cautious around him until she knew more about where his loyalties lay.

"Your Majesty, we've been made aware of the situation. I am very sorry about it, and while I am staying for the coronation, I am sending most of my staff home."

"I understand." He was staying. He wasn't so much a friend of Fitzy's that he'd disrespect his new queen, then.

Martindale glanced at the members of her team, who were brushing off snow and stripping off their coats, then back at her. "Is it safe to go out there?"

"I wouldn't linger, but it should be." She looked at Harper. "Don't you agree?"

Harper nodded. "I do agree. In fact, we warded the area around the covered driveway, too, because we thought people might be leaving. As long as the vehicles are pulled under that section, it will be safe. For a time, anyway."

"How thoughtful. Thank you." Donna turned her smile on Martindale. "There you have it. Feel free to let the others know."

He nodded. "I will. Thank you."

One of the household staff offered to fetch any non-vampire help available to bring the vehicles around and he gave them the go-ahead.

With that, she turned back to her team. "Thank you for your hard work. I'm sure that wasn't fun. Why don't you all come into the great hall?"

They seemed to understand that the foyer wasn't the most private of areas and followed her into the big room.

As soon as the doors were shut, she asked the rest of her pressing questions. "What did you mean the covered driveway will be safe 'for a time'? How long will this ward last? Will the snow interfere?"

Harper sighed. "What I mean is that I can't really say how long the ward will last. The snow could definitely degrade it." She looked at the floor, shaking her head. "I'm really sorry. There's not much I can do about the snow."

"I understand that. No one blames you for the weather." But Donna needed to know more. "Will it degrade because the snow will cover it up?"

"No, that won't affect the ward line. The problem

will be if enough snow falls for the weight of it to break the ward line. Then we're in trouble."

Will spoke up. "But there's a second issue. Both salt and ash melt ice. That's why they're used on roads. If the ingredients of the ward line melt the snow, that water could potentially wash some of the line away."

Donna sank her hands into her hair, trying to think.

"We can prepare for an attack," Pierce said.

She stared out the windows at the falling snow. "How? This place is enormous. There are a lot of people here, but not enough to cover every possible entry point. And I need to be able to protect everyone in this house. I'm responsible for them."

Her temper was rising, but her anger wasn't with those around her. It was all for Lillis and Yavi. "We need to find the Daemon Twins." She tried to channel her emotions into figuring out a solution. "We need to cut off the head of the snake."

# CHAPTER 20

"I'm with you, boss. But *finding* the snake is the problem," Temo said. "Too bad Rixaline's not nearby."

"If only. But the Daemon Twins must be somewhere close," Donna said. "After all, why go to the trouble of trying to take me down if they weren't going to stick around to watch?"

"Agreed," Charlie said. "Pierce, didn't you and some of the guys go through their rooms after they left?"

Pierce nodded. "We did, but we didn't find anything useful."

"Nothing?" Charlie asked. "Was there any trash in the trash cans?"

Pierce looked at Will, who shrugged and looked at Temo, who shook his head like he wasn't sure. Pierce frowned. "Sorry, I don't think we looked."

"Charlie, what are you thinking?" Donna asked.

"I don't know exactly, but there might have been something we could have used. Some kind of clue. Would housekeeping have cleaned those rooms already?"

Donna didn't know. "We'll have to ask Marcus. He's upstairs with Dr. Ogden."

Rico stepped forward. "They left their contact information with him. Phone numbers are traceable, as are cell phones. Of course, that's not legal, unless you're a law enforcement officer and you've got a court order."

Donna snorted. "I don't care about legal and I don't need a court order. I have Neo." Who was also upstairs.

Temo tipped his head. "She still with Francine?"

"Yes. Would you text her and ask her to come down? One of the household staff is with Francine, so she won't be alone. Charlie, text Marcus. Get the Daemon Twins' numbers from him." Donna looked around. "Anyone else have any ideas?"

Charlie answered without looking up from her phone. "There can only be so many places a couple of daemons could hole up around here. Rico, put some of that FBI training to use and see what you can find out in whatever way you can that won't violate your standing as an agent. Neo can handle the stuff that will."

Donna grinned as Rico looked at her. "What she said. Get to work."

"I thought you wanted me to handle that interview with Fitzhugh."

"I do," she said. "Right after you locate Artemis's children. Or sooner, if Neo beats you to it."

With a smirk, he held up his hands. "I'm off to get my laptop."

"About getting to work," Harper said. "If you don't

mind, I was going to create small bags filled with the warding material for all of you to wear. Protection talismans, basically."

"That's fine, Harper." Donna wasn't sure how much good something like that would do if a demon managed to get up close and personal, but she also understood the woman's need to feel useful and busy.

"Thank you. I'll be in the library if you need me."

"Harper, wait just a moment longer," Donna said. She wanted to make sure nothing else came up that might require the witch's attention.

Harper stopped by the door. "Sure."

Sitting idly by while they were basically under attack was inexcusable. Unless you were Francine or Bunni. Or the host of remaining funeral guests. Donna didn't want any of them helping. She couldn't afford to have their blood on her hands if something went wrong.

Charlie's phone buzzed. She read the screen. "Marcus is on his way down. He'll give me the numbers."

"Excellent."

One of the doors opened and Neo slipped in. She went straight to Temo's side and took his hand. "Good to see you guys are back."

"Francine doing all right?" Donna asked.

Neo shrugged. "The doctor gave her some stuff to help her sleep. She tried to fight it, but the doctor said sleep would help her heal. Michael promised he'd stay with her while she slept, and she finally gave in."

"Good." Michael was definitely earning his bonus. "As you might have guessed, I have a job for you. Use whatever skills you have to trace the Daemon Twins' numbers or cell phones or whatever and see if you can locate them. Can you do that?"

Neo grinned. "I live for that kind of stuff. Bring it on."

Marcus entered next, Dr. Ogden with him. "I take it the warding went well?" Lots of nods answered him. "Good. I have those numbers for you, Charlie, but then I have to go see to some of the guests who are leaving."

"By all means," Donna said. "And while the warding was completed, it may not hold all night. The more people we can see safely off, the better."

Marcus's brows lifted. "It may not last the night?"

"Snow complicates things," Harper answered with a frown.

He took that in. "I see. Well, perhaps I can hurry some of the departures along." He went to Charlie, his phone out. "First, those numbers."

Neo joined them while Marcus shared the info.

Donna took it upon herself to introduce Dr. Ogden. "For those of you who haven't yet met him, this is Dr. Ogden. He's looking after Bunni and Francine."

Dr. Ogden gave them all a nod and a wave.

"There's a fresh pot of coffee for you behind the bar, doctor."

"Thank you, Your Majesty." He went to get himself a cup.

"Temo, Will, Pierce. Get with the security team and set up regular patrols through the house. All floors. I want doors and windows checked. Let's not get complacent."

"You got it, boss," Temo said. The other two men joined him.

Donna took a breath. They were going to be all right. It was going to be a long night, no doubt about that, but they'd get through it.

Then the lights went out.

Deeper within the house, a few shrieks could be heard. Donna felt a burst of panic but not enough to stop her from rolling her eyes. Some of the guests were a little dramatic. The fire in the great hall put out plenty of light and vampires had excellent vision. She imagined any guest in rooms without fires in the hearths or candles would be left in pitch black. "What do you think, Marcus? Branch down on a power line somewhere?"

He nodded. "Probably. The generators should kick on any—"

The lights came back on.

He smiled. "All of the generators are well-maintained and fueled. Nothing to worry about there." His smile faltered, and he looked around the room. "You did include the generators in the ward line, didn't you?"

No one answered him right away. Then Cammie spoke up. "Are these generators big square units that look like HVAC?"

Marcus nodded. "Exactly."

She asked another question. "Where are these generators?"

"There's one for the south wing, one for the north wing, and one for the garage."

Cammie exhaled. "The north and south wing generators were definitely included. Not sure about the one for the garage, but that's probably not a big deal, right?"

No trace of a smile remained on Marcus's face. "It might be. The garage generator also powers all of the exterior and landscape lighting."

The words were barely out of his mouth when complete darkness fell outside.

"Get every light on in the house and a fire going in every fireplace," Donna commanded. "Go. All of you. Spread out through the house and tell everyone you meet to do the same."

Everyone scattered.

Donna started for the great hall's doors, but Hector stopped her. She'd almost forgotten he was there. "Pardon my intrusion, but should you really be alone, Your Majesty?"

"I'll be fine. Thank you for your concern." She hesitated. "Is there any way you can use those powers of yours to help us? Can't you cast some kind of sleep spell over these creatures hiding in the shadows? My sister said they don't sleep, but isn't there anything you could do?"

He let out a reluctant sigh. "Hard to make the sleepless sleep. Even for me."

"Hard. But not impossible?"

"I'd have to be close to one to try anything."

She grimaced. "I don't want to put you in that situation. Just keep yourself safe, then, all right?"

He nodded. "You, too, Your Majesty."

She headed out again, looking for light switches to turn on. Staying safe was starting to seem harder and harder to do.

# Chapter 21

For two hours, with the house blazing bright and the multiple fireplaces crackling away, Marcus and a slew of other household staff managed to get almost every funeral guest into their cars.

All that remained in the house were five governors, not including Fitzhugh in the basement cell, Claudette, who refused to leave on the grounds that she had no means of transportation to France yet, the emissary, who'd agreed to stay in his quarters, and Donna's staff and friends. That included Queen Francesca and her staff. The other monarch had decided she was staying no matter what.

Donna found that incredibly kind and supportive, if not an unnecessary risk, but she knew better than to push Francesca too hard to leave. She was the kind of woman who did exactly what she wanted. That was a big part of why she and Donna had become such fast allies.

Thankfully, Francesca had decided she and her staff were better off in their quarters, working on the advancement of the Allied Vampire Nation, than underfoot when Donna had other issues to attend to.

Of course, Francesca was only a text away if Donna needed her.

The governors were all in their rooms, where they'd been advised to stay for safety reasons. Claudette hadn't left hers since speaking to Donna. Some of Donna's team were patrolling the house as she'd requested, making sure there were no issues on any of the floors. Another handful of them were in the library.

Donna had no clue what the emissary was doing.

Francine and Bunni were in their rooms. Dr. Ogden had taken his coffee upstairs to be close to them and better monitor their progress.

All in all, Donna felt all right about how things were going. It was certainly good to have fewer people to look after.

Unfortunately, neither Rico nor Neo had made any headway on finding the Daemon Twins. Not the news Donna had hoped for, but both had told her it was going to take time.

Time she felt like they might not have.

She and Cammie were alone in the great hall. Cammie had brought in a book from the library. Something on ancient cleansing rituals.

Donna mostly paced. She couldn't stop herself from staring out the windows, but with it being so dark outside and so bright inside, it was like looking into a mirror. She was tired of seeing her own worried face staring back at her.

Finally, she turned away. She wished they could turn off all the lights. She'd love nothing more than to sit quietly in the great hall, lit only by the fire, and just relax.

But that wasn't her life. She wasn't sure it ever would be again, despite Marcus's reassurances that there were times of calm. She thought about calling Christina, but her daughter was probably asleep, and Donna wasn't sure she could pretend nothing was wrong.

Christina didn't need to worry about her mother right now.

A strange scrabbling sound came from near the bottom of one of the French doors. At least that's where Donna thought it was coming from. "Do you hear that?"

Cammie looked up, seeming to listen. "Yes. Does this place have mice?"

"I have no idea. Sounds like it's coming from one of those doors, though." She made a face. "I wish we could turn these lights off. I can't stand feeling like I'm in a fishbowl. We can't even close the drapes."

Cammie put her book aside. "I get that, but it's for everyone's safety. Demons hate light. Won't stop them entirely, but it will at least aggravate them."

"Oh, good," Donna said. "I'd hate for them to be in a good mood."

Cammie snorted. "Don't be such a wise—"

The scrabbling started up again. Louder. Cammie

got up as Donna started toward the door. Cammie held her hand out. "Stay back."

The sound grew louder. More insistent. Donna shot her sister a look. "I'm not afraid of mice."

Cammie fired up the flashlight on her phone and turned it at an angle to see through the reflection on the glass.

A split-second went by as they stared at the undulating wave of black that was climbing the door's glass exterior. There was something familiar about it.

Donna's brain abruptly made sense of what she was seeing. She let out a shriek and jumped back. "Mary and Joseph. I *hate* spiders. Where on earth could they be coming from? How could they even survive in this cold?"

"They couldn't," Cammie said as she scanned her light across the wall of French doors. Every single one was covered in a mass of the eight-legged nightmares. "This is the work of the demons. Trying to scare us out of the house. Trying to get us to break the ward. If it hasn't already been partially broken."

"What do you mean?"

Cammie looked closer. "The spiders are actually on the glass. That means some of the demons' magic has been able to penetrate the ward. Or it's weakening." She held her phone very close to the glass, tapping it lightly to knock enough spiders off so she could see out. After a few seconds of looking around, she glanced at Donna. "That's not a good sign, but in a way it is.

The demons have tipped their hand by letting us know the ward is losing its power."

"The house being covered in spiders is a good sign?"

Cammie shrugged. "If they were smarter, they would have waited until the ward was completely broken and attacked in full force. But this? This was a stupid, impetuous move. Thankfully, demons aren't known for their great reasoning skills or abundance of patience. Probably helps that they're being driven by the Daemon Twins."

Donna thought about that. "Because the Daemon Twins want the house breached before the sun rises."

"Yes," Cammie said. "They need their daysleep. In fact, based on what Marcus told us about them when they arrived, they might need it more than your standard vampire, since they have the double whammy of demon blood to deal with, too."

Marcus came running in with Charlie. The two had been in his office, working on coronation plans. "We have a problem," he said.

"It's not good," Charlie added.

Donna nodded at the French doors. "You mean the spiders? We know."

"Spiders?" Charlie asked.

Marcus frowned and stared at the glass. "No, that's not why we ... how very awful."

"Wait," Donna said. "That's not the problem you came in here about?"

"No. It was because of this." He went to the bar sink

and turned on the faucet. The water ran red. The warm, metallic scent hit Donna instantly. He grimaced. "It's been the same at every faucet I've tried."

Her fangs descended involuntarily. "Is that blood? They turned our water into blood?"

Charlie nodded. "It is. And they did."

Donna wrested back her self-control and tucked her fangs away. "They know we're vampires, right?"

He turned off the faucet. "I'm sure that's the point, because it's probably drugged or poisoned. Either way, we need to make sure no one drinks this."

Temo and Pierce came in. Both men looked slightly alarmed. Their gazes went directly to the wall of glass doors behind Donna and Cammie.

"If you're here about the spiders," Donna said. "We already saw them."

Cammie wiggled her fingers. "Just a demon trick. I take it you saw them on the upstairs windows, too?"

Temo's lip curled as he nodded. "Why'd it have to be spiders, man? I hate those freaking things."

Pierce walked over to one of the French doors. "Am I the only one who can hear them? All those tiny feet…"

Temo groaned. "I couldn't until you said that."

Kace and Will ran into the hall next. Will shook his head. "I'm guessing you already know."

Cammie nodded. "Demon trick."

Kace narrowed his eyes. "So the spiders aren't real?"

"No," Cammie said. "They're real. But the demons

are trying to trick us into freaking out and leaving the house. Or doing something to break the ward."

Kace frowned. "It's a complete shame I can't breathe fire, otherwise I'd fly over the house and toast those furry invaders."

Marcus tilted his head. "There are flame throwers in the arsenal."

Donna thought about that. "Something to consider, but that would require leaving the house, which we don't want to do."

Charlie wrapped her arms around her torso. "Maybe I could try a scream with just enough banshee power in it to fry their little nervous systems."

"That has promise," Donna said. "But are you sure that wouldn't break the glass?"

Charlie scrunched up her face. "No. That's a hard thing to judge."

"Then I think we'd better skip it unless absolutely necessary," Donna said.

Cammie cleared her throat softly. "Just so all of you know, the ward is probably only an hour or so away from being completely penetrable."

"An hour?" Pierce looked incredulous. "After all that hard work of spreading it around the house?"

Cammie glanced at the faucet. "Could be longer, but the snow hasn't let up. Those big flakes are heavy and full of water. It's just a matter of time. And the demons know it. Otherwise, why would they have bothered to turn our water into blood?"

Kace scowled. "They turned our water into blood?"

Marcus twisted on the faucet to demonstrate. "It's like this at every sink I've tried."

"That's just nasty. I know you people drink that stuff, but how are we going to make coffee?"

Donna almost laughed. "I'm sure there's plenty of bottled water, isn't there, Marcus?"

He nodded. "There is. But we need to make sure no one drinks this, as it's probably poisoned or drugged."

Temo sighed. "Come on, guys. Let's spread the word, then get back to patrolling. The last thing we need is for those spiders to find a way in."

As they started to head back out, Donna called after them, "Keep the fires going in the fireplaces. I don't want any spiders coming down the chimneys."

"On it," Temo answered, giving her a thumb's up.

She sighed and looked at Marcus. "I hate to ask this, but have you checked on Fitzhugh lately?"

"No. I'll go down there now."

Cammie leaned against the back of the couch, her eyes on the glass. "Maybe he's all wrapped up in webbing and the spiders took care of the problem."

Donna snorted. "I don't think we're going to get that lucky."

On his way out, Marcus said, "I'll be back with a report shortly."

"Thank you." Donna went over to lean on the couch beside her sister. "Which of the ten plagues do you think they'll try next?"

"Let's hope it's not boils." Cammie crossed her arms, her gaze pensive.

"Gross. Yeah, let's hope it's not that." Donna recognized the look on her sister's face. "You're thinking about something."

"I am." Cammie nodded. "But it's a last-ditch effort."

"Would it get rid of these demons?"

"It would, but I'm not ready to talk about it until I'm sure it's the only thing left for us to try. Besides, it wouldn't do anything about Artemis's children, and I don't think they're going to let up anytime soon."

Donna exhaled slowly. "I don't think they are, either. Which means we really need Rico or Neo to come through."

Cammie leaned forward and used her thumb to crush a small spider that was creeping up the inside of one of the doors. "And fast."

# CHAPTER 22

Rico shook his head as Donna looked over his shoulder at his laptop screen. "They're not using credit cards, I can tell you that much. Or at least they're not using cards in their own names. Any chance you know of other names they might use?"

"No. And I'd think if Marcus did, he would have mentioned that." She thought a moment. "What about recent check-ins under any name in the last week? Since we don't know when they arrived."

He looked up at her. "You want me to check every single hotel, motel, bed-and-breakfast, and Airbnb in the area? Do you know how many possibilities that is?"

"In Lebanon, Kansas? It can't be that many. Besides, they wouldn't stay in anything but the best. I don't see Lillis with her Louboutin boots and Chloe handbag staying at the Motel 6, you know what I mean? In fact, I'd bet they're renting a place. Something private. Start your search there. Work from the most expensive places on down."

He started tapping away. "Will do."

A new, half-formed thought popped into her head. She couldn't quite grasp what her brain was formulating, so she moved on, going next to where Neo was working. Neo had headphones on and was bopping her head side to side. Donna sat on the library table next to Neo's laptop.

Neo pushed the headphones back. "Nothing yet. Sorry. I'm thinking those numbers they gave Marcus belonged to burner accounts, because there's no history on them. None. Which is pretty indicative of a burner."

"Agreed," Rico said.

"The good news is," Neo continued, "you're right about them being close. At least they were, based on the last tower the phones pinged off. That was hours ago, though. Probably when they had the phones on to give Marcus the numbers. So maybe search within a ten-mile radius." She looked at Rico. "Does that help you narrow things down?"

"It does." He smiled at Neo. "Did you ever think about going into the FBI? With your skills—"

She grunted like that was a crazy idea, then raised her brows and pursed her lips with a full serving of attitude. "They couldn't afford me."

Donna chuckled, but her amusement soon faded. "You guys, we have to find them. Shutting them down would shut down these demons. And if these demons get into the house…"

She took a deep breath as the possibility of what could happen became very real. "I don't think they'll leave any of us alive."

Rico pushed his seat back. "Let me call in help from

the Kansas pack. They said they were ready and willing."

"Against demons? Seems like asking them to join a suicide mission. Have you ever fought a demon?"

"No." He propped his right ankle on his left knee. "But can they be any worse than any other creature?"

Cammie walked in, carrying the book she'd been reading. "Yes. Because they aren't of this world. They're stronger than any supernatural I've dealt with, faster, too, and although they're not the most intelligent creatures, they have us in numbers. Let's not forget the poison they carry, too. How is the search for Artemis's children coming?"

"It's not." Donna hated the sound of everything Cammie had said. She wasn't crazy about how quickly her sister had changed the subject either. "How many demons do you think are out there?"

Cammie slid the book back onto a shelf before answering. "I've never faced a horde before, but I've read enough accounts and heard plenty of stories to know that's what we're up against. A full-on horde. They'll be like grains of sand."

Neo leaned back in her chair and crossed her arms. "How do you know for sure it's a horde? Couldn't it be just a couple out there?"

"It could be," Cammie answered. "Except earlier when I used my phone's flashlight to look outside, the snow around the house was completely trampled. Not an inch of fresh snow. Not a sign of a single, clear footprint, but so many that none of them were distinguishable. Trust me, it's a horde."

Neo swallowed. "And when the ward breaks?"

"The instant that ward falls, they will swarm the house. Most likely kill every last one of us. I'm sure that's what they've been tasked to do. Clean out this house to make way for Lillis and Yavi."

Neo's eyes widened. "Then what the hell are we supposed to do?"

"Exactly right," Cammie said. "We need to fight fire with fire. The Venari way."

"Meaning?" Donna asked.

"We may have no option but the last-ditch effort I spoke of. We need to open a hellmouth."

They all stared at Cammie without saying anything. Finally, Donna broke the silence. "A hellmouth?"

Cammie nodded. "It's exactly what it sounds like. A gateway to hell. Once it's opened properly, the demons will be drawn to it and sucked into the depths of hell, where they came from. As soon as they've all gone through, we'll close it and the threat will be gone."

"Sounds pretty neat and tidy," Rico said.

Neo nodded. "For reals, though—if it's so easy, why haven't we started doing this already?" She made a face. "There must be a catch, right?"

Cammie lifted her chin, but her expression grew oddly uncomfortable. "There is. The reason opening a hellmouth is a last-ditch effort is because the key ritual requires a soul."

"Whoa." Donna put both hands up. *Whoa*. This really feels like something we need to discuss as a group. Let's get everyone in here before you say another word."

It took almost fifteen minutes to gather everyone in the library. Donna's team, the household staff, and, of course, Marcus. Donna called Francesca to join them. This seemed like information she needed to know.

Donna stood beside Cammie as everyone got settled. "As you all know, this is my sister, Cammie. What some of you might not know is that she spent most of her life in service to the Venari, as a hunter."

That changed a few expressions, but no one ran from the room screaming. Donna kept talking. "We're very fortunate she's with us because she knows more about demons than any of us. And she's got a plan for getting rid of them. I'm going to turn the floor over to her and let her explain."

Donna gave Cammie a nod and went to sit by Queen Francesca.

Cammie stepped up. "My sister is right that I know a lot about demons. I've killed or dispatched more of them in my time with the Venari than I can count. The most I've ever faced in one fight was three, and that was with two other Venari alongside me. I have a scar on my left shoulder from that fight."

She shook her head. "This battle isn't going to be that easy. We're facing a horde situation here. That means there are more of them out there than any of us could count. Artemis's children must be especially strong to have called a horde. Or their father is a high-ranking demon, because summoning a horde takes power."

Donna watched the faces around her. Expressions had turned bleak.

Cammie must have noticed that. "What I'm suggesting would take out the entire horde in a very short time. At least in a way that, once begun, would render them almost powerless against us, then gone. It's just getting to that point."

"Tell us," Temo said. "We'll do whatever it takes."

Cammie nodded. "Good. Because it's going to take a lot. What we need to do is open a hellmouth to draw the horde in and take them back to hell. That ritual is going to require a lot of work. I know the incantation necessary to do it, but we have to open it far enough away from the house that no one inside feels its pull."

"Is that possible?" Neo asked. "You didn't say that could happen."

"Well, I'm saying it now. Hellmouths are strange, temperamental things. They have an unnatural kind of allure that can seduce even the sanest mind. We'll need to distract the horde in some way so we can get at least fifty yards from the house before performing the ritual."

"We?" Charlie asked. "How many people do you need to do this?"

"At least three. Plus the sacrifice."

That word caused a deep silence to settle over the room.

Pierce broke it. "Explain exactly what you mean by sacrifice, please."

Cammie took a breath. "Opening a hellmouth like this requires a soul. There's no other way around it." She glanced at the shelves behind her. "I've been searching for another option and can't find one. And we're running out of time."

Quite a few heads turned to look at the windows, Donna's included. It was impossible to see out of them, but she felt like she could see the spiders all the same.

Temo stepped forward. "I'll do it."

Neo let out a soft sob. "Temo, no."

Charlie stood up. "I'll do it."

Donna had had enough. She got to her feet. "Neither of you will do it. I am not about to lose either of you. I'll be the sacrifice."

Francesca muttered something in Spanish, then quickly switched to English. "You cannot."

"Of course I can. I'm one of the few people here who can give up their soul without dying."

Cammie shook her head. "Donna, I don't think this is a good idea."

"Neither do I," Pierce agreed. "I'll turn my scythe in and get my soul back. Then I can be the sacrifice."

She smiled. "It's very sweet of all of you to volunteer. But there's no need. I can and will do this. That's the end of discussion."

Marcus took a step forward. "Your Majesty, please don't think for a moment that I would argue with you, but your sister is right. If something happens to you and things don't go as we expect, then Lillis and Yavi will get exactly what they were after in the first place."

Donna understood that. It wasn't like this was a spur of the moment decision, but she'd known the moment Cammie had said the hellmouth would require a sacrifice that she was the only one capable of being that sacrifice.

She smiled at Marcus. "Then we just need to make sure nothing unexpected happens."

# Chapter 23

The buzz of conversation that followed her statement was almost deafening. Donna put her hands up and gestured for silence. "Please. I know you all have a lot to say and I'm sure many questions, but if we let Cammie finish, maybe some of those questions will be answered. The only discussion we won't be having is about someone else serving as the sacrifice. Cammie? Please continue."

Cammie nodded, but shot Donna a look of unhappiness.

Donna sat back down. She understood her sister didn't want Donna to give up her soul, but there really was no other way forward. She wasn't about to lose one of her friends when she could handle the job herself and at no cost other than her mortal soul.

Something she could afford to lose, unlike the rest of them.

Cammie cleared her throat. "Once we figure out a way to get outside and get a distance from the house, opening the hellmouth won't take long. It'll take a few minutes, however, and it would be best if we're undisturbed while that's going on. Because of that, we need to not only figure out how to get out of the house, but how to stay off the demons' radar long enough to open the hellmouth."

She looked around as if expecting suggestions. When no one spoke up, she went on. "Something else we need to be prepared for is the possible arrival of Artemis's children. They'll be able to sense the horde's dispersal as it happens. I imagine that could bring them back to the property pretty quickly. It might not, but we need a plan in place for dealing with them."

Donna stood again. "As far as I'm concerned, they are guilty of murder and attempted murder, and they should be dealt with appropriately." She looked at Francesca. "Would you like to weigh in on this?"

Francesca nodded. "Murder and multiple attempts to murder you and more of your people. They need to be eliminated. King Lucho will agree. The Allied Nation stands behind you."

"Thank you," Donna said. She looked at Marcus next. "We need to arm everyone. I trust the royal armory can handle that?"

"It can. Would you like to see it? It's on the first floor of the south wing."

"Not just yet." She turned toward her sister. "I can handle getting you and me out of the house undetected and far enough away to open the hellmouth."

"You can?" Cammie looked surprised.

Donna nodded. "Trust me on this one." Jerabeth's invisibility potion was about to be put to the test.

"We'll still need a third person."

"Okay. Who would work best for your purposes?"

Cammie's gaze went straight to Pierce. "You would, Pierce. A reaper is of no interest to the horde, as you are not a vampire for them to attack and you have no soul."

He nodded. "I'm in."

"Perfect," Donna said. "And thank you. I'd also really love it if we had a distraction on the other side of the house. Something to draw the horde's attention. Who's willing to help with that?"

She looked at Cammie before anyone could respond. "Do you know the best way to distract them? Something that will keep them busy until we can get into place and get the hellmouth open?"

Cammie nodded. "Sure. Send a vampire out."

Marcus and Neo raised their hands at the same time.

"Hang on just a second," Donna said. "We need to figure out a safe way to do this. I was thinking maybe Kace could fly out there and distract them."

Kace nodded. "I could. What if I put Neo on my back?"

"Not without me," Temo answered. "If she goes out there as bait, I'm going along to protect her."

Kace shrugged. "I can take them both."

"All right," Donna said. "Marcus, you can arm them? Give them something that will work against demons?"

He seemed puzzled by that request. "I might need

your sister's help with that. I'm not sure what would do the job."

"Shotguns with salt shells." Cammie gave him a nod. "If you don't have any of that ammo, we can make some."

Donna clasped her hands together in front of her chest. "Then we have our plan. Anyone who isn't going outside should consider themselves part of a patrol unit. Marcus, you're in charge of the inside of the house. Anyone who wants to know what they should be doing, see Marcus."

He raised his hand. "Come see me for a team assignment." He raised his eyes to Donna again. "How soon before you head out?"

She deferred to Cammie. "We're on your timeline."

Cammie thought it over. "If you need help making salt shells, maybe half an hour. If you don't, we could leave in probably ten minutes."

"There you go," Donna said.

Charlie raised her hand. "Your Majesty? If I may?"

"Sure, go ahead."

"At full force, I'm sure my scream could knock the horde back. I'd like to come with you. To help open the hellmouth." Charlie looked like she might scream if Donna said no. She'd never seen such determination on her admin's face.

Donna nodded. "We'd be happy to have you."

As everyone began to gather around Marcus to be put on a patrol team, Donna spoke to Queen

Francesca. "I would feel best if you were safe in your quarters. I hate to ask you to confine yourself like that, but if anything were to happen to you, it wouldn't be good."

Francesca stood. "I understand. My heart will be with you." She smiled. "And my security team will help Marcus. The rest of my staff will be with me, and we brought our own weapons, so we'll be fine. I don't want you to have to worry about any of us right now."

"Thank you."

Francesca nodded. "And if it helps ease your mind at all, Lucho and I have a list of new council members ready for your approval. We'll be up and running before you know it."

"That's good to hear." She laid her hand on Francesca's arm. "Be safe."

"I promise, I will." Francesca kissed Donna on the cheek. "You do the same."

As she swept out of the room with her staff around her, Donna noticed Pierce in deep conversation with Will. Maybe asking what power reapers had against demons? Getting some pointers? She wasn't sure.

Another member of the household staff came into the library and went straight to Marcus. They had a brief conversation, then Marcus looked at Cammie. "We have five cases of rock-salt shells. We're ready to go."

Cammie took a deep breath. "In ten minutes, I'd like everyone who's going outside to meet in the great hall."

Donna went to her sister. "I have to go up to my rooms and change. I'll be as quick as I can." She also had to get Jerabeth's potions.

"Okay. Wait. You said you could get us away from the house undetected. How?"

"Before we left New Jersey, Jerabeth gave me two vials of a new concoction she's working on. It gives the user about fifteen minutes of invisibility. That should be enough, right?"

Cammie nodded slowly. "It's going to be tight. But I think so."

Donna's brows went up. "You think so? Are you sure you can't do better than that?"

"I've read the incantation twice, just to practice. The first time it took me eleven minutes. The second, it took me nine and a half. And that's without me prepping the ground. Or taking your..." Cammie's mouth bent oddly. "Soul."

Donna leaned in. "About that. How is that going to work exactly?"

Cammie paled. "With my holy dagger, I need to draw a circle on the earth. Using your heart's blood as the ink. Good thing I hung onto that dagger."

Donna knew what she'd heard, but she asked anyway. "My heart's blood?"

Cammie nodded.

"How exactly is my heart's blood going to get on your holy dagger?" But Donna already knew.

Cammie just stared.

Donna wiped her hand over her face. "Won't that kill me?"

"It...shouldn't."

"Um, once again, if you could just sound a little more certain about that."

Cammie nodded in short, rapid movements. "Right. Well, I've taken out vampires that had their mortal souls and I can tell you that a direct hit to the heart only works on the second try in those cases."

Donna didn't feel as confident as she would have liked. "Okay, great. So as long as you only stab me through the heart once, we're good."

Cammie frowned. "You don't have to do this."

Donna made herself smile, although her insides had just turned to Jell-O. "I'm the reason we're in the mess. I should be the one who takes the biggest risk to get us out."

# Chapter 24

Donna went up to her new apartment to get Jerabeth's vials. Donna had tucked them away in her hard jewelry case for safe keeping.

It took some doing to find that case, since the staff had apparently unpacked her things for her. She found it in the closet, on top of a built-in set of drawers. She took the vials out, then realized she still needed to change into something more appropriate.

What exactly did one wear to the opening of a hellmouth?

She went with jeans, her good old lug-soled boots, a long-sleeved black tee, and her Ferris & Coven leather jacket. She tied her hair back in a ponytail. A face full of wayward hair wasn't going to help her. She was going to need every advantage she could get.

She pressed her fingers against the spot under her T-shirt where her crucifix was, taking as much reassurance from it as she could that what they were about to do was the right thing. And that it would be a success. Meaning she didn't die for real *and* the demons were eradicated.

Thinking about any other outcome sucked the breath out of her lungs. She wasn't ready to be done with this life. Not because she was queen. A crown and a title and a whole lot of responsibility that she'd never asked for weren't things she'd miss. But being a mother? And a soon-to-be grandmother? Those things mattered.

Her family and her friends were her life. The idea of never seeing them again made her eyes hot with impending tears.

She blinked and tipped her head back until she calmed down. She needed to focus on the positive outcome. Facing her own possible death made that tough.

With a sigh, she headed out, but stopped at the closet's entrance to take one last glance around. There was no guarantee she'd ever see this apartment again and something inside her wanted one more look.

Had Artemis realized the last time she'd walked out of these rooms that she'd never be returning? That she'd never see her friends and family again?

Maybe she hadn't seen her children in a while anyway.

Another second or two ticked by before Donna turned the lights off in the closet and went back downstairs, the vials snug in her pocket.

Pierce and Charlie were waiting in the great hall. As Donna entered, so did Kace. Temo and Neo came in holding hands. Neo was in her Ferris & Coven jacket, too.

Donna smiled at her. "Looks great on you."

"Thanks."

All they needed now was Cammie. The tension of the coming mission seemed to hang in the air. To distract herself, Donna kept talking. "Has anyone been up to see Francine and Bunni lately?"

Kace nodded. "I just checked in on Bunni. Still sleeping. No change."

"Oh." Donna had hoped for better news. "And Francine?"

"She's awake," Neo said. "She's watching a movie with Michael. Some dancing and singing thing with Jim Kelly."

Donna frowned. "Jim Kelly?"

"*Gene* Kelly," Temo corrected.

Donna laughed. "I take it she's doing all right?"

"Yeah," Neo said. "She seems to be."

Donna exhaled. "Good." If only Bunni would follow suit.

The doors behind her opened and Marcus came in, carrying two black shotguns. He had a small bag over his shoulder. He held the guns up. "Temo and Neo, these are for you."

Temo came right over and took them. "Mossberg 930. Semi-automatic. Ghost sight." He stared down the barrel. "Nice."

Marcus nodded as he slid the bag off his shoulder and handed it to Temo. "Each gun holds seven shells plus one in the chamber, but I brought you extra shells, just in case. Not sure how easy it'll be to reload midair, but better that you have more than you need than not enough."

"Agreed," Temo said as he took the bag.

"There's a walkie talkie in there, too." Marcus patted the one clipped to his belt. "In case you need to reach us."

"Good idea." Temo looked at Neo as he held up one of the shotguns. "Are you going to be able to handle one of these?"

She stared at the weapon. There was uncertainty in her eyes, but Donna doubted Neo would admit to anything that sounded like a weakness. Neo shrugged one shoulder. "Sure. It's just aim and shoot, right?"

"Yep," Temo said. "That's the beauty of a shotgun. You don't have to be accurate to get your point across. But let's make sure you've got it positioned correctly. I don't need you getting hurt from the recoil."

"They're best at about twenty yards," Marcus added. "Kace, will that work for your flying purposes?"

He nodded. "I can manage that until we get to the tree line, then I might have to go higher. Of course, I don't really know how high demons can jump. I should ask Cammie about that when she gets here."

"I'm sure she'll be here soon," Donna said. She went to stand by the fireplace with Pierce and Charlie. Both of them offered her tight, quick smiles, but there was enough worry on their faces for her to understand how they really felt.

In another two minutes, Cammie entered, wearing

the chainmail shirt prototype that the Ferrises had come up with. Donna prayed it was as tough as they thought it was. Cammie didn't have the same kind of supernatural protection that the rest of them did.

Cammie looked around. "Everyone's here. Good. Are we ready?"

They all nodded, except for Kace, who raised his hand. "How high off the ground should I be? I don't want demons jumping all over me and being able to get to Neo."

"I've never seen one jump more than twenty feet," Cammie answered. "But go thirty if that makes you feel better. Be safe first. Understood?"

"Yes."

"All right. We get one shot at this, so it has to be done right. And remember, do your best to keep them from making contact with your skin," Cammie said. "You've all seen what they can do."

Donna's mind went to Bunni and Francine.

Cammie continued. "I just checked the warded area beyond the front doors. It seems to be holding reasonably well, so that's the exit we'll all use."

She pointed at Kace. "You need to shift and get Neo and Temo mounted up before you leave the house. If you don't fly out of here, you might not make it off the ground. Will you be able to clear the doors?"

He considered it. "Those are pretty big doors. With both of them open, and if these two duck, I should be able to. I've never taken off in such a short space, though."

"Do your best. Temo, you have the walkie talkie. As soon as the horde is following you, radio in." Cammie looked at Donna, bracketed by Pierce and Charlie. "Once Temo does that, we'll go out. Pierce, I want you in reaper form. It'll reenforce for them what you are, but your wings will also give Donna additional cover to hide behind. Charlie, you and I will follow her. You all have weapons as well?"

Pierce patted his scythe. "I do."

"Just my voice," Charlie said. "Unless there's something else you think I should carry?"

Cammie nodded. "We should all have a couple of blades on us. Swords would be nice, but these things move so fast that any combat is most likely going to be up close."

"Me, too?" Donna asked.

"Yes. All of us." She turned to Marcus. "Can the armory supply us with a few blades each?"

"Absolutely. Do you have a preference?"

"The strongest weapons you've got. Damascus steel, if you have it."

"I'll be right back."

As he left, Cammie faced them all again. "Any more questions?"

Donna didn't really have any, but the silence was worse. It let her think too much. "Do you have everything you need to open the hellmouth?"

Cammie reached into a sheath strapped to her thigh. She pulled out a slim dagger with a crystal blade and a gold handle. "My holy dagger."

Just seeing it made Donna's stomach roll over. She put her hand to her belly and stared, unable to say anything. That was the blade that was going to take her mortal soul.

Pierce's hand cupped her elbow as he leaned in. "Charlie and I will be right beside you the whole time. And listen, as someone who just lost his soul, it's not that bad. I promise you. You're going to be fine."

She nodded, voiceless.

Cammie tucked the blade away, frowning with deep regret. "I'm sorry. You're so brave that I keep forgetting how scared you must be." She came over to Donna and put her arms around her sister. "I promise you're going to survive this. I wouldn't do it if I had any doubts. I would never hurt you in a million years."

Donna leaned against Cammie and nodded. "Thank you. That helps."

Then Cammie whispered in Donna's ear. "You have your crucifix on, right?"

Donna nodded again.

"Then I'm not the only one looking out for you." Cammie leaned back and smiled. "I love you. You know that, right?"

"I do," Donna said. "I love you, too. And I know we have to do this, or we're all going to die."

Harper ran in, a handful of little pouches dangling by black cords from her hand. "Here. I made as many as I could. Please take one and wear it. I know it probably doesn't seem like much, but if it causes a demon a few seconds of hesitation, those few seconds could be all you need to stay safe."

They all helped themselves to one of the talisman bags she'd made, slipping it on and tucking it under their shirts.

Donna nodded at her. "Thank you, Harper. I appreciate you giving us every advantage possible."

"I just wish I could do more."

Donna gave her a smile. "You did a lot. You bought us the time we needed to figure out a plan."

Marcus came back in with a large roll of black suede. He unfurled it on one of the couches. The roll had pocket after pocket, each one filled with a blade. "Help yourselves."

Pierce, Charlie, and Donna each took a few, finding spots in their belts or jackets to tuck the blades away.

As they finished that up, Marcus said to Donna, "Your Majesty, I wish you the greatest success and the utmost protection. If anything were to happen, which I don't believe it will, I just wanted to say that it has been my pleasure to work for you."

She smiled, doing her best not to tear up. "Thank you, Marcus. You're an incredible help and a fine person. But nothing's going to happen to me. After all, we can't waste all of those coronation plans now, can we?"

He smiled back. "No, Your Majesty."

With that, she looked around the room. "I suppose it's time to make this happen."

## CHAPTER 25

Kace shifted into his gargoyle form in the middle of the foyer, which was an enormous space. Filled with a large, winged, stone creature, the room didn't seem quite so big, and Kace seemed twice the size Donna remembered.

Neo stared up at him with obvious skepticism. She poked him with a finger like she was checking to see if he really was made of stone. "Um, dude. I know you can fly, but you must weigh as much as two or three elephants. Adult ones. Not the babies. How do you stay in the air?"

Donna understood completely. She'd had some of the same thoughts herself before she'd taken to the air with him.

He turned his head to look at Neo. "Magic. I don't question how blood sustains you, do I?"

"No, but me drinking blood isn't the same thing."

Temo, who was standing beside her, gave Neo a nudge. "It'll be all right. Kace has done this before."

"Yeah," she said, eyeing the gargoyle. "I know, but still. He's stone."

Cammie arched a single eyebrow. "Are you changing your mind, Neo?"

Neo glanced over like she'd been caught with her hand in the proverbial cookie jar, a clear sign that while Cammie might not officially be a nun, she hadn't lost the stern tone capable of filling people with guilt and reminding them of their obligations. "No."

"Good," Cammie said with a jerk of her head toward Kace. "Then mount up. Our time is running short."

Temo laced his fingers together to make a step for Neo. She put her hands on his shoulders, her foot in his grasp, and up she went.

Temo followed, using sheer strength and a good jump to get himself into position behind her. He patted Kace's back. "We're in place."

Marcus and Cammie went to the doors as Kace lumbered backwards to get as much launching space as possible.

When he was almost touching the rear wall, he lowered his shoulders. "Stay low," he told Neo and Temo in a voice that seemed to rumble out of him.

They crouched down as much as they could.

Then Kace gave Marcus a nod. A second later, he launched himself forward, pumping his wings.

Cammie and Marcus yanked the doors open wide as Kace sped toward them. Donna glanced outside. The snow had stopped. At the very edge of light beyond the door, eyes filled the darkness. Red, glowing eyes with elongated pupils like snakes. They moved and shifted almost as if they weren't connected to bodies.

Donna held her breath and squeezed Pierce's hand. It was better to keep her eyes on Kace. His feet came off the floor, but there was no way his outstretched wings were going to fit through the doors.

Donna grimaced. Impact seemed certain.

At the last instant, Kace pulled his wings in, sailed through the door, then thrust them out again, pumping hard as he banked toward the sky.

Donna exhaled as she watched them go. "Did you see the eyes?"

Pierce nodded. "I did."

As Kace disappeared into the night with Neo and Temo, Cammie and Marcus shut the doors. Marcus unclipped his walkie talkie from his belt and adjusted a few of the knobs, making it squelch.

He spoke into it. "Can you hear me?"

The walkie talkie crackled and Temo's voice came through loud and clear. "Yep. They're definitely following us. Looks like a sea of red eyes and black bodies below us. And even though it's dark out here, the horde is somehow darker. These things are creepy."

Cammie pointed at Pierce. "Time to go."

He let go of Donna's hand and shifted into his reaper form, his wings spreading out behind him.

Donna couldn't shake the feelings of fear and dread that welled up inside her. She'd never been a fan of haunted houses, and that's what this felt like—as if she was about to walk through the worst haunted house of them all.

One where the things hiding in the dark truly wanted to kill her. And then, at the end, the sister she loved with all of her heart was actually going to do just that.

Her mind began to spin, making her palms sweat and her breath come in short pants. She struggled to get control of herself. To push those thoughts down.

The idea of being surrounded by demons terrified her. Maybe it was her Catholic upbringing and what she knew about those creatures. They were fallen angels, cast from heaven with no hope of ever returning. And a being with no hope had nothing to lose. "I'm not sure I can do this."

Pierce took her hand. "You can. Without any question, you can do this. You're the strongest woman I've ever known. Belladonna, you survived the Mob."

Her gaze strayed toward the door. "But these are demons. Worse than the Mob."

He shook his head. "You also survived the fae. And you're a strong, fast, lethal killing machine yourself. Don't lose sight of that. Just because those abilities haven't been put to the test doesn't mean they don't exist." He took her other hand, drawing her attention to him. "Focus on your children. And the grandchild you've yet to meet."

She nodded. He was right. Her breathing slowed.

He smiled at her. "And just think, when this is all over, maybe we can take a vacation down to Mexico to visit Francesca. Or just pick one of Artemis's houses in some exotic country and go there. She's got places all over, right?"

Donna nodded. His distraction had worked. "That sounds like a plan. Thank you." Her courage was back, but if she hesitated another second, she might never walk through those doors. "We need to go. Right now. Or I'm going to lose my nerve."

She fished the potion vials out of her pocket and held them out. Cammie came over and took one. Together, they pulled the corks and drank down the pale pink liquid. The taste was slightly herbal and a little floral. Not bad, actually. Donna had expected much worse.

Marcus frowned. "That worked fast."

"Does that mean you can't see us?" Donna asked. She could see all of them, including her sister, which had to mean Cammie could see her. Thankfully. If that hadn't been the case, they'd have been in big trouble. So much for thinking ahead on that one.

He looked through her as he shook his head. "No, Your Majesty. Not a trace of you or your sister."

Charlie stared through them as well. "Jerabeth is really onto something with this one."

"Come on," Cammie said. "We're wasting time. Remember, Pierce, four minutes out at a good pace, then stop us."

"You got it," he answered.

Marcus opened the doors. "Be safe."

Pierce smiled at where Donna had been. "Use me for cover."

Donna nodded, realizing a second later that he couldn't see her. "I will."

Cammie and Charlie fell into place behind her. And out they went into the cold. There were no eyes in the darkness anymore, a small comfort that Donna clung to, because once Marcus closed the door behind them, much of the light disappeared.

Slowly, her eyes began to adjust, finally picking out more than just shapes by the time they were beyond the covered driveway. Maybe that was true for the rest of them, too, because that's when Pierce picked up speed, taking longer steps and breaking into an easy run.

Everyone followed.

It was eerily quiet with just the crunch of snow under their feet and the soft sounds of their breathing. Talking would draw attention and Cammie had warned them to say as little as possible.

Donna couldn't see anything in front of her. Pierce's wings were too wide. And she wasn't sure she wanted to see what might be alongside her. She focused on what was visible, the gleaming ebony feathers of his gorgeous wings and how they shivered and fluttered with his movements.

On they ran. She counted off minutes by sixty-second intervals, trying to time when they'd be stopping. She was short by a few seconds when Pierce slowed.

"Here," was all he said.

They were in a stretch of field a couple of yards from the tree line near the property's eastern edge. She scanned the sky. There was no sign of Kace or his passengers. That didn't mean the horde wouldn't lose interest and circle back. They had to move fast.

Which meant Donna's sacrifice was about to be required.

Somehow, Charlie stood beside Cammie, who stood beside Donna. Pierce positioned himself next to Charlie. He stared into the darkness like he was trying to find Donna.

Donna watched her sister, knowing what was coming next but not how it was going to happen.

Cammie slipped the holy dagger from its sheath, then raised it into the air and whispered a few words of Latin. At the sound of her voice, Charlie and Pierce moved closer. Cammie crossed herself with the dagger in her hand before turning to Donna.

Pierce and Charlie seemed to be watching the footprints they were making in the snow.

Donna crossed herself, too, then squeezed her crucifix. *Please let me live through this.*

The wind picked up, howling through the trees. It brought the stench of sulfur to them. Instinctively, Donna knew it was the stench of demons.

Cammie looked at Donna and spoke quietly. "The sacrifice is necessary now. Are you ready?"

Was she ready? Not really. But this wasn't about her anymore. Donna let go of her crucifix to open her jacket. She was glad neither Pierce nor Charlie would have to witness this. Her voice came out in a ragged whisper. "Yes."

# CHAPTER 26

Donna thought about closing her eyes, but she didn't want her last image to be nothing but darkness. She'd volunteered for this. She might as well see it through.

Cammie raised the holy dagger high, with both hands wrapped around the hilt. Then she brought it down. The crystal blade slipped easily into Donna's chest.

She heard Charlie gasp and Pierce let out a soft cry.

Donna gasped, too, at the first sharp bite. For a moment, the pain seemed like it was going to swallow her whole. It consumed her, mind and body, until that was her existence.

Then the pain became a distant thing. There, but almost like it was happening to someone else. Was she the one choking? Trying to breathe? She was. Maybe that was her soul leaving and taking her breath with it.

Frozen in place, she felt like she was watching it all unfold from above herself. There was a fog around her that she couldn't quite break through.

Pierce took her arm. She must be visible again. She realized she was staggering backward, drifting toward the ground.

Cammie pulled the blade free, dripping red. She immediately began to draw a circle with the blood, speaking the incantation necessary to open the hellmouth.

All of that was in Donna's periphery. She wasn't sure if she was in her own body or not. The floating felt real. The pain was increasing. It was waking her up. Bringing her back to herself.

Cammie's invocation kept going. None of the words made sense to Donna but they reminded her of being at Mass. It was almost like she could see the flickering lights of the candles. The smell of incense filled her nose and replaced the metallic scent of her lifeforce leaving her body.

She fought the urge to close her eyes. What if she couldn't get them open again? But her lids were so heavy. Pierce had hold of her. Or maybe she was on the ground.

Nothing meant anything except the throbbing ache in her chest. Her T-shirt was sticky with blood. Her blood.

Was she dying? Or was she already dead?

Her eyes closed. Maybe the darkness had answers. It called to her, like a warm, comfy bed. She let it take her under.

She woke to a loud crack and came to like a person who'd been drowning, sputtering and coughing. She was on the ground, Charlie and Pierce crouched beside her. Firelight flickered over their faces.

"I can't breathe," she wheezed. She clutched at her chest. So much blood.

Charlie shook her head. "Stop trying. You don't need to anymore."

Donna stared at her. Then nodded in understanding. She was dead. Undead. Breathing was no longer a requirement. "You can see me?"

"Yes," Charlie said.

"Okay." She blinked a few more times as it all came back to her. She tried to sit up. "What was that sound? Did something break?"

"Yes," Pierce said as he helped her to her feet. "The earth."

The hellmouth was open. The ground had split wide in a jagged gash with smaller cracks running away from it. The snow surrounding it was completely melted, leaving bare, parched earth. The firelight Donna thought she'd seen came from the hellmouth. From deep down inside it. Every now and then, a flame jumped high enough to be visible, licking at the hellmouth's edge.

Which was where Cammie stood, arms outstretched. No sign of her dagger now, but she continued to speak in Latin. Finishing the incantation, maybe. Or keeping the hellmouth open. The light set Cammie's eyes on fire, too. A gust of air wafted up from the cracks in the earth, blowing Cammie's hair around and making her look like a holy warrior come to do battle with everything dark and evil that walked the world.

Donna swallowed, gulping down air, unable to help herself. The stench of sulfur had increased threefold. There were other smells, too. One that could only be described as burned flesh. Another that seemed very much like decay.

Donna was glad she no longer needed to breathe.

Cammie stopped speaking to stare into the darkness beyond the flickering light. "They're coming. Stand next to me, hands on me."

Pierce hooked his arm around Donna's waist and helped her to Cammie's side. Charlie went around to flank Cammie, putting her hand on Cammie's arm.

Donna did the same. Pierce stayed slightly behind her, letting her lean on him while he put his hand on Cammie's shoulder. The urge to move closer to the hellmouth emerged in Donna's mind. Was that the seductive power Cammie had spoken of?

"Don't flinch," Cammie said. "They have to come close enough to lock onto the soul."

She pulled out her holy dagger from somewhere. Through the traces of blood, the crystal blade glowed with a clean, pure light that seemed oddly beautiful against the backdrop of the hellmouth's dark flames.

Donna couldn't take her eyes off it. "Is that my soul?"

"Yes," Cammie answered. Her gaze never wavered from the distant darkness. "They're here."

Donna looked into the darkness on the other side of the hellmouth. Once again, it was filled with eyes, red and glowing. There were teeth, now, too. Sharp and pointed and crowded into mouths too wide to be human.

Row after row of demons appeared. Too many rows to count.

"Just a few seconds more," Cammie said.

Donna stared into the hellmouth. It seemed to go on forever. She inched toward it to get a better look.

"Then what?" Pierce asked.

The demons crowded closer to the hellmouth. The wind had begun to howl louder, although Donna felt no breeze.

"Then I toss the dagger in, and they follow it," Cammie answered.

"Donna's soul," Pierce said. "Gone forever."

Cammie didn't budge. "There's no other way."

"I suppose not." He kept his hand on Cammie's shoulder but moved to stand on the other side of Donna, pressing her closer to her sister.

Was he feeling the draw of the hellmouth?

As the demons came closer, the flames made the front line visible. It wasn't something Donna ever wanted to see again. Their skin was black and mottled like it had been melted over long, twisted bones.

Their arms and legs and fingers were stretched, their spines curved, their features exaggerated. Jaws that hinged just under their ears. Eyes twice the normal size, irises red and luminous.

They reached out toward the dagger, hands grasping. Long, curved nails tipped their fingers and toes. The claws that had hurt her friends.

Cammie raised the dagger. The eyes followed it. "*Ad Infernum*," she shouted. Then she tossed the dagger in.

The demons followed, flowing into the hellmouth like a poisoned river.

Cammie stepped back.

"Is it done?" Pierce asked. "They can't stop, right?"

"It's done," Cammie answered. "Nothing can stop it now."

He kissed Donna's cheek. "I'll be back. I promise."

She frowned. "What do you mean?"

But he was already moving past her. Two big steps, a leap into the air as he spread his wings, then he dove down into the hellmouth.

Before Donna could say another word, he disappeared into the flames.

She sank to her knees, screaming his name. "Pierce, no! Come back! Pierce!"

Behind her, Charlie yelled for him, too.

"Pierce!" Donna moved toward the hellmouth as the demons continued to pour into it. Her fingers found the edge. She peered in, trying to see him, desperate to go after him. The heat was nearly unbearable and the putrid aromas wafting up turned her stomach. She wept, her heart broken. Why had he done that?

Cammie crouched beside her, holding onto her. "You can't go after him. I'm so sorry. I never thought he'd succumb to the hellmouth's pull."

Donna shook her head, tears dripping off her face. "Pierce," she whispered. "Why did he do that? What was he thinking?" she managed to ask through sobs.

"I don't know," Cammie said. She crossed herself. "The hellmouth is a dangerous thing. He was a good man."

Charlie knelt beside her, her own soft sobs echoing Donna's. "The best," she whispered.

Donna thought she might throw up. She felt worse than when Cammie had stuck a dagger in her heart. If she weren't already dead, this would have killed her.

The man who'd saved her life, the man she'd only just come to realize how much she loved, her friend, her confidant, her right hand, her love, was gone.

# CHAPTER 27

The stream of demons into the hellmouth began to taper off, though Donna was only vaguely aware of it as she knelt by the edge. The heat and stench blasted her, but she was numb with grief, her thoughts mired in the why of it all.

Her stomach churned as she continued to weep. Her emotions were as raw as an open wound, and she didn't care. She hurt too much to care.

Kace landed a few feet away, Temo and Neo on his back. They slid off and walked over.

"What happened?" Neo asked.

From Donna's side, Charlie answered her. "Pierce went through the hellmouth. We don't know why."

Donna rocked herself back and forth. "He's gone."

Neo rushed to Donna. "Was it an accident? Did one of the demons pull him in?"

She just shook her head and cried harder. Those scenarios would have been easier to take. If he'd fallen. Or been dragged down. But he'd *jumped*.

Charlie pressed her hand to Donna's back, then stood. "No, none of those. It seemed very much deliberate on his part. Like the pull of it got to him."

"Why would he do that?" Temo asked.

"I don't know," Cammie said softly. "The hellmouth is a terrible thing. Kace, could you fly over the property and look for any stragglers?"

"Sure," he said. "I'm really sorry, Donna." He took off.

Temo went to his knees beside Neo, his big hand coming to rest on Donna's shoulder. "I'm really sorry, boss. Pierce must have had some reason."

Donna just nodded and wiped at her face. She felt wrung out. This couldn't be real. She stared into the hellmouth, expecting him to come back any second.

Kace returned a few minutes later. "I didn't see any stray demons. Looks good to me."

"Thank you," Cammie said. "I should close the hellmouth now."

"*No*," Donna snapped, looking at her sister. Her fangs had punched through her gums, and she knew her eyes must be ablaze with the anger she was feeling, but she didn't care. "He might come back through."

Cammie hesitated, then took a few steps closer. "Nothing can come back through. This hellmouth was opened with a soul. That makes it a one-way street."

Donna glared at her sister. "Then you don't need to close it, do you?"

Cammie backed away. "I know you're upset—"

"Leave me alone." Donna went back to staring into the hellmouth. "He said he'd be back."

Cammie said, "He had no way of knowing..." She seemed to think better of finishing her thought.

Around Donna, a soft, whispered conversation began about how cold it was and how they should really go back to the house and how Lillis and Yavi could be on their way.

It wouldn't have mattered to Donna if the Prime suddenly showed up. She wasn't leaving the hellmouth until Pierce returned.

"I'll stay with her," Temo said.

"Me, too," Charlie seconded.

"I'm sorry, Donna," Cammie said quietly.

Donna ignored her. She wasn't mad at her sister so much as mad at the world. She was mad at herself. Her sister might have opened the hellmouth, but Donna had provided the soul. The very thing that was keeping Pierce from returning to her.

She was vaguely aware of Kace taking off with Cammie and Neo on his back to return to the house.

She put her face into her hands and began to sob anew. This was her fault. Once again, she'd been the catalyst that had caused trouble. Being queen was a stupid idea. She didn't need that in her life.

She didn't need to be governor, either. She didn't need to be anything. She just wanted to be left alone and not have to be responsible for anyone but herself.

Temo put his arm around her. She leaned into him as she cried. He pressed his cheek to the top of her head. "I can't imagine how much you hurt."

She nodded and wiped at her eyes. "How can he be gone? Why would he leave me?"

"I don't know, boss. I'm sure he had a good reason."

"There's no good reason for jumping into a hellmouth."

"Maybe there was," Charlie countered. "Maybe we won't know what it was until he gets back."

Donna sat up straighter and looked at her. "You think he's going to come back?"

Charlie shrugged and tried to smile. "Look at this life we live. Crazier things happen every day."

"They do," Donna said. She clung to that.

"This isn't your sister's fault," Charlie said quietly. "It's not yours, either. I know you well enough to know you're probably blaming yourself."

Donna clenched her teeth to keep from bursting into fresh tears. "It *is* my fault."

"No, it's not." Charlie's tone was firmer, more insistent. "Stop saying that. This is Lillis and Yavi's fault. *They* unleashed this horde. *They* created this mess. *They* put us all in danger. You and Cammie put an end to all of that."

"Didn't help Pierce, though, did it?" Donna didn't want to feel better about any of this. She needed to wallow in the pain and heartbreak, to really feel it. That wasn't punishment enough, but it was something.

Temo shook his head. "Charlie's right. The blame for this falls on Lillis and Yavi. That's it. End of story."

"Then why do I feel so responsible?"

"Because you love him. And he loves you. And

wanting to blame yourself is natural. But it's not productive, boss."

Donna crossed her arms, pulling her jacket tighter against the cold at her back. "I don't care."

Temo narrowed his eyes. "Don't you?"

"No," Donna spat out.

"So you don't care that Lillis and Yavi are out there? What if they call another horde? Or don't you care about that, either?"

She did care. She hated those two. "Of course I care about that." She closed her eyes for a moment. "But I can't leave until he comes back."

"I know you're hurting. We all are. Pierce is a huge part of all of our lives." Charlie put her arm around Donna this time. "Wouldn't it be nice to be able to tell him when he gets back that Lillis and Yavi have been taken care of?"

Donna knew what they were trying to do. And it was working. A little. The pain in her heart felt like it would be there for the rest of her life. Even if she lived to be a thousand. "If I'm not here when he comes through, he'll think I don't care."

Charlie tipped her head. "Ma'am, I mean no disrespect, but there's no way he'd ever think that. For one thing, you're covered in blood from sacrificing your mortal soul in a pretty dramatic way. I'm sure he'd understand if you wanted to get cleaned up. Maybe take a minute to yourself to process what you just went through. He'd want you to feed, too, to make sure you keep your strength up."

Donna opened her mouth to say something, but Charlie wasn't done.

"For another thing, if he came back and found out that you'd done nothing about Lillis and Yavi, he'd be pretty surprised. You're not the sort of person who lets a wrong that terrible go undealt with. He'd expect you to deal with them, I promise you that."

He'd have expected to be by Donna's side, too, but she couldn't argue because Charlie wasn't wrong. Donna took a breath, purely a reflex action at this point. "I know you're right. But part of my world is *gone*." A new tear slipped down her cheek. "I love Pierce. I need him. How am I supposed to get through this life without him? How am I supposed to be queen without him by my side?"

Charlie sniffed. "I understand. I wish I had those answers for you."

"Pierce would," Temo said.

That caught Donna off guard and made her laugh. Just a short, quick burst to acknowledge the truth of what he'd said. Then she sighed as one last sob shuddered through her. "I know I can't just sit here. I have to do something. And that something might as well be taking care of Lillis and Yavi."

She got to her feet and brushed herself off. She really did need a shower. She was covered in blood and it was starting to dry, which was making everything she had on stiff and uncomfortable. She was sure she didn't smell so great, either.

Temo and Charlie stood up with her. Temo nodded. "Neo and Rico have to be close to finding them, right? And as soon as they do, we're going to take them out. Or at least take them into custody. Whatever you think is best."

Donna shook her head. "The time for mercy is over. There won't be a council hearing or any kind of trial. They've caused too much pain already. Not just to Bunni and Francine. To all of us, by putting us through this." She looked at Temo and Charlie. "And they meant to kill me and everyone close to me. That's all I need to know."

"Then all we have to do is find them," Charlie said. "And work out a plan."

Donna stared into the fiery hellmouth, sending all the hope and love she had inside her to Pierce. *Stay alive. Wherever you are, whatever you're doing, stay alive. And come back to me. Soon. I miss you. I want to take that vacation together.*

His words in the foyer came back to her. A lightbulb flipped on in her brain. "I don't know about the plan, but I have a pretty good idea of where to find them."

# CHAPTER 28

Donna knew what she must look like as she walked back into the house.

The way Marcus's eyes rounded proved it. "Your Majesty. Are you all right?"

"I'm fine. Just down one mortal soul. Where's Rico?" She needed to keep moving and to focus on the work that remained. Once that was behind her, she could collapse and mourn Pierce properly.

"Still in the library working, the last I saw."

"Good. Walk with me. Anything new?" She started in the direction of the library. Temo had already texted Neo that they were on their way back and that she should get ready to search for the Daemon Twins again.

Marcus fell in step beside Donna. "The spiders are gone. We'll be on generator power until Kansas Power and Light can come out. The demons chewed through the main line. The maintenance crew is working on getting the garage generator back up so we can have exterior lights again. The demons did a number on it, too, but the maintenance crew is very capable."

Donna nodded. "Fantastic. How are Bunni and Francine?"

"Miss Francine seems very well. Michael hasn't left her side except to run errands for her. I'm sorry to say there's been no change in Bunni."

Donna frowned. "Is there anything else Dr. Ogden can do for her? I don't care about expense or anything like that. Make sure he knows that."

"I will, Your Majesty. I'm sure he's doing everything he can. What else can I do for you?"

Donna's needs could wait. "Does Artemis own any other properties in this state?"

"Yes. Three. One is an apartment building that's strictly an investment property. It's handled by a local management company. The other two are houses she intended to remodel and turn into more available guest space for when there was overflow."

"Get me all three addresses." She wasn't taking any chances.

"Right away." A gleam came into his eyes. "You think Lillis and Yavi are holed up in one of those?"

"Yes. And not just because we haven't had any success finding them anywhere else. They believe those properties are part of what belongs to them. Why wouldn't they stay there?"

"I should have thought of that. It's my fault."

"Marcus, nothing is your fault. You've been managing a house the size of a resort, numerous guests, political intrigues, a new queen, and all while mourning the loss of the previous one. Never missing a beat, either. The fact that you haven't turned tail and run is downright amazing."

He smiled. "I would never leave you like that."

"I know you wouldn't. And I appreciate it."

"I'll get those addresses and meet you in the library."

"Thank you." She kept going with Temo and Charlie behind her as Marcus took off. Probably for his office or wherever records like that were stored. Charlie needed to get brought up to speed on all of that so she and Marcus could share the load.

The three of them walked into the library. Rico was at his computer. Neo was opening her laptop. Donna greeted them with an announcement. "I've got three good leads for you."

Rico glanced over, and a look of horror crossed his face as he took her in. He stood up. "Did the demons get you?"

"No, just my sister. And while I'm missing one mortal soul, it's thankfully not something vampires need. I'll be fine."

"Good. But you look like you lost a fight."

She felt that way. Like she'd lost the most unfair battle of her life. "I just need a shower."

Quietly, he said, "Cammie told me about Pierce. I'm really sorry."

Donna steeled herself for how his sympathy would make her feel. She didn't want to cry anymore. Not in front of people, anyway.

Fortunately, Marcus came in, keeping her from having to talk about how she looked or felt one second longer. He had a glass of blood in one hand and his tablet in the other. He handed her the glass. "I have the addresses."

"Give them to Neo and Rico and let them go to work on them." She emptied the glass in a few swallows, set it aside, then looked at the pair. "You have about half an hour to vet those locations and tell me which one the Daemon Twins are most likely at. Maybe less time. Depends on how long it takes me to shower this blood off."

They both nodded.

"I expect results. I want those two turned into ash before the sun rises."

Charlie looked at her watch. "That gives us less than three hours."

Donna put her hands on her hips, the movement causing her T-shirt to peel away from part of her stomach where it had dried and stuck on. She couldn't get into the shower fast enough. "I want at least three teams of five each."

Temo nodded. "I'll make sure we're armed and ready."

"Perfect. Marcus, do we have vehicles fueled up?"

"We will by the time you're out of the shower. Do you have a preference? Sedans, SUVs, trucks?"

"SUVs are fine."

"Very good. Only two of those are UV proof. The new Escalade hasn't had the glazing done yet."

They'd need all three for the number of people and weapons they were going to take. "That's fine. We'll make sure no vampires use that one."

He nodded. "I'll see to the vehicles. Is there anything else I can do for you?"

She took her jacket off. "Pretty sure this needs cleaning. Maybe ask Will or Harper if there's something specific that should be used."

"I'll take care of it."

That was all the answer she needed. "Then I'm headed to the shower." She left them to their work and went upstairs.

She thought about going to see Bunni and Francine, but with the way she looked, that probably wasn't a great idea. Francine didn't need a heart attack from shock. And even if Bunni wasn't awake to notice, Donna didn't like the idea of risking it.

When Bunni woke up, a bloody nightmare shouldn't be the first thing she saw.

Donna went straight to her apartment and directly into the bathroom. She leaned on the counter to get her boots off, then went to see about the shower.

The shower was like an entire room all by itself, it was so large. A room with a marble seating area, multiple shower heads, and both steam and waterfall options.

All Donna wanted was hot water and strong soap. She turned the water on, and in a few tries, managed to get two of the three heads going. Close enough.

She went back to the main area to get undressed and find towels. Being in that bathroom meant she was right next to the closet, where Pierce had helped her look through the dresses. She didn't go in. She didn't want to get blood on anything. Instead, she stood at the door and inhaled, searching for a faint wisp of him. A trace to remind her that he had been in her life just a short time ago.

Her sensitive nose found it. A hint of his cologne. A new wave of pain washed over her. She closed her eyes as she held onto the door frame. He wasn't really gone, was he? She refused to believe that.

But if he wasn't gone, why did she hurt so bad?

She turned away and shed her blood-soaked clothing with a sudden frantic urge to have it off, tearing her T-shirt in the process. When the last shred of fabric was gone from her body, she looked at herself in the mirror.

She ran her hands over her chest. There was no wound where the dagger had gone in, but it was clear where the epicenter of the bloodletting had begun.

Even her crucifix was caked with it. She rubbed some of the blood off , but the pendant and chain would probably both need a good soak.

She pulled the ponytail holder out of her hair and tossed it on the pile of clothes on the floor. She never wanted to see any of that again, never wanted to be reminded of what had happened while she'd been wearing them. Maybe she'd toss the whole lot into the fire.

Steam was beginning to waft out of the shower. Nothing was going to happen until she got clean. She found some towels, hung them on the bar near the shower, then stepped in.

She went straight under the water to soak. Maybe a little too hot, but she didn't move. Let it scald the blood right off of her. As she stood there, the tears came back. She gave in, hoping to get them out of her system before she had to rejoin the others.

It was extra hard to grieve when the person whose comfort she wanted the most was no longer here. She wanted to fall into his arms and have a good cry, but if she could do that, she'd have nothing to mourn.

She backed out of the spray to get soap and made the mistake of looking down. A puddle of red covered the shower floor and more blood had spattered the walls. She felt like she was standing in the middle of a crime scene.

It was horrifying, even for her. She grabbed one of the handheld sprayers and began washing the blood off the walls. When it was finally gone, she put the sprayer back in its holder. Most of the blood was off her, too.

She pumped a couple squirts of bodywash into her hand. It smelled nice. Tart and a little sweet. The label said grapefruit and honey. Had that been Artemis's favorite? Didn't matter. Anything was better than the way she smelled. Like demons and blood. That wasn't a fragrance anyone should have to inhale.

She lathered her entire body head to toe, twice, making sure to suds up her crucifix. Then she shampooed her hair, conditioned it, and rinsed it out.

As she got out of the shower and wrapped her hair and body in towels, she realized she wasn't quite ready to go after Lillis and Yavi.

First, she needed to apologize to Cammie. Donna had lashed out at her sister in anger. And none of this was Cammie's fault. Everyone in this house was safe because of her. Donna owed her a heartfelt apology.

She just wasn't sure where her sister was. Still wrapped in her towels, she walked through the apartment to the guest room.

The door was closed. Donna could hear a heartbeat through it. "Cammie? Are you there? Can I talk to you for a minute?"

That was about how long it took for the door to open. Cammie was in a bathrobe, looking very much like she'd showered, too. Her eyes were red-rimmed and puffy. "I'm so sorry about Pierce. I didn't mean for—"

"Don't apologize," Donna said, her own eyes filling again. "I'm the one who needs to do that. You did nothing wrong. You saved us all. I'm really sorry I snapped at you. Forgive me?"

Cammie pulled Donna into her arms and for a long

moment the sisters embraced and cried and said nothing.

At last, Donna pulled away and wiped her eyes. "I need to get dressed and go back down. We're going after Lillis and Yavi."

"You found them?"

"Not yet, but I think we're about to. Artemis owns three other properties in the area. I believe they're at one of them."

Cammie nodded. "Makes sense. Do you want company?"

"I'll take all the help I can get on this one. I do not want them getting away."

"I'll suit up and come down." Cammie took a breath and studied Donna. "I'm so glad you're okay. If anything had happened to you, I'd never forgive myself."

Donna gave her a weak smile. "Be honest with me. Do you think there's any chance Pierce will come back?"

Cammie's face darkened, telling Donna everything she needed to know. "I guess anything is possible, but you understand where that hellmouth leads, don't you?"

"I do."

"It's not a place people generally come back from. I suppose if anyone might find a loophole, it would be a lawyer."

Donna sniffed, smiling a little too. "I can't stop wishing for that to be true."

"Nor should you. I'll say some prayers for him before bed."

"Thank you." Donna wasn't about to give up hope. She took a few steps back. "I really need to get dressed. See you down there?"

"Yes."

Donna went back to her room. She never thought she'd get to a point in her life where the thing she wanted most was a get-out-of-hell-free card.

# Chapter 29

"Mary and Joseph. Those two are absolute garbage." Donna ground her teeth together as she looked at the confirmation Rico showed her on his screen. Neo stood on his other side, looking on as well. "Of course they'd hide out in an apartment building where there would be more potential for collateral damage."

"We're going to have to clear the building before we go in," Rico said.

Donna glanced at the time. "At four eighteen a.m.? Not only would that inconvenience the tenants, but can you imagine how slowly that's going to happen? And how much commotion it'll cause? The Daemon Twins will know something's up, and with the cover of night, they might slip away."

"Uh-uh," Neo said. "Can't happen."

"I agree," Donna said. "So instead of that, we're going to wait for daylight. I know I said I wanted them ashed by sunrise, but this changes things. I'm not letting one more person get hurt because of them."

Rico nodded. "Good call."

"Plus, a lot of those people will leave for work by nine, and Lillis and Yavi will be asleep." She narrowed her eyes. "Maybe it's underhanded to attack when they're the most vulnerable but seeing as how they sent a demon horde after me, I'm not going to let a little ethical grayness bother me."

Rico smiled. "One person's underhanded is another person's tactical operation."

She nodded. "I'll take everyone who's daylight capable. That means you. In fact, you just became a team leader."

She looked at Neo. "Can you get me specs on that building? I want to know all possible escape routes."

Neo went back to her laptop. "I'm on it."

"Any chance you snuck that drone of yours onto the bus?"

Neo's mouth hitched up in a half-grimace. "No, sorry."

"It's all right. But you've just been commissioned to build one for me."

Neo grinned. "That's what I'm talking about."

Donna said to Rico, "I want nothing left to chance."

"Understood."

Cammie came in. "Did you find them?"

Donna nodded. "Yes." She pulled out her phone and sent a text to the group. *Anyone who's available and willing to run a daylight raid on the Daemon Twins, please come to the library.*

Didn't take long. Temo and Charlie showed up first.

For a second, Donna expected Pierce to walk in behind them. For a second, she felt happy, looking forward to seeing him. Then reality smacked her, hard. Her anger returned.

That's where she was now. Mired in anger. It simmered deep down inside her, hidden under the responsibility of what needed to be accomplished. But it was there. Waiting to be let out.

Kace and Hector came in next, Marcus and Will behind them.

Donna was surprised to see the tour bus driver. "Hector, you don't have to be part of this. It's not your fight."

"They hurt Miss Francine. That makes it my fight. Besides, I can be useful."

"I know you can." She just wasn't sure how. She smiled all the same, because she didn't want him to feel bad.

Harper walked in as Hector approached Donna, stopping a few feet away. "Ma'am, if you don't mind me asking, how are you going to handle these daemons? They're hard to kill."

She blinked. She hadn't been expecting that. "We're working on a plan."

"He's right," Cammie said. "They are hard to kill."

Donna looked at her sister. "How hard?"

"Stake to the heart plus decapitation hard. Which means you have to sever the head before they pull that stake out of their chest."

Donna hadn't realized that. "Okay, so it's going to be hard. But not impossible."

Hector's eyes narrowed. "There's another way."

"Tell me. I'm open to anything."

"You said it would be a daylight mission, right?"

Donna nodded. "Yes. I want as few occupants in that apartment building as possible so that no one else gets hurt."

"Then the safest way to do that is to dreamwalk. Slip into Lillis and Yavi's dreams and kill them while they sleep."

Donna stared at him as she tried to sort out what he'd said. "I know you're a sandman, but how would I get into their dreams? Dreamwalking isn't something I've ever done. Or could even begin to know how to do."

"Easy," he said. "I'll take you."

"You can take me into their dreams?"

"Yes."

"And you've done this before?"

"I have. But just because it's easy doesn't mean it will be pleasant. Dreams are strange places. The dreams of creatures like these? There's no telling. But if you do this, it means they won't wake up again and they can't be a threat to anyone."

"I like the sound of that. And I don't care how strange or weird the dreams are." She'd had more than her share of strange dreams. She'd manage. "All I need to do is get in, do the job I came for, and get out. How hard is it to kill them in their dreams?"

"Not hard at all. You die in your dream, you die in real life." He smiled. "Unless I'm there to save you."

That was both terrifying and reassuring. "I can't do both of them at once, obviously. Right?"

"Right. No one can be in two places at once."

"Then we'll start with Yavi. He seems like more of a threat than his sister."

"Hold on a second," Cammie said. "How safe is this?"

"Safe," Hector said. "The only thing a dreamwalker needs to be is fully intent on their objective while they're in the dream. They must not lose focus."

"I can do that," Donna said. She'd never been more focused.

Charlie chimed in. "What happens if Yavi wakes up while you two are in there?"

Hector looked at her. "Then we get kicked out. Not the most pleasant experience, but not life-threatening."

"Except," Temo said, "that we end up with a very unhappy daemon on our hands who might become life-threatening."

Hector nodded. "Sure. Which is why you'll need to have a team in place to deal with that possibility. But I promise, doing this while they sleep will be far easier than having a battle in the middle of that apartment building."

"How?" Temo said. "Won't you have to get into the apartment?"

"No, that's the beauty of it. We'll need to be nearby,

but that could be in the parking lot. They never have to see any of us face to face if this goes well."

Temo thought about that, then looked at Donna. "That is a pretty sweet deal." He asked Hector, "How many can you take into the dream?"

"Just one besides me."

Temo frowned. "I don't like her going in there without someone to watch her back. No offense to you, I mean someone trained to protect her."

"No offense taken," Hector said. "And I understand. She is your queen." He glanced at Donna. "Do you wish to send someone in your place? It doesn't have to be you."

"Yes, it does," she said. "I'm the one they want dead. And they took Pierce from me. They should die by my hand. Just tell me what I need to do to prepare."

"There isn't much," Hector said. "Just be well-fed. And open-minded."

"I can do that. Can I take weapons into the dream with me?"

He narrowed his eyes and made an odd face. "That's a bit of a gray area. Sometimes you can take things into dreams, but there's no guarantee. We will try, though."

"If I can't take a weapon in, how will I deal with them?"

He smiled. "You can make just about anything you need in a dream, even if the dream isn't yours. You'll see."

This was all starting to sound trippy to Donna, but

what was one more weird thing in her already weird world?

Harper held up her finger. "Actually, I might be able to help with that. I've cast dream spells before. Maybe I could enchant a blade with a dream spell so that it would more easily cross between the two realms."

"Worth a try," Will said.

"I agree." Donna looked at Marcus. "Take Harper to the armory. I want several daggers and at least one sword."

Marcus's brows went up. "The Queen's Sword?"

"No. I'm not risking anything happening to that before I'm even crowned. Just give me the next best thing."

"Yes, Your Majesty." He and Harper left.

Charlie crossed her arms. "I'd try to talk you out of this, but it would be a waste of breath. Besides that, I think it's safer than you going into their apartment with the team."

"Thank you, Charlie." She looked around at her friends. "We'll need teams in place to cover all exits. We can't assume Lillis won't figure out something's going on and attempt to get away while I'm dealing with her brother. Or decide to unleash another demon horde. Or something."

Temo nodded. "Agreed. We go in ready for anything."

"Anything," Rico said.

"I wish I could send the main security team with

you, but they're all vampires," Marcus said. "And not a daywalker among them."

"It's all right," Donna said. "I'll need a team here, too, just in case Lillis and Yavi have some kind of Plan C in place for the house now that Plan B didn't work. Again, we need to be ready for anything."

Dr. Ogden appeared at the door. "Pardon the interruption, Your Highness."

Donna glanced at him with a sense of breathless anticipation. "No worries. What's going on?"

"Bunni has woken up. I thought you'd want to know. She's not out of the woods yet, however."

"That is good news, though, right? That she's awake?"

He nodded. "It means she can feed directly. That will help her tremendously."

Donna headed toward the door. "I'm going up to see her. The rest of you do whatever you need to do to get ready."

Kace fell into step beside her. "Mind if I come with you?"

"Not at all, come on."

This was good. Bunni needed to survive. It would make losing Pierce easier to take, in a way. Not that Bunni was any kind of substitute. But Donna couldn't take any more death right now.

Unless it was Lillis and Yavi's deaths.

# CHAPTER 30

Bunni's room was dark and smelled like illness. It reminded Donna of a hospital ward with a touch of the hellmouth thrown in—stringent, metallic, and not so fresh. "Bunni?"

She was pale, despite the blood transfusions. Even her lips were pasty. For a woman who was usually dressed in the brightest colors possible, she seemed nearly invisible against the white sheets. Her cheeks were sunken and dark, bruisy shadows made crescent moons under her eyes.

All because Bunni had thrown herself in the path of the demon attacking Francine. That wasn't something Donna was going to soon forget.

She tried again. "Bunni, you awake?"

Bunni finally opened her eyes to look at Donna. "Hey." Her voice was raspy and weak.

"You don't have to talk," Donna said as she moved farther into the room. "I just wanted to see you and let you know that we're all pulling for you. I'm so glad you're awake."

Bunni's mouth curved in a little half-smile before flattening again. Her eyes closed. "Yeah."

"Kace is here with me." Donna waved him in.

He stopped beside Donna but made no move to go closer to the bed. He seemed hesitant, though he'd been here with Bunni earlier.

"Mm-hmm." Her eyes stayed shut.

Kace looked concerned. "Bunni, do you mind if I sit with you?"

"'Kay."

Kace shook his head, voice lower than a whisper. "She doesn't seem that much better to me."

Donna thought the same.

Dr. Ogden came in. "She needs to feed. Bunni, do you feel up to feeding?"

Without much real effort, she rolled her head back and forth enough to say no.

Thankfully, Dr. Ogden was persistent. "Feeding would make you feel better, Bunni. I promise. It did wonders for Francine."

"Please, Bunni," Donna said. "Just give it a try."

Kace glanced at Dr. Ogden. "Does it matter what kind of blood?"

"Not really. At this point, a fresh supply is what matters most."

Kace went to the chair beside the bed, settled in, then dug her hand out of the covers to hold it. "Come on, Bunni. It'll make you feel better. Help you heal. Please."

Her eyes flickered open.

"Do it for me?" he asked.

She stared up at him, eyes glazed. Donna wasn't

sure if Bunni thought she was dreaming or understood this was real.

Kace pushed up the sleeve of his Henley, then put his forearm right in front of her mouth. "Go on. Bite me. You know you want to."

That seemed to wake her up. Her nostrils flared. Her lips parted, showing her fangs. She hesitated and looked at Kace's face.

He nodded. "It's okay." He took her hand and put it on his wrist.

She held onto his arm as he touched it to her mouth. She bit down.

"Excellent," Dr. Ogden said. He picked up the thermal scanner to check Bunni's temperature.

Donna agreed with his assessment. It *was* excellent. She couldn't believe Kace was doing this, which made her appreciate him that much more. She knew firsthand just how healing Kace's blood was. Drinking from him had saved her from fae poison not that long ago.

Maybe he didn't dislike Bunni as much as he'd let on. Certainly seemed like he cared for her now. Or was this just his way of helping her get better?

Either way, Donna was pleased. She put her hand on his shoulder. "I'm going to see Francine. Thank you."

He held up his free hand in acknowledgement.

Donna slipped out, leaving Kace and Dr. Ogden

with Bunni, and went across the hall to Francine's room.

She could hear the television before she even opened the door. Michael was asleep in the upholstered chair near the bed, but Francine was awake. The movie looked like *Bringing Up Baby*. Cary Grant, Katherine Hepburn, and a wayward leopard. Seemed like the perfect recovery comedy.

Francine smiled brightly as Donna came in. "Hi, honey." Her smile turned sympathetic. "I heard about Pierce. Are you okay?"

"No." Donna mustered a smile. "But I don't have time to collapse right now." She sat on the edge of the bed. "Bunni's awake. Did you know that?"

Francine gasped. "That's wonderful news. No, I didn't know. Is she going to be all right then?"

"Dr. Ogden says she's not out of the woods, but she's feeding from Kace right now, so that has to be a good sign."

"Absolutely." She patted Donna's hand. "He's going to come back, you know."

"Dr. Ogden?"

"Pierce. He's going to come back."

Pain shot through Donna's heart like an arrow. She forced herself to get past the ache. "I sure hope so."

"Don't lose faith, honey. You'll see."

Donna nodded, afraid to speak past the sudden knot in her throat. She cleared it away, softly, then found her voice. "We've located Lillis and Yavi. We're going after them in a few hours."

Francine's brows went up, which was when Donna realized they'd been penciled in recently. Had Michael been helping her with that? Francine leaned in. "Daylight raid? Smart move. Much more stealthy."

"You don't think it's kind of sneaky to go after them when they're the most vulnerable?"

Francine snorted. "You think they'd even waste a moment worrying about a thing like that if the situation were reversed?"

Donna smiled. "No."

"Then neither should you." She squeezed Donna's hand. "You're too nice. You're queen now. Sometimes you can't be nice because you have to be just."

"I know. But that's not always an easy change to make. Trust me, though, I won't be nice when it comes to them. The havoc those two have caused, not to mention the injury to you and Bunni and the death of the security team member…" Donna shook her head. "Their sentence has already been determined. I will not risk further death or injury to my people by letting them live."

"Good," Francine said. "They give vampires a bad name."

"I agree. I'm pretty sure if Cammie were still Venari, they're exactly the sort she'd be going after."

"Is she going with you?"

"Yes. Since it's a daylight mission, I'm the only

vampire going. But it's not going to be the kind of raid you think. Hector's taking me into their dreams."

Francine's mouth rounded. "Oh, that'll be something. Dreams are crazy when you get in them."

Donna furrowed her brow. "Have you done it? You sound like you're speaking from experience."

She nodded. "Once, a while back. Lionel was having these recurring dreams where his father kept telling him he'd never amount to anything. Hector suggested he needed an advocate to speak up for him in his dream because he felt so intimidated by his father he couldn't do it himself. Lionel agreed and Hector took me in."

"What was it like?"

"Sort of like falling asleep, but when you wake up, you're in a place where the standard laws of physics don't really apply." Francine laughed. "Mostly what I remember is that the room it all took place in was our library. You remember that room?"

"I do," Donna said. How could she not? It was where the big fight between her, Fitzhugh, and Pierce had taken place during the party Francine had thrown to celebrate Donna becoming governor of New Jersey.

"I guess you would. Anyway, all the books had eyes and ears and it seemed completely normal."

"That is weird. How did it go? Were you able to be the advocate Lionel needed?"

"I was. I told his father all of the marvelous things Lionel had done, how popular he was, what a great partner he was to me, how good our life was, and by the end of the dream, his father actually apologized to him." Francine rested her hand on Donna's arm. "He's never had that dream again."

"I'm glad to hear that. Gives me real hope that this dreamwalking thing is the right way to go."

"You're going to kill them in their dreams, aren't you?"

"I am. Which also seems unfair, but—"

"They would do the same to you. In fact, if they knew a sandman willing to help them, they would have tried it already, mark my words. Get them before they get you, Donna. If they'd go to all the trouble of sending a demon horde after you, do you really think they're just going to pack up and go home?"

"No. That's why I have to put an end to them. I know that. But it's not in my nature to take a life like that. I guess it's something I need to learn to deal with as queen." She'd known it was going to be a hard job.

She just hadn't expected it to be this hard. Or to come with so much loss.

## CHAPTER 31

Donna hung out with Francine a little while longer, then returned to look in on Bunni. She'd fallen back to sleep, Kace seated at her side. Her color looked better.

He glanced up when Donna opened the door. "Time to go?"

"Not yet. I'll make sure someone texts you."

He nodded. "Thanks."

Donna went downstairs. The sun was creeping toward the horizon, she could feel it on her skin. Soon the house would quiet as the remaining vampires went to bed. She really wanted to see Francesca before they went off to deal with Lillis and Yavi, except Donna had no idea where in the massive house Francesca was.

She sent the queen of Mexico a quick text. *Are you still up? I'd love to see you for a few minutes, but I don't know where your rooms are.*

Francesca texted back right away. *Second floor, south wing. I'll send Benito to meet you.*

*Perfect.* Donna headed in that direction. A couple of minutes later, she spotted Benito in the hall.

He bowed.

"Nice to see you again, Benito."

"The pleasure is mine, Your Majesty. Her Royal Highness awaits you."

"Lead the way."

He took her two doors down to a set of double doors in a small alcove. He opened one of them, then bowed again and stepped back to let her through.

She walked in, admiring the brightly colored apartment. It was nothing like her new one. These rooms were an explosion of color, red and blue mostly, with accents of yellow and black. Lots of tropical greenery, too, which gave the space a feeling of being elsewhere. "This is lovely."

"It is," Francesca said as she walked toward them. She was in a cobalt blue and white caftan trimmed with matching blue pompom fringe. "Reminds me of home. How are you, my friend? I heard what happened."

"I'm holding up. Preparing to go to war and make sure those two never hurt anyone else."

"Good," Francesca said. She gestured to a small seating area in the lounge. "Please, sit with me. Can I get you anything?"

Donna was about to say no, then rethought it as she took a spot on the floral sofa. "Coffee actually. If you have any."

"Benito will make some. Cream and sugar?" Francesca glanced at her assistant in silent command, and he nodded and left to do her bidding.

"Yes, please. Listen, I apologize that I haven't

approved that list of council members yet. I will, I swear, as soon as I have two minutes."

"Don't you dare apologize. You've been busy. Busier than any of us should ever be."

"I have been, but getting the new council seated is important."

"It is. And it will happen when it can happen." Francesca leaned in, a sly smile spreading across her face. "Tell me. What is it like to walk in the sun? It's been so many years. You are so fortunate to have acquired that gift."

"You're right, I am blessed. It's wonderful. But it's not like it used to be. I don't take it for granted anymore. The heat of the sun on my skin never fails to remind me of that." Donna smiled wistfully. "I always wonder if one day that ability will disappear. I hope it doesn't, but one never knows. So when I can be out during the day, I try to absorb what it's like. Just in case."

"Very smart." Francesca had taken the end of the couch. She turned to see Donna better. "Tell me about the raid."

Donna nodded. "Daylight, as you know."

"Also very smart," Francesca said. "Any advantage you can get over those two, you must take. Go on."

"Teams will guard all possible exits, but we don't plan on entering the apartment until cleanup is necessary. Which it will be, if everything goes according to plan."

Francesca seemed thoughtful. "Do you think they killed the occupants in order to take over that apartment?"

Donna's mouth came open. "You know, it's very possible. I never thought to ask Rico if that apartment was listed as occupied. I should find out."

"You should," Francesca said. "You can add it to their list of crimes."

She shook her head, angry all over again. "One more reason to dispatch them. In fact, I was just saying that if Cammie was still in the Venari, this would be a job for them. Especially now that the Daemon Twins might have killed humans."

Francesca's brows arched. "You could call them."

Donna frowned. "And turn the Daemon Twins over to them? No, I don't think so. We can handle this without anyone else getting hurt. I feel certain of it."

"You don't think the Venari could do that?"

Benito returned with Donna's coffee on a silver tray, along with cream and sugar in matching silver vessels. She smiled at him as he set it down, then fixed her cup the way she liked it. "I suppose they could. But I don't think I want to start my reign by turning over my problems to someone else to handle. Besides, what if people started to think there was something more going on?"

Francesca nodded, listening.

Donna went on. "What if they thought that the Venari were somehow working for me in some capacity? With Cammie's history, that wouldn't be a far reach."

"It wouldn't be, you're right. And it would give people reason to talk." Francesca smiled. "Well done. I agree with all of that."

Donna sipped her coffee. It was very good. Maybe better than what she'd had here so far. She wondered if Francesca traveled with her own special brand. "Was that a test of some kind?"

"Not at all. And I would have backed whatever decision you made. I was merely curious as to your thoughts. You've made a wise decision." Francesca traced one of the red hibiscus flowers on the sofa's fabric. "Artemis knew what she was doing when she named you queen."

"Thank you for the support." Donna held her cup in both hands. "This has been a real baptism by fire, I have to say." She drank more of her coffee, figuring the caffeine would do her good. "Bunni woke up for a bit."

"That is excellent news. She's recovering then?"

The lights went off. "Not again," Donna said as she looked up at the ceiling. "I thought that was taken care of."

"We can light some candles," Francesca said.

The lights came back on. Donna shrugged. "I'm sure they'll tell me what that was all about later. Anyway, about Bunni. I guess she's recovering. Dr. Ogden was cautious about her prognosis, but she fed while she was awake and he thought that would be a great help."

Donna stared into her cup, thinking too much about what might have been. Or what might still be. "It would break me to lose anyone else."

A long stretch of silence passed between them, but Donna didn't mind it. Francesca was good company whether or not they were talking.

At last, Francesca spoke. "I don't want to upset you by speaking his name, but Pierce was a good man. I don't know the details of what happened, other than the fact he went into the hellmouth. Is it true that he said he'd be back?"

"Yes." Francesca had been right about speaking his name. It caused everything inside Donna to hurt.

"If he said it, I believe it."

Donna glanced at her. "How can you be so sure? I want to be that sure. I keep thinking that if he isn't really gone, I wouldn't hurt like this." She swallowed as new emotions threatened to spill out of her. "But I hurt so much."

"Of course you do," Francesca said. She reached over and took Donna's hand and held it. "You love him. You know what kind of pain that causes. Or haven't you ever been in love before?"

Donna's almost laugh was bitter and short. "I thought I was, once. But no, not like this. Not with a man who cared more about me than himself. Not with someone who genuinely wanted the best for me. Never with a man like Pierce."

"My people believe that you never really die until

your name is no longer spoken. As long as you remember him and talk about him, he will always be with you."

Donna smiled as best she could. While she appreciated the sentiment, she wanted to cry all over again. She didn't want memories of Pierce. She wanted *him*.

A knock at the door turned both their heads. Benito went to answer it.

Marcus stood on the other side. He bowed briefly. When he straightened, his gaze flicked toward Donna. He looked concerned.

Donna got to her feet, leaving her cup on the table. "What is it, Marcus?"

"I'm sorry to interrupt, Your Highnesses, but ma'am, I need to speak to you as soon as possible."

Francesca stood. "Go on, Donna. I can feel the sun scratching at my back. I'd best go to bed."

Donna took the other woman's hands and smiled. "Thank you so much for listening, and for your counsel. I am so thankful for it."

"Anytime. Be safe on your mission."

"I will be. I'll tell you all about it tomorrow."

Francesca smiled. "I can't wait."

Donna went straight to Marcus and began to walk with him down the hall. "What's going on?"

As soon as the door to Francesca's apartment closed, he spoke. "I don't know if you saw the lights flicker—"

"I did."

"The maintenance team was checking to make sure everything was up and running properly, including refueling the generators. In the course of all that, they accidentally kicked the power off."

"So that's what happened. No big deal, right? It's not like the horde is back." She scanned the expression on his face. "Right?"

"No, Your Highness, it's not. However, it seems the disruption caused a power surge, which normally wouldn't have been an issue, but we just had one surge because of the horde. The second one shorted out some important components of the house's security system."

"Marcus, I appreciate the explanation, but can you just tell me what the bad news is? I'm not sure how much more suspense I can take."

A muscle in his jaw twitched. "The bad news is Fitzhugh is no longer in his cell."

# Chapter 32

Donna stopped walking and stared at Marcus. If her heart could still beat, she was pretty sure it would be pounding. "Fitzhugh is loose in the house?"

"As far as we know, ma'am."

She put her hand to her forehead. "Okay, listen, for future emergencies of this kind, you can text me along with everyone else at the same time. You don't have to come get me and tell me first. I will never get mad about that."

"It's not royal protocol to—"

"Screw royal protocol. When something like this happens, you spread the word to everyone immediately. That man knows he's on death row. He could do just about anything and we need to put people on their guard. Have you secured the grounds?"

Marcus nodded. "Yes. The exterior lights are back on and there are several teams patrolling outside. All of the vehicles are locked, and the keys are with the valet, who's locked them in his office."

"All right, that was a good response." Not as bad as she'd first assumed. "Do you think he's in the house or just somewhere on the property?"

"Most likely in the house."

"Most likely doesn't sound like a hundred percent." She glanced up at one of the cameras in the hall. "Can't you just check the closed-circuit feed and figure out where he is?"

Marcus frowned. "Normally, yes, but the security cameras are part of what we lost in the power surge."

Donna realized no one else knew yet. She yanked out her phone and sent a text to the group. *Fitzhugh is loose. Be on the lookout. Assume very dangerous. Partner up. Great hall asap. Except for Kace. Guard Bunni & Francine, please.*

She put her phone away and started walking again. "Great hall, now. This is not good, Marcus."

"No, ma'am, it isn't. I'm sorry." He kept in step with her, his head down. "I understand if you're angry."

"Not at you. It's not your fault. It doesn't sound like it's anyone's fault except a system that couldn't handle being overloaded twice. Actually, if we're going to blame anyone, it should be Lillis and Yavi for knocking over the domino that started all of this." Donna kind of wanted to punch something. "You know he's going to try to escape."

"I'm not so sure, ma'am. The sun will be up in about thirty minutes. The sky is starting to lighten."

"Doesn't matter. He'll get out if he can. Better to take his chances trying to find shelter than to face certain death by staying here. In fact, he might think he's better off waiting until daybreak to try to escape. He probably thinks that once we're all asleep, his odds of getting free improve. If he can keep from going up in flames once he's outside, that is." She glanced at Marcus. "I bet he risks it. He knows full well what awaits him here."

"I'm sure he does."

She sighed in frustration over the situation. There was no part of her that blamed Marcus. "This has to be dealt with and fast. I don't want to leave with this going on." A new thought popped into her head. "How exactly did he escape?"

"The cell has an electronic lock that can be operated from a main booth, just like in most prisons. When the power surge went through, it turned all of that off, disengaging the lock."

"Like in most prisons?" She narrowed her eyes. "Just how large is the holding area down there?"

"Eight cells in all."

"Eight?" She stared at him. "Do they get used a lot?"

He shrugged. "With more frequency than you'd imagine. The queen's house has been used as a holding and transfer facility for a long time. Because it's centrally located, it's worked well in that capacity." He hesitated. "Some executions have taken place here, too."

"Lovely." Might be time to make some more internal changes. When she could actually think about that. Her phone was practically shaking out of her pocket with incoming messages. She took it out and had a look. Nothing that couldn't be answered when they were all together in the great hall.

A new thought came to her. "Wasn't there a twenty-four-hour guard on him?"

"There was. I found the man unconscious and injured, but alive."

Donna felt relieved by that news. "Good. I'm glad about that."

Getting to the great hall took another five minutes, during which she didn't talk so much as think. Her biggest problem was she didn't know the house well enough to determine where the best escape route might be. No one else in her group did, either. They were going to have to rely on Marcus and the household staff to help them search.

Everyone was assembled in the great hall when she entered. "Close the doors."

As Marcus and Temo did that, she kept talking. "Kace isn't here because I asked him to guard Bunni and Francine, as you saw in my message. Fitzhugh escaped his holding cell due to a power surge that caused the locks to disengage. Best we know, he's still in the house. Where, we have no idea. But he needs to be back in custody before we leave for the apartment building, because I'm not leaving a house full of sleeping vampires with a criminal who's very awake and desperate to escape."

Charlie nodded. "Not to mention one who's capable of just about anything."

"You got that right," Neo said. "Plus, you know how hard it's going to be to stay awake after the night we've had? At some point, some of us won't be able to. Daysleep's gonna hit us like a ton of bricks."

"You can say that again." Will shook his head. "I thought it was just because I'm new to being a vampire, but yeah. Daysleep is like a double dose of Ambien."

"I know," Donna said. "And unfortunately, Fitzhugh's had too much time to rest and sleep and prepare. There's no telling how long he'll be able to resist the daysleep, or what he'll be willing to do to get out of here. Especially running on adrenalin like he probably is. So, thoughts? Suggestions? Ideas? Nothing's off the table."

Cammie shifted. "I would treat this like a hunt."

Donna listened with interest. "Go on."

"He's in this house somewhere, right? And while it's big and it's a lot to cover, it's not impossible. We start at one end and sweep through. At some point, he'll pop up. Then we deal with him."

Donna nodded. "Straightforward. I like it. Unless anyone has a better suggestion, I say we arm up and get going."

Rico stepped up. "It's not a better suggestion, more like an additional one. If you can get me a piece of his clothing, I might be able to track him."

Donna wasn't against that, but it seemed almost impossible, all things considered. "He's been all over this house, and there have been vampires everywhere in here. For years. You really think you can pick him out?"

Rico shrugged. "I should have no problem following his scent, but if I can't, its only wasted a few minutes. And if I can, I've saved us time. Your call. Obviously."

Donna glanced at Cammie.

Her sister nodded. "Let's try it. Werewolves can track like nobody's business."

Donna turned to her deputy. "Marcus? Can you get Rico something of Fitzhugh's?"

"I'll be right back, Your Majesty."

"Meet us at the armory."

"As you wish." He left while the rest of them filtered out of the room to get weapons.

That meant they were all headed in the same direction. The armory was on the first floor of the south wing while many of the guest rooms were on the second and third floors. Marcus veered toward the stairs.

Once in the armory, they all milled about finding a weapon they felt comfortable with. Cammie stood beside Donna, looking up at the queen's gleaming gold sword. Cammie had already helped herself to a crossbow. "You really ought to take that."

Donna gave her the side eye. "Do you have any idea what that thing is worth? I don't want to be the queen that damages it."

Cammie rolled her eyes. "It's the Queen's Sword. You're the only one who *can* carry it, so you should. It's literally named after you. Sort of. You know what I mean. Plus, think about how poetic it would be to dispatch Fitzhugh with that."

Donna stared at the gold blade. "There is something kind of sweet about that thought."

Cammie leaned in. "By the way, we really need to close that hellmouth. The longer it stays open, the greater the possibility that it could draw more demons. Won't be a horde, of course, but even the singletons can cause problems. And without a soul to draw them in, they'll just gather in the area and cause problems."

"I don't care." Donna glanced at her sister. "It's not getting closed until Pierce comes back."

Cammie's smile was tight and pacifying. "Donna…"

A soft thunk drifted down from the floor above them, followed by a louder one, then the muffled sound of what might have been a word. Maybe the word, "No." At the very least, it was the sound of a voice being cut off. Everyone went quiet at once and looked up.

Charlie frowned. "That's probably nothing, right?"

Temo shook his head. "Probably. But then again…" He shrugged.

Donna grabbed the Queen's Sword and ran for the stairs. Everyone else followed. She had no idea where Fitzhugh's room was, but she'd figure it out when she got to the second floor.

Didn't take much figuring. The third door on the left was open. As she slowed to approach and looked in, she saw Fitzhugh in the darkened room, his form silhouetted by the pink dawn. His back was to the windows. And he had Marcus.

Fitzhugh held a blade to Marcus's heart, the tip already burrowing into his flesh so that blood dampened the front of his shirt.

There was a significant amount of ash on the floor.

Donna locked eyes with Fitzhugh's as her team circled around her. "Let him go and we can talk this out."

Fitzhugh laughed. "I don't think so, Queenie. Not until there's a UV-proof SUV ready to take me to the airport, where your royal jet will be fueled up and waiting. Then he's going to ride along with me. Once I get home safe, you can have him back. Understand?"

She did. "It doesn't have to be like this."

"No? So you *don't* intend to sentence me to death?"

"I won't be sentencing you to anything." She didn't want to lie to him, but not answering directly was fine. "We are in the process of seating a new council. One that will be fair and impartial. You'll get a hearing that will be unbiased. I promise."

"Sure, that sounds *great*." He jerked Marcus back, causing him to let out a small noise of discomfort.

Losing Marcus was unacceptable. So was letting Fitzhugh leave. Donna's hand went to her crucifix while she tried to think fast. She went with the first thing that came to her.

With a shake of her head, she did her best to look as

imperious as possible. "A house servant isn't going to get you very far."

She handed the Queen's Sword to Charlie, who was now beside her, then spread out her arms to show she was weaponless. "Take me instead."

# CHAPTER 33

"What?" Charlie turned toward Donna. "No."

"Yes." Donna kept her gaze on Fitzhugh. She could tell by the gleam in his eyes that he liked the idea. "I'm not going to lose anyone else."

Marcus tried to shake his head. "Please, Your Highness, don't."

Fitzhugh gripped Marcus tighter, making his mouth bend in pain as the dagger seemed to dig deeper. The bloodstain on his shirt spread. "Shut up, or you'll end up like Claudette."

Donna glanced at the ash on the floor. "Is that who that is?"

"Yes," Fitzhugh snarled. "In case you don't think I'm serious about getting out of here, that should be proof enough. Get in my way and you'll find out for yourself."

Desperation took hold. She'd had a troubled relationship with Claudette, but the woman *had* been her sire. Fitzhugh had to be stopped. Donna took a step forward. "You really have no choice but to let me take Marcus's place."

"I have all kinds of choice," Fitzhugh snapped back.

She shook her head. "Not if you want a car and a

plane at your disposal. Who do you think organizes all that?" Fitzhugh loved to think she was stupid. Might as well use that. "You really think I know how to make that happen? Because I don't. Not a clue. That's Marcus's job. You either let him go or your attempt to get out of here ends now."

Fitzhugh's expression blanked, probably because he was thinking, then he frowned in frustration. "Fine. Do a slow turn and lift your shirt so I can see your waistband."

"I said I was unarmed."

"Do it."

Donna relented, moving slowly enough that she had a chance to wink at her team, to let them know this was her plan and to let it play out.

Too bad she didn't know what happened after she took Marcus's place, but she'd figure it out. One thing she could count on was Fitzhugh underestimating her. He had from the very first time they'd met. That weakness would give her an opening eventually. Then she'd turn that to her advantage.

None of her team looked happy about what she was doing. She understood. But if anyone was going to be held hostage, it should be her.

She finished turning, coming back around to face him as she dropped her shirt. "I'm completely unarmed. Just like I said."

Fitzhugh nodded. "Tell your staff to leave."

"You heard him," Donna said. "Go. All of you."

"Boss," Temo started.

"Now." Donna didn't want them to leave, but she saw no other way to save Marcus. The upside was it got them all out of danger.

"He'll kill you," Cammie said.

Donna stared directly into Fitzhugh's eyes. "No, he won't. He doesn't want to be hunted by my Venari sister for the rest of his life."

Anger burned hot in Fitzhugh's gaze. Maybe some embarrassment, too, since Cammie had used her Venari status against him not that long ago. "*Get out.*"

Donna twisted toward her friends. "Do it."

One by one, they started to drift out of the room, all of them shooting visual daggers at Fitzhugh.

She faced him again. The sky filling the window behind him continued to lighten. "You'd better hurry," Donna said with a nod at the window. "Sun's about to come up."

"I'm aware," Fitzhugh said. "Come closer, hands on top of your head."

She put her hands on her head and took a few steps in his direction.

As soon as she was within reach, he shoved Marcus away and grabbed her, pulled her against him and dug the blade into her chest. "You're a fool, you know that?"

She winced. The pain was more tolerable than he was, but she ignored him as a plan started to form. "Marcus, get the Escalade ready. The new one."

He narrowed his eyes, then nodded in understanding. "Yes, of course. The new one. I'll have it out front."

Fitzhugh's arm tightened around her body. "And the plane."

Donna nodded. "Call the pilot. Let him know we need him. Have the jet fueled up and ready to go."

"Right away." Marcus backed toward the door. "Anything else?"

She stayed silent.

Fitzhugh snarled, "Just make sure no one interferes with us on the way out or Queenie here gets it."

"Understood," Marcus said. Then he left.

Fitzhugh laughed and tipped his head toward hers. "Alone at last. Must be a thrill for you, eh?"

Donna's skin crawled at the feel of Fitzhugh's toxic breath on her neck, but at least it distracted her from the pain of the blade digging into her skin. "Sun's coming up."

"Move."

Together, they went forward in an awkward half-walk, half-stumble made necessary by his close grip and Donna's best attempt to keep the blade from piercing her body any further. Instead of taking her to the stairs, he turned her toward the elevator.

Smart decision. On the stairs, she could have pitched herself down and shaken him off, giving Temo or Cammie or someone else a chance to put a bolt through Fitzhugh's heart.

They rode down and when the elevator doors

opened, there was no sign of anyone in the foyer except Marcus. Donna was glad of that. There was no telling what Fitzhugh would do if he thought he was about to be ambushed.

Marcus spoke as Fitzhugh dragged her off the elevator. "The Escalade is out front. Key fob is in it. Tank is full. The jet is about twenty minutes from being ready but should be fine by the time you get to the airport. Anything else?"

Donna looked through the front windows. Based on the growing brightness and the prickle on her skin, the sun had almost reached the horizon. Unfortunately, the covered driveway would keep Fitzhugh safe from its rays.

Sooner or later, however, the car would not.

Fitzhugh nodded at Marcus. "Get out there and open the driver's door and the passenger door behind it."

That wasn't going to work the way she wanted. She needed him up front, where he could get full exposure. "Really," she scoffed. "You're going to sit behind me? You think you can keep that blade on me from the back seat?"

"Don't worry about where I'm going to sit." As Marcus headed for the Escalade, Fitzhugh prodded her forward.

"You're going to miss all the beautiful Kansas scenery." And all the wonderful UV light that would be streaming through the windshield.

"Shut up and walk."

They started their odd shuffle again, keeping at it until they were out the door and on the way to the SUV. The wind whipped past but so far the sky was only slightly cloudy, allowing for good light. Only the faintest hint of sulfur remained in the air.

"Remember the speed at which I can move," Fitzhugh whispered into her ear. "And how fast I can shove this dagger into your heart. Try anything and you'll find out firsthand."

She nodded. He pushed her toward the driver's seat. "Get in. Leave the door open."

She did as he asked, leaving her seatbelt off. If this worked, getting out fast was going to be important. "I don't know where the airport is."

"That's what GPS is for." He got in behind her and shut the door, leaning forward to position the blade over her heart again. "Close your door, then program the navigation."

As she reached for the door handle, she took one more look at Marcus. He was watching from the open doorway of the main entrance. There were some familiar faces in the side windows. None of them looked happy.

She mouthed the words, *I'll be okay.*

Marcus gave a short nod.

She smiled to reassure him, then closed the door and used the vehicle's touchscreen to call up directions for the private airfield. She hit start and a computerized voice directed her through the vehicle's speakers, urging her to drive forward.

"Go on," Fitzhugh said.

She started the car, shifted it out of park, and slowly moved forward. Another minute, maybe two, and the sun would be up. He wouldn't get much of it in the backseat, but the hand that was holding the blade was fully exposed.

Or it would be, once they were free of the covered part of the driveway.

"Step on it," he snarled. "Quit stalling."

"I'm not stalling. I haven't driven a car in ages and I'm not used to something this big. Or, you know, driving with a knife in my chest." She glared at him in the rearview mirror, which was when she realized just how smart Marcus was.

The sunroof was closed, of course, but the sunshade that should have covered it wasn't.

Even sitting in the back, Fitzhugh was about to get a nice tan. Just as soon as the sun was properly up. She glanced at the skyline. It had to be any second. She almost needed sunglasses.

A fiery ball breached the horizon, causing her to squint. She grinned. Time to light this fire. Literally.

She sped up, moving the car out of the shadows and into the blazing sun.

"That's better," Fitzhugh grunted. "But no speeding. If I see police lights behind us, it won't go well for you."

The first rays hit Fitzhugh's hand. For a second,

nothing happened. Then she smelled smoke. She almost laughed but kept herself contained. This wasn't over yet. Pretending like she had no idea what was going on would be best.

There was something she could do to help things along, though. She slammed her foot down on the gas, kicking in the overdrive and making the car lurch forward.

The force of it pushed Fitzhugh back into his seat. Unfortunately, he kept hold of the blade as he got jerked away, but at least it wasn't threatening her anymore.

"Son of—ow!" Light poured through the sunroof, filtered only by the smoke that had begun to fill the car.

Fitzhugh seemed to catch on that something was wrong. As he cursed and muttered under his breath, he tried to scramble into the very rear of the vehicle, where the windows were tinted the darkest.

Which was when Donna reversed tactics, slamming on the brakes. That threw him back into the sun, halfway into the front seats. He'd lost the blade along the way. As she brought the car to a stop, she hit the buttons to automatically put all of the windows down and raise the rear liftgate.

Sunlight flooded the vehicle.

Fitzhugh began to howl. The smoke thickened and, here and there, flames danced on his skin. He clawed at his collar, as if loosening it would alleviate the heat. "What have you done to me?"

"What should have been done ages ago." She opened her door and jumped out, running to put distance between her and the SUV.

Fitzhugh burst into flames with enough force to knock her to the ground. He cried out, cursing at her. She rolled over to keep an eye on things. Even if he managed to get out, where would he go?

A swift breeze churned the flames higher and hotter, making certain there would be no escape for him. In moments, the car was engulfed. The cries stopped. She got to her feet, watching it burn. A perverse sense of satisfaction filled her. Ash drifted through the air.

Fitzhugh was no more.

She couldn't say she was happy, exactly, but she was glad he would never be able to torment anyone else ever again. Despite that, she shook her head at the waste as she turned to walk back to the house.

Shame to lose a brand-new SUV like that.

# CHAPTER 34

As she walked into the house, she was greeted by applause from the staff, and her friends and family. She put her hand up to stop them. "I know what just happened needed to be done, but it doesn't feel right to clap for a thing like that."

Cammie stepped forward. "Then let's just say we're applauding your bravery and your courage and your safe return."

Donna nodded, relenting. "Okay." After a few seconds of new applause, she raised her hand again. "Thank you. But we have work to do."

She made a face as she looked at Marcus. "And now we're down an SUV."

He smiled. "We'll figure it out, Your Majesty. Thank you for saving my life."

"You're welcome. I'm very glad I could." She glanced toward the second floor. "Poor Claudette."

Charlie walked toward her. "Not to be unkind, but she knew who she was getting involved with."

"I know," Donna said. "But still." She found Marcus again. "Maybe her ashes could be gathered and put into an urn? She was my sire, after all."

"I'll get someone on that right away."

"Get yourself cleaned up first. You all right? No lasting damage?"

"No, Your Highness. Thank you for asking."

She smiled at him. "Thank you for pushing the sunshade back on the sunroof."

He grinned. "I thought that might be helpful."

"It was. Tremendously." She ran a hand through her hair, loosening a few bits of ash. "Ugh. Nasty."

She gave herself a shake, sending more particles into the air.

Temo joined them. "I need a little more time to get the teams set up, then we're ready to head to the apartment building whenever you are."

"Perfect. We just need one more vehicle."

"There's a Hummer you can use," Marcus said. "With the two remaining SUVs, that should give you enough space, don't you think?"

"Should be," she answered. "Temo? How much gear space are you guys going to need? Will that do?"

"We'll make it work."

"Thank you." She looked at all those around her. "If you're not on one of the teams going to the apartment building, that probably means you're a vampire. And in that case, please, go get some sleep." She smiled. "It's safe now."

Neo grinned back. "Think I'll go check on Francine and Bunni before I turn in." She gave Temo a kiss. "Go get 'em, baby."

He nodded after he'd kissed her back. "Sleep tight. See you soon."

Still smiling, Neo bounded up the steps toward Francine and Bunni's rooms.

Will yawned. "You be safe, Donna." He touched Harper's hand. "You, too, sweetheart."

"I will, Dad. Promise."

As the vampires left, Kace came downstairs. "Neo says Fitzhugh has been taken care of. Bunni's still sleeping. Figured I'd better come down and see when we're leaving."

"Soon," Temo answered. "Get geared up and meet us out front at the vehicles in half an hour."

He nodded. "Will do." He walked over to Donna. "I think you have something in your hair."

"It's ash," she said, combing her fingers through the front pieces again.

"Ash?" His brows went up. "What did I miss? Neo didn't give me any details."

"I need to go change my shirt, but the short story is Fitzhugh became one with the sun, thanks to the queen's new Escalade not being UV-proofed yet. Which is why it's sitting halfway down the drive on fire. Unless it burned itself out already."

Kace narrowed his eyes. "So, how did you get covered in ash?"

"He took me as his hostage so he could get back to New York safely." She shrugged. "Guess he didn't think that one through."

Kace snickered. "Yeah, I guess not. Glad you're unharmed."

"Thanks. Me, too." She looked at Cammie. "I'm going upstairs to change and get cleaned up. Be right back."

"Okay." Cammie's hand went to rest on the strap securing the crossbow to her body. "I'll be right here."

---

Getting everyone into the vehicles took a few minutes, especially with the gear that had to be loaded. Not just weapons, but some body armor Temo wanted to bring in case the apartment had to be breached.

Cammie was in her chainmail and Donna had put her Ferris & Coven jacket, now cleaned of all blood, back on.

The ride took about thirty minutes, putting them outside the apartment building a few minutes before nine. The urge to sleep was strong in Donna, but the pull couldn't compare to the desire to remove the problem of Lillis and Yavi.

Especially now that Fitzhugh had been dealt with.

She was so close to being able to focus on her new role as queen. And even closer to finally being able to mourn Pierce the way she wanted. The way he deserved.

She lifted her face to look out the window. When she'd gone upstairs to change, she'd gone to his room near her apartment and taken one of his pocket squares. It carried the scent of his cologne. She'd tucked it into one of her inside jacket pockets, close to her heart. Every once in a while, she caught a whiff of his familiar fragrance.

It made her feel like he was here. That he'd be with her on this mission. There was some comfort in that. Pain, too, but what was love without pain? The two went hand-in-hand.

Cammie was their driver, with Harper in the front passenger seat, Donna and Hector in the back. On the floor between her and Hector was a cooler with a couple of containers of blood. Hector said she'd want to have it.

Cammie parked across the street from the apartment building, then twisted to look back at her sister. "This all right?"

Donna nodded. "It's perfect. We shouldn't be too close, in case something goes down. Rico and Temo's teams can be in the parking lot. They need to be close. Now we wait."

The other two teams got into position, one in the front parking lot, one in the alley behind the building. A team member had been assigned to do some recon to be sure that Lillis and Yavi were in the apartment and asleep. Marcus had supplied a master key so they could access the place without issue.

Temo's report came about twelves minutes later via group text. *We have confirmation. Good luck, boss.*

"You got this. And don't worry," Cammie said. "If anything happens, Harper and I have your backs."

"That's right," Harper said. She reached into her jacket. "Here are those spelled blades I promised. One for you and one for Hector."

She held the slim daggers out to them. They were simple weapons, but there was no need for anything more elaborate. They'd do the job they were required to do. Donna took one. She already had a sword on her hip, although it hadn't been spelled.

Harper offered the other to Hector. "Not only are they spelled to make them slip through realms more easily, but I added a familiarity spell to both of them, meaning if you drop them, they'll come back to you of their own doing."

"Very cool," Hector said. "It can be easy to lose track of things in a dream. That might be useful."

Harper smiled. "Good. I hope they are."

Donna tucked the blade into one of the many sheath pockets in her jacket. She had a few others in it already, but knew there was no guarantee they'd get through. "I guess I'm ready. Any final words of advice, Hector?"

"Stay focused on the reason you're there. To find and kill Yavi. When that's done, we'll come out of his dream before we go into Lillis's. Not only will it give you a break, but I want to make sure it's not taking a toll on you. Dreamwalking can be exhausting. Among other things."

She slanted her eyes at him. "Is that likely? That the dreamwalking is going to affect me in some way?"

"I won't know until we're in there. If you feel like it's becoming too much and you want out, just say the word pineapple."

She laughed softly. "Pineapple?"

He grinned. "I figured it wasn't a word you'd say otherwise. Is that okay?"

"It's great. Pineapple is my safe word. Got it."

"Then we're ready to begin."

Donna nodded. "Cammie, text the group. Tell them we're starting."

"Will do."

Donna expected to be nervous. She wasn't. Just filled with anticipation and the feeling that soon this would all be behind her.

Hector took out a tan leather pouch and opened the drawstrings. "Remember what you're there to do. Remember your safe word. And stare into my eyes."

She nodded, keeping eye contact with him.

He slipped two fingers into the bag, then brought out a pinch of powder. He lifted his hand above his head and sprinkled it over both of them. "Here we go…"

The small grains floated down, sparkling little stars, drifting sideways and looping around like tiny fireflies dancing to unheard music.

The bright, glittering specks filled her vision until all she could see was Hector before her.

The specks got brighter and brighter until there was nothing but undulating light shining in her eyes.

Then everything went black and quiet, but the darkness felt peaceful. Not like anything to be afraid of.

She realized her eyes were closed. She opened them. Hector was at her side, but they were no longer in the car.

All around them was a strange, bleak landscape painted in muted colors. Black, leafless trees clawed at a gloomy purple sky. Hard dirt and short, nubby grass burned brown stretched out before them. The wind whistled past like the distant cry of a lost child, bringing the smell of ozone and wet earth. Thunder rumbled in the distance.

The sky was so dark it was hard to say what was a cloud and what wasn't. "Storm coming?"

Hector shook his head. "Maybe. More likely his subconscious trying to warn him we're here."

"That's a cheery thought." She felt the front of her jacket and the sleeves, then reached for her hip. The only weapon that remained was Harper's spelled blade. She checked the interior. Pierce's pocket square was still there. She zipped her jacket up. She wasn't sure if she could lose things permanently in a dream, but it seemed like anything was possible. Especially considering she was here to kill someone.

But having that blade and his pocket square made her feel better. Like they tethered her to her own world.

"There." Hector pointed toward a small cabin on the crest of a hill in the distance. Bright yellow light shone from the single window. Had that been there before? She didn't think so. He nodded. "That's where we'll find Yavi."

# CHAPTER 35

As they walked, Donna looked down at herself. Her hands were rough and red, like she'd been doing hard labor with them. She was dressed in dirty, worn dungarees, and had work boots on her feet. One was held together with twine and tape.

She glanced at Hector. He looked the same as she remembered. "Do I look different to you? Or just to myself?"

He shook his head. "You and I will not always see the same things. Everyone interprets dreams differently."

"Then you don't see a cabin on a hill?" He'd pointed to it, after all. "Or hear that thunder?"

"No, I see the cabin and hear the thunder. But there will be subtle differences based on what our own minds bring to the experience." He smiled. "I promise it's not that different. And won't affect anything that matters."

"Okay." She looked around. "This wasn't what I expected to see in Yavi's head."

"Me neither. Makes me think…well, I don't want to say in case I'm wrong."

"No, go on. Please. You know this realm better than I do."

Hector glanced around before answering. "I thought Yavi was the one in charge, the one pushing Lillis to take the throne. I believe you thought that, too."

"I did," Donna confirmed.

"I don't think that after seeing this. This isn't the dream of someone who's in charge." He dug in as the hill they were climbing suddenly became steeper. "This is a prisoner's dream. I'll know for sure once we're in the cabin."

Donna didn't know what a prisoner's dream was, but this was Hector's area of expertise, so she believed that he knew what he was taking about. She pushed harder against the ground. "If we get there. Why did this hill become so hard to climb?"

"We're anomalies. On some level, Yavi's subconscious knows that. An easy way to get rid of us is to make our passage more difficult. Once we get through this, his mind will begin to believe we belong, and things will smooth out."

"I hope so, because if this gets any steeper, I might not—"

They were standing in front of the cabin door.

Donna looked behind her. There was no evidence of any hill. The ground just swept away from the cabin with a subtle rise and fall. "Okay, that's weird."

"That's how dreams work."

"Do I knock?"

"No. This might be Yavi's mind at work, but you need to be in control as much as possible. You can shape the dream to your will that way."

"Good to know." She opened the door.

The cabin wasn't as bright inside as the light shining through the window led her to believe. A small fire crackled in a potbelly stove. Pushed up against one wall was a single metal cot with a thin mattress and a tattered blanket. Yavi, or at least the person she guessed was Yavi, sat on the bed, staring into the flames.

Other than a rickety table with two chairs and a sink affixed to the wall, there was nothing else in the cabin.

Donna shook her head. "Is that him? He looks like a child."

Hector nodded. "That's him."

She took a step back. "I can't kill a child."

"It's only a dream, Donna."

She shook her head again. "I don't care. I'm a mother. There are lines you just don't cross."

"Then do something about it."

She frowned at him. "Meaning?"

"Find a way to make him an adult. Get him to change. Make him listen to you. This is your mission. Bend the dream to your needs."

"Can't you do it?"

"No, I'm sorry. All I can do is transport you in and out. Anything else would make me complicit."

"Oh. Right. Okay." She wished she'd known that ahead of time, but it made sense. She took a few steps toward the little boy on the bed. He continued to stare into the fire.

"Yavi?"

He looked up at her, cheeks sunken with hunger, eyes too large for his face. "Are you my mother?"

"No. Your mother was Artemis. Can I speak to Adult Yavi, please?"

"Can you tell my mother I'm hungry? Tell her my sister won't give me anything to eat."

"Did your sister put you here? Is she keeping you in this cabin?"

He nodded. "Yes. She's very mean to me."

Odd. He really had seemed to be the one in charge when they'd been at the house. Donna crouched down to talk to him on his level. "You know, if you become Adult Yavi, you can walk right out of this cabin and get anything you want to eat. As much of it as you like."

The little boy looked at her. Then he shifted, expanding and growing until a more-than-life-size adult towered over her. Yavi had become a monster version of himself. His fangs were twice as long as normal, and his eyes gleamed like angry red beacons. "How dare you invade my dreams?"

She fell back onto her butt in shock. "What the—"

He grabbed her by the jacket and hauled her to her feet, twisting his hand into the leather. "Who do you think you are?"

She just barely got Harper's blade out as he lifted her higher and her feet came off the ground. She couldn't quite get her grip right, not while her air was being cut off by his grip. Then she remembered she didn't need to breathe. Stupid dream. She made herself calm down and think. She needed to stay in control. And to buy herself time. "I'm just here to check on you, Yavi. Lillis sent me."

The anger left his face, replaced by…fear?

"She did?"

Donna nodded. "Yes. She wants a report on you."

His eyes widened. "What are you going to tell her?"

Donna finally got her grip right on the dagger's hilt, then lifted it high. "That you're dead." She plunged it into his chest.

His face registered the shock of being stabbed, then he exploded into ashes.

Donna closed her eyes instinctively against the shower of soot. When she opened them, everything had changed. She was back inside the safety of the SUV. Hector was beside her, Cammie and Harper in the front seats. "Is that it?" She blinked again, trying to get her bearings. "Is it over?"

Hector nodded. "Yavi has been dealt with. Only Lillis remains. But I have a feeling she's not going to be that easy. Especially now that we know she was the one behind all of this."

Cammie's brows shot up. "You mean Yavi wasn't running the show?"

Hector shook his head. "Based on what we saw in his dream, no. He might come off as the one in charge but it's an act. Lillis is the boss. Which means she's the most strong-willed of the pair. Her dream will be trickier to navigate."

"Trickier how?" Donna asked.

"We won't know until we get in there, but the more confident and in control the dreamer is, the harder it is to dreamwalk through their subconscious."

Donna nodded. "That's all right. I've had practice now. I feel like I'm better equipped to take her on." Although she did feel tired.

"Did my blade make it through?" Harper asked.

"Yes." Donna patted the sheath where the blade had been only to find it was there again. The rest of her weapons and the sword were also where they belonged. "It's what took Yavi out."

"Good," Harper said. "I'm glad about that."

"Same here," Donna said. She looked at Hector. "When can we take on Lillis?"

"As soon as you've had some nourishment. You probably feel energized right now because you were successful but trust me when I tell you that's temporary. Dreamwalking is exhausting. Feed. Then we'll go in."

"All right." Donna opened the cooler and took out a bottle. She wasn't going to argue. If taking on Lillis was going to be a challenge, she wanted to be ready. "Cammie, send a group text. Let everyone know Yavi is gone."

"On it." Cammie pulled out her phone and began typing.

Donna almost smiled. Cammie seemed pretty happy to be able to share that info. Donna tipped the bottle back and drank. Didn't take long for her to feel better, which made her realize she had been low on energy.

She wiped her mouth on the back of her hand. "Hector, you have been invaluable on this trip. I'm so glad you're here."

He smiled. "Thank you. But I'm here because of Lionel. After all, he's my boss. And a very good man. I'm lucky to work for him."

"Then you're about to get even luckier." Donna grinned. "This isn't information you can share because it hasn't been made public yet, but Lionel Prescott is about to become the new governor of New York."

"Hey," Cammie said. "Good choice. Does he know?"

Donna chuckled. "Yes, he knows. I talked to him first to make sure he was interested in taking on that much responsibility."

Hector's smile went from ear to ear. "Miss Francine is going to be great at being a governor's wife."

"She absolutely will be," Donna said. "And I think they're exactly what New York needs after Fitzhugh." She rolled her shoulders. The blood was kicking in, filling her with energy. "I don't know about you,

Hector, but I'm ready to go. If we don't get rid of Lillis, I may never make it to my coronation, and if that doesn't happen, Lionel won't be the governor of anything."

"I am definitely ready," Hector said as he pulled out his pouch of magic sand.

"Go get her," Cammie said.

"Stay safe," Harper added.

Donna nodded and looked into Hector's eyes like she had the first time.

He took out a pinch of sand. "Here we go."

# CHAPTER 36

Donna woke up to a familiar sight. The queen's mansion. *Her* home. The great hall, specifically.

Apparently, Lillis wasn't wasting any time planning for her future. She was so confident that she was going to be queen that she was dreaming about the home she thought she'd be living in.

The nerve.

Hector appeared beside Donna. He looked around, his expression bleak. "I knew she was going to be harder."

Donna didn't get that. "Why does seeing this house make you think that?"

"She's dreaming about it and it's not a warped reimagining. Look around. How close of a replication is it?"

Donna scanned the room. Everything was the way she remembered. "It seems almost identical," Donna answered.

"Which means she's not just projecting, she's imagining her life as it will be. If this was a cartoonish replica, it would imply her subconscious knew what an impossible goal being queen was. But it's not. It's very real. And that's how she sees it."

"Awesome," Donna snarked. "But it gives us an advantage, too. After all, I know my way around this place better than she does. At least I should." Donna hoped that was true.

"Good. Then you can take us to the queen's quarters, because that's most likely where we'll find her."

"Hang on. Are you saying we just go in there and surprise her?"

"I guess I was. What do you think we should do? Bear in mind, her subconscious knows we're here. It's only a matter of time before she starts to test us, just like Yavi did."

The great hall doors opened, and Marcus walked in. He looked almost the same, except for a smattering of gray hair and a noticeable gauntness. His brows arched in obvious condescension. "The queen is waiting for you."

Okay, the attitude was different, too.

"Like I said," Hector muttered.

"Right," Donna muttered back. She returned Marcus's haughty gaze. "We're waiting here to see the queen."

He stared at her as if he hadn't expected that.

"Go on," Donna said. "Tell her we're here and we expect to see her."

He shook his head. "But she's the queen. People are supposed to do what she says."

Donna stepped into his personal space. Hector told her it was important to stay in control, and she'd definitely learned the importance of that while she was in Yavi's head. "We both know I'm the queen. So you tell her to get her skanky little daemon butt down here, or I will set this mansion on fire and burn it to the ground with her inside it. Is that clear enough for you?"

Marcus stared at her blankly. He turned and headed out of the room without another word.

Donna looked at Hector. "Think that will work?"

He smiled. "It just might."

The lights dimmed and the room began to twist and shift. Walls disappeared. The fireplace vanished. Large shards of glass grew out of the floor.

Donna moved just in time to keep from being sliced in half. "Hector, look out."

He sidestepped, missing another one.

At last, everything went still. Balls of fiery sparks appeared throughout the room. Roughly the size of a penny, there were too many of them to count. Or maybe it was just a few and she was seeing their reflections.

It was impossible to tell. The light from the fireballs bounced off every piece of glass, turning the space into a demented house of mirrors. Donna gaped at Hector through several layers of glass. Hard to guess how many, but she didn't like being separated from him. And not just because it felt deliberate.

"Didn't work the way I'd hoped," Donna whispered. "Mary and Joseph, I did not see that coming."

"Welcome to the realm of dreams," he said. "It's all right. You can navigate this. Just be careful."

"What do you mean me? Aren't you coming with me?"

He raised his hands to press against the glass walls surrounding him on all sides like a prison cell. "I can't."

Donna fumed. "She did that on purpose."

"Absolutely. But you can do this. I know you can. You must believe that, too."

With a nod, Donna concentrated her attention on the direction that felt like forward. She knew she had to remain confident and focused, but that was easier said than done. The fireballs buzzed around her, and there was no telling what might happen next. "Maybe I shouldn't have threatened her."

"No, that was good. If you'd backed down and we'd gone to her apartments, it probably would have been worse."

"Worse?" Donna turned to look at him and brushed against one of the shards, putting a deep slash in the sleeve of her jacket. "Yikes."

"Did you get cut?"

"No, I'm okay." She examined her sleeve as best she could in the weird, fiery lighting. "It didn't go through. Pretty sure the iron in this thing makes it wear like armor."

"Good. Remember, stay strong. Trust your instincts. And above all, don't forget that this is a dream. You *can* control it."

She nodded. "Thanks, but if that's the case, why can't I just get you out?"

"Because I'm a sandman. I'm not as much of an interloper in this realm as you are. If the dream is water, you're oil. I'm ink. I might be noticeable to the dreamer's subconscious at first, but after a short while, I blend in. You never will."

"Got it. All right, here goes." She started forward again, carefully. This might just be a dream, but she didn't need to be sliced to ribbons while she was here.

Maneuvering a path through the maze of glass shards was slow going. That alone worked on her nerves. She also wasn't interested in being here any longer than necessary. She tried to focus on the shards so her frustration didn't become a distraction.

All of the glass fragments were taller and wider than she was, and on more than one occasion she worked herself into a dead end. That only aggravated her mood. On the third dead end, she paused, took a deep cleansing breath, then thought about doing something reckless. Better to run it by the expert first, though.

Hector was several yards behind her and hard to see clearly through the warped reflections.

"Hector?" She tightened her hands into fists.

"Yes?"

"Couldn't I just smash through this glass?"

"You could. But how would you protect yourself

against the broken pieces? You saw what happened to your jacket when you brushed against the glass."

She growled softly and relaxed her hands. "Right. Good point."

She went back to picking her way through the glass maze and came face to face with one of the snapping, sparking fireballs. It hovered directly in front of her at chest level.

"Out of my way."

The ball didn't move. Just floated there with what Donna felt certain was arrogance. This whole dream reeked of it. Lillis thought she was better than Donna. Better than everyone, probably.

Donna put her thumb and index finger together and flicked the ball out of the way.

The moment she made contact, electricity zapped her. Every inch of her body came alive with the sharpest pins and needles she'd ever felt.

If she'd had breath, it would have been sucked from her lungs. As it was, she fell against the flat surface of the shard behind her as she tried to ride out the pain.

"Are you all right?" Hector's voice sounded far away.

Was she blacking out? She could not do that. Not here. Not now. *Get control.* She held her hand up, the only answer she could give.

The pain subsided and she collected herself. Instead of seeking calm, she gathered up the anger she'd been suppressing. The pain of what had happened to Pierce.

The disgust at Fitzhugh. The resentment at how the council had treated her. The fury at her father, the emissary, for leaving her and Cammie all those years ago. For acting in the present like that past didn't matter.

She stopped pushing all of that hurt and pain and resentment down and let it rise.

A tempest grew within her, filling her until a strange calm took over. She was in the eye of her own personal storm.

Perhaps this was what real control felt like. No more pretending she was fine. It was time to be exactly what she was. Her fangs descended and in the glass before her, she saw her eyes begin to glow. Dream or not, the real Donna was here to stay.

She funneled all of that violent serenity into the word, "*No.*"

The glass shards shook with the sound of her voice, even though it hadn't come out with any volume. The word echoed off them, vibrating through the room until the glass began to crumble and disintegrate.

The great hall returned.

The fireballs survived to gather in front of the doors. As if they were intent on keeping her from getting to Lillis.

Donna wasn't about to be that easily deterred. If this was a dream and she could control it, then it was time to see just how much she could actually manipulate. With her cool, calm, furious mindset, she focused on what she wanted to happen. She took a deep breath and blew hard at the fireballs.

They sputtered and pulsed, sparking hard, then they all went out like candles on a birthday cake.

"Very good," Hector said with a small amount of awe in his voice.

"Thanks." She pulled the blade from her sleeve and anchored it in her fist. "Now let's go find Lillis."

## CHAPTER 37

Now that their surroundings looked like the queen's mansion again, Donna's confidence grew. What she'd just done to the glass shards and the fireballs helped, but knowing where she was going was a big deal.

As she and Hector went up the stairs, because she didn't trust getting into the elevator's enclosed space, she asked him a question. "Could the fact that we're back in the queen's mansion mean Lillis is weakening?"

"Maybe. It's more likely that since you showed her how powerful you are, her subconscious isn't treating us like so much of a threat. More like part of the dream than intruders. Whether that's good or bad will have to play out. But I don't believe we'll run into too many more obstacles that prevent us from getting to her."

"I hope not. This is starting to feel like one of the video games my son Joe Jr. loves to play. Which would make Lillis the final boss."

Hector smiled. "That it would. Especially because once we reach her and you defeat her, the game will be over."

"I can't wait." Finding Lillis was the point, after all. Donna was glad Marcus hadn't returned. She'd been afraid Lillis would turn him into an enemy and force her to fight one of her own people as one of the obstacles. Donna would, of course, but it wasn't something she wanted to be forced into.

They reached the top of the stairs. The hall before them looked the same as the real one, although there was no way Lillis could know what the queen's apartment looked like beyond the doors. Unless she'd been to Artemis's house before.

Donna imagined that had to be true. Otherwise, how could Lillis recreate all of this with so much accuracy and detail? One brief trip wouldn't have been enough.

She tipped her head toward the doors. "That's the entrance to the apartment up ahead. Stay behind me, okay?"

He nodded. "As you wish."

She glanced at him and saw he had his blade in hand. "I do. I can't have anything happening to you. If I can't do what I need to do, you're my only way out of here."

"Nothing will happen to me, I promise."

"It better not." They reached the doors and she put her hand on the knob. She had no idea what she was about to face. There was no way Lillis was going down without a fight, but Donna was prepared for that as best she could be. All she could do was pray this went as easily as it had with Yavi.

She reached for her crucifix to reassure herself. It

wasn't there. She clenched her jaw. She would *not* read anything into that. This was just a dream. Made sense that daemon Lillis wouldn't want any religious symbols around. Nor would she know Donna wore such a thing. But could Lillis control what was on Donna's person? Or had the crucifix not made it through just like her sword and the unspelled blades hadn't?

Dreams were confusing. Even more so being inside one.

She opened the apartment door and went in. The apartment seemed exactly the same as it was in reality. Same colors, same high-end spa feel. There was no sign of Lillis in the living room or kitchen area. Where was she? Maybe she wasn't in here after all.

Donna heard soft voices. Laughter and sounds of pleasure. Her bedroom. What kind of nonsense was Lillis up to?

Donna glanced down at the blade in her hand. It wasn't really the weapon she wanted. She wanted something more impressive. Something that made a statement about why she was here. She'd just proven she could control her surroundings. Could she do the same with her personal belongings?

She decided to start small by focusing hard on her crucifix. She put her hand to her chest where it should be and with all of her mental strength imagined it there.

Just like that, the hard metal was under her fingertips. She smiled. She could do this.

She concentrated again, this time on the blade in her hand. The metal changed in her grip, lengthening, and turning from silver to gold as it morphed into something much more recognizable. If there was ever a time to wield the Queen's Sword, this was it. She smiled. Having it in her hand gave her confidence another boost.

"Perfect," Hector said softly.

"Thanks. Now let's go find her and end this." Donna opened her bedroom door. Shapes moved under the bed linens, and she heard soft laughter muted by the fabric.

Donna didn't care what new game this was. She wasn't participating. She was here to kill Lillis and end this nonsense once and for all.

She leaped onto the bed, sword raised high, prepared to slide it into Lillis's heart.

The covers flipped back, revealing Lillis in a tiny ivory lace negligee, her bedmate beside her.

Donna's jaw dropped.

"Pierce?"

At the sight of him, she went numb with grief and confusion. The sword dipped as her grip on it loosened. Her stomach rolled over and her heart ached worse than when Cammie's blade had penetrated it. "How..."

This wasn't real, she reminded herself. Just a dream. That's all it was. Even so, he looked so real. And the way he smiled up at her nearly broke her in two.

Lillis snickered. "Come to kill me, have you? In my mother's house? With my mother's sword? You must think you're awfully clever."

Donna wasn't thinking much of anything right now. "I—"

Lillis was suddenly where Pierce had been, and he was in her place. The shift happened in the blink of an eye. Lillis laughed. "Which one is really me? I guess you'll have to kill us both to find out."

Donna shook her head. She couldn't do that. Fighting Marcus was one thing, but Pierce? Dream or not, she couldn't run him through. What if that killed him for real? Or was his appearance in this dream proof he was already dead?

Neither of those questions had good answers.

In her heart of hearts, she knew logically that this was just a dream. That there was no way the man in front of her was Pierce.

But that same heart was broken by her love for him and that made it nearly impossible to side with logic. Her grief over losing him was too fresh. Her need for him too great. Her pain trumped reason.

She jumped off the bed to get some distance, hoping that would help. She needed to figure this out before she did something there was no coming back from. "Hector, what's going on? What happens if I kill them both?"

"Lillis dies," he responded.

"Do I, though?" Lillis asked with mock innocence.

"Or do you just get to live with the memory that you killed the man you love? Assuming you haven't already killed him by forcing him into that hellmouth."

How did she know about that? Had Lillis and her brother been there, watching? "No," Donna said. "I didn't force him into the hellmouth."

"Didn't you?" Lillis tossed off the covers and hopped out of the bed, stalking toward Donna. Her ivory teddy changed to a filmy black peignoir set that billowed behind her despite the fact there was no wind in the bedroom.

Empowered by her anger, Donna pointed the sword at Lillis. "You caused that hellmouth to be opened. It was the only way to deal with the demon horde you sent after us. It was your fault, and you know it."

Lillis canted her head to one side. "Just like it's your fault Pierce is here now."

"No, it's not. This is your dream. Your sick mind at work."

She wagged a finger at Donna. "But you're the one who brought a piece of him with you, aren't you?"

"No, how could I—" Pierce's cologne wafted up from the pocket square tucked into her jacket. A shudder went through Donna. *Had* she done this? *Was* she responsible?

"Of course you did. Now look what you've done." Lillis made a clucking sound with her tongue. "Poor sad vampire. So confused. Is your lover alive, or isn't he? Are you willing to kill him or not? Will anyone remember you, the queen-who-almost-was, after you die? So many hard questions."

The mocking tone in Lillis's voice dug into Donna's heart and mind like an ice pick. Her confidence began to erode, slipping away drop by drop. She had to do something. She had to figure this out. "Pierce, is that really you?"

He sat up in the bed and the covers fell to his waist. He pulled his knees to his chest and smiled at her. "Of course it's me. Doesn't it look like me?"

It did look like him. But wouldn't the real Pierce be telling her to save herself?

Lillis came closer.

Donna brandished the sword higher. "Not another step."

Lillis and Pierce changed places again, putting Lillis in the bed and Pierce directly in front of her. He wore pajama pants and nothing else. The smell of his cologne intensified. It looked very much like him. It *smelled* very much like him. But this was just a dream.

Or was it? Everything seemed so real it was hard to be sure.

He took a step toward her, putting the tip of her sword inches from his heart. "Do you really want to kill me, Donna?"

She chose her words carefully. "I need to kill Lillis before she kills me. She's the reason Francine and Bunni were hurt. The reason a member of the security team died. The reason you ended up in the hellmouth."

He narrowed his eyes and his expression hardened into one of disappointment. "We both know you're the real reason I ended up in the hellmouth. Does that mean you should die, too?"

He moved another step toward her, pressing himself into the tip of her sword. A single drop of blood trickled from the wound and ran down his bare chest.

That proved he was real, didn't it? No, that was just how dreams worked. Anything could seem real. She had to get control again. But seeing Pierce had thrown her, and it didn't feel like something she could easily pull herself out of.

Something Lillis was no doubt counting on.

Desperation set in. Time was ticking away. This had to end. Now. The longer she remained in this alternate reality, the harder it was to separate fact from fiction. "Hector, what do I do?"

"You know what to do," he said from behind her. "That might seem like Pierce, but it isn't. You know that. Find the courage you need and get it done."

That was the answer she'd been afraid of. She was trembling. And fighting the urge to speak the safe word and get out of here as fast as she could.

If she did that, Lillis would win this round, which would give her the upper hand. And there was no doubt in Donna's mind that Lillis would come for her again and again and again until Donna was dead and Lillis was queen.

That couldn't happen. Too many more people would be hurt or killed because of her. Donna's friends for sure. The staff that supported her. The visitors who expected her to keep them safe.

Lillis began to laugh. "What was my mother thinking to make you queen? You don't have what it takes, and you never will." She rose up out of the bed, a sword of her own in her hands. A gold one, just like what Donna held. She pointed it at Donna. "Prepare to die, pretender."

Tears spilled down Donna's face. She knew what had to be done. She just had to find the strength to do it. And then the ability to live with what she'd done. Because this wasn't a dream so much as a nightmare.

With a guttural cry of pain and anguish, she shoved the sword into Pierce's heart.

# CHAPTER 38

Another explosion of ash, another involuntary closing of her eyes, and Donna found herself back in the car with Hector, Cammie, and Harper.

This time, she was sick to her stomach and brokenhearted. She stared out the window but all she could see was Pierce, dissolving in front of her, a look of shock and surprise on his beautiful face. "Home. Please. Now."

"What happened?" Cammie asked. "Did you get Lillis?"

Donna swallowed. She was in no shape for conversation.

Thankfully, Hector answered for her. "She did. It's done."

"Okay, good," Cammie said. "Maybe now we can close that hellmouth and call it finished."

"Not yet," Donna snapped as she turned toward her sister. "Please, just stop with all of that."

Cammie frowned.

"Shouldn't we go check the apartment for ourselves?" Harper asked. "Just to be sure."

Donna pulled herself together enough to speak a few more sentences. "Temo and his team will do it. Just let them know. Then get a cleaning crew in there to erase any signs of Lillis and Yavi."

"What happened in there?" Cammie asked as she took out her phone. "You don't seem okay."

"I'm not," Donna choked out. "Please, let's just get home."

"I'm sure she's exhausted," Hector said. Then he spoke to Donna. "It probably wouldn't be a bad idea to feed again."

Donna shook her head. She didn't want to feel better. She didn't deserve to. She might have put an end to Lillis, but at what cost to her mental health? Lillis might have lost the war, but she'd left Donna with wounds that weren't ever going to heal.

Donna closed her eyes and leaned her head against the window. Lillis had known exactly what she was doing. Donna couldn't shake the last images she'd seen. Of putting that blade through Pierce. Watching his eyes round in betrayal. Then the way he went to ash.

That should be enough to prove to her the person she'd killed in that dream wasn't him. Reapers didn't go to ash like that. But what her head knew and what her heart believed were two very different things.

It was impossible to feel otherwise. Not when a being that looked and smelled and sounded exactly like Pierce had been right there in front of her.

That had to be what Lillis had intended. To cripple Donna with guilt and remorse and grief. She'd never forget what she'd done or how it made her feel.

She heard the sounds of texting, then the car started, and the GPS guided them back to the house. Donna only became aware they were home when Cammie woke her.

She stood in the open passenger door, shaking Donna gently. "Hey, we're here. We're back at the estate."

It was blazing bright outside and bitter cold. Donna squinted and held her hand to her forehead like a visor. She grunted in understanding, released her seatbelt, and slid out of the vehicle.

Her knees buckled as her feet touched the ground.

Cammie grabbed her before she fell. "Whoa. I've got you. Hector said you'd need a lot of rest after what you went through. Come on, let's get you up to bed."

Donna nodded. She was exhausted. Mentally, physically, emotionally. All three tanks were on Empty. She knew she should have fed in the car, but she hadn't had it in her. She leaned against her sister and made it a few more steps before dizziness swept through her and her knees gave out a second time.

Her lids opened again, her only indicator that she'd passed out. She was vaguely aware of being carried by Kace, Cammie at his side. "Right up to bed," her sister was saying.

They were in the house, where the lighting was dimmer and easier on her eyes but she closed them anyway. She didn't care what went on around her. She just wanted to sleep and forget. And, hopefully, not dream.

She never wanted to dream again.

Kace deposited her on her bed. She drifted in and out, hearing the door shut, then Cammie mutter something about getting changed.

"What?" Donna asked, squinting up at her.

"I was just saying we should get you changed into something more comfortable."

"Yeah." Donna closed her eyes and rolled over, hands tucked under her cheek.

"Come on," Cammie said, trying to ease her out of her leather jacket. "You can't sleep in this. It's covered in blades and it can't be comfortable."

"It's fine," Donna mumbled.

Cammie wasn't about to let that happen, clearly. She finessed one of Donna's arms out of a sleeve, then rolled her to tackle the other one. Before Donna knew it, her sister was lifting the jacket away.

And taking Pierce's pocket square with it.

Donna came awake. "No, give that to me." She grabbed the jacket and dug the silk square out of the inside pocket.

Cammie frowned at her. "What is that? And what's going on with you? You're kind of a mess. Why won't you tell me what happened?"

Donna clutched the fabric to her chest, inhaling his fragrance and replaying the scene from Lillis's dream in her head. She stared at her sister while she realized how right Cammie was.

Donna *was* a mess. Inside, anyway. Hot tears streamed down her face. "She made me kill him."

"Who made you kill who?"

"Lillis. She made me kill Pierce." Donna got the words out as best she could without completely dissolving into a sobbing snot-monster. "She split herself into two parts in her dream. One was her, one was Pierce. Then she put me in a situation where I had to kill him to kill her."

Horror filled Cammie's eyes. She pulled Donna into her arms. "Oh, Donna. That's beyond awful. I'm so sorry that daemon cockroach put you through that. I hope she's enjoying the hellfire she deserves right now."

Donna sniffed and pulled back. "Do you know if Temo found anything in the apartment?"

Cammie nodded. "Two piles of ash and one decomposing human, the former tenant. No doubt dispatched by Lillis and Yavi."

Donna shook her head. "They deserved to die."

"Yes, they did. But you didn't deserve to go through that. You've been through so much in such a short amount of time."

Donna lay back and stared up at the ceiling. "What's done is done. I'm exhausted and I want to sleep, but I really don't want to dream."

"I can get Hector if you want. He might be able to help with that."

Donna rolled her head back and forth on the pillow. "No. I'm sure he could but I don't want to see him again so soon. Nothing against him. The man deserves a medal. He's probably exhausted. But after what we just went through…"

"I understand." Cammie patted Donna's leg. "How about you take a quick hot shower, get into some pajamas and meet me back here, where I'll have a big glass of red wine waiting for you. Then we can find an old movie and I'll stay right beside you while you sleep. If you seem like you're having a nightmare, I'll wake you up."

"You will?"

Cammie nodded. "You bet."

"Okay." Donna swung her feet off the bed. "If I can stay awake during a shower."

Cammie shrugged. "Then don't. Just get into a nightgown."

"No, a shower would be good. After all of that, I don't feel so clean." Donna stood, putting the pocket square on the nightstand.

"What is that piece of fabric?"

Donna glanced at it. "One of Pierce's pocket squares. I just wanted something of his to keep with me. Lillis hinted that bringing it with me into her dream is what triggered his presence there."

"Sounds like garbage if you ask me. Sounds like her

trying to make you feel guilty." Cammie stood up, scowling. "I'm glad those two are gone. They were evil to their cores. The world is better off without them, so if you're handing out medals to Hector, give one to yourself."

Donna couldn't quite make herself smile. Pierce was too much on her mind. "Listen, about the hellmouth…"

Cammie shook her head. "Whenever you're ready. Just takes a few words in Latin to close it. You can even do it yourself if you want."

Donna couldn't do it just yet, but soon, she'd have to. She couldn't leave a hellmouth open on the property. "Would you write them down for me?"

"Sure."

"Thanks. Be right back."

She grabbed a nightgown out of her dresser, then went straight to the bathroom. She turned on the water, then stripped. She was happy to see her crucifix gleaming around her neck. She clipped her hair up and got into the steamy shower.

The last time she'd been in here, she'd been covered in blood. This time, she felt like she had a layer of ash on her, even though she didn't. This beautiful, luxurious shower had become far more utilitarian than she was sure it had been meant to be.

She soaped up, rinsed off, and got out. She dried herself, then pulled on her nightgown and went back to bed.

Cammie had the TV on and was searching for a movie. She'd closed the curtains so the room was wonderfully dark. A big balloon goblet of red liquid sat on Donna's nightstand, next to Pierce's pocket square. A folded piece of paper was stuck halfway under the goblet's foot. No doubt the words to close the hellmouth.

Cammie smiled at her. "Feel better?"

"Cleaner." That was all Donna could answer to honestly. She wasn't sure if she'd ever really feel better.

Cammie watched the screen as she flipped around. "How about one of the Thin Man movies?"

"Perfect." Donna sat on the bed and tucked the pocket square under her pillow. She opened the slip of paper. The necessary words in Latin, as she'd requested. She refolded the paper and got under the covers, propping herself up on some pillows. She'd think about the hellmouth tomorrow.

She took a few big gulps of the wine, emptying half the glass. It was good and certainly not meant for gulping, but who cared? What did it matter? Did anything anymore?

She set the glass aside, dug out the pocket square to hold in her hand, and prayed for dreamless sleep.

# CHAPTER 39

Donna woke to a dark room, lit only by the flickering gray tones of whatever movie was playing. She looked around for the time and found it on the cable box. A few minutes after three a.m. She'd slept a long time.

She looked over her shoulder. Cammie was beside her, snoring softly.

Donna smiled briefly. Her sister needed rest. They all did. They all needed a vacation, really. Maybe they'd take Francesca up on her offer to visit Mexico. Someplace warm and balmy and far away from here sounded pretty good right about now.

Although going without Pierce would be hard.

She got up and went to the windows, pushing the curtains aside to look out.

The glow of the hellmouth burned in the distance like a bonfire. Flames shot up into the night, daggers of light and destruction threatening to slice through anything that dared come close enough.

She glared at it for a long, hard moment. Her anger was back. Not with the same kind of punch it had before. She'd used up some of that anger dreamwalking.

But a good portion remained.

She pulled on jeans, a sweater, her leather jacket, and her boots, then grabbed the slip of paper from her nightstand and tucked it into the pocket of her jeans. She grabbed the pocket square, too, and put it back inside her jacket. Then she finished the remaining wine in two long swallows.

On her way downstairs, she zipped up her jacket. She knew she must look like a nightmare. Makeup smeared, hair wild, and the kind of crazed look in her eyes that had to be present.

With the way she felt inside, there was no way it wasn't showing through.

She passed one of the housekeeping staff in the hall, carrying towels. The woman kept her eyes down and Donna said nothing, just kept going. She didn't want to interact with anyone. She just needed to be left alone so she could do what needed to be done.

She made it to the front door without running into anyone else, although she could hear people in rooms she passed, and more voices coming out of the great hall, which she avoided.

With a quick look behind her, she slipped outside.

The cold was good. It braced her for the job that lay ahead, slapping sense into her. Pierce wasn't coming back. As much as she didn't want to believe it, she knew it was the only logical conclusion. Cammie said no one came back from what he'd done. Donna just hadn't wanted to face that truth because it held a deep pit of pain.

Pain seemed to be her new normal. If that's what her life was meant to be, then at least she could be honest with herself.

It was time to close the hellmouth.

She marched toward it, the crusty snow crunching under her steps. The first walk out here had taken four minutes at a pretty good clip, but time didn't matter. She'd get there when she got there.

Something dark seemed to lurk in the shadows behind the hellmouth's light. Another demon, maybe? Drawn to the intoxicating stench of the hellmouth?

Maybe Donna would help him in before she closed it. She found a blade in her jacket and gripped it firmly. The smell grew worse as she got closer. With her free hand, she pulled the pocket square from inside her jacket and held it over her nose, muting the stench with bittersweet memories.

The smell of Pierce's cologne made her tear up, her emotions raw and on the surface after what she'd just been through. And what she was about to do.

The closer she got, the more the demon at the dark edge became a long, rounded lump on the ground, but the dancing light and grasping shadows made it hard to figure out what she was seeing. Was it two demons crouched together? The constantly shooting flames and bursts of light in the hellmouth made it hard for her night vision to adjust.

What was it? Could be a pile of dirt. Donna didn't remember it being there.

There was no snow on it either, so it couldn't have been there long.

She should have brought the sword with her, but she'd been so focused on getting this done, she hadn't taken the time. Dumb decision. One she would not make again. Blade in front of her, she went in to investigate, tucking the pocket square away.

The light and dark swirling around her made the lump seem almost human-shaped. She moved closer, blade out. Were those wings? They looked scorched and possibly melted. An injured demon?

Maybe it was dead.

She nudged the shape with her foot, pushing it over.

The wings unfurled, revealing the creature inside.

Pierce.

With a gasp, she dropped her blade and fell to her knees beside him. His face was covered in soot and his clothes were ragged. He reeked of smoke and sulfur. "*Pierce*, speak to me. Is it really you? Are you okay? Pierce!"

Clearly, he wasn't okay. She wasn't sure he was even alive. She cupped his face in her hands. He was warm and clammy. He didn't feel dead. *Wait*. He was a reaper. He couldn't be dead.

She leaned in, kissing him softly while whispering to him. "Pierce, say something. Tell me you're okay. Tell me it's really you."

"I told you I'd come back."

If she hadn't been so close to him, she wasn't sure she'd have heard his words. With a sob, she wrapped her arms around him and held him tight, tears of joy glazing her face. "Yes, you did."

Francine had known, too. But Donna had been about to close the hellmouth.

Flames roared suddenly, dancing higher like they'd done when she'd looked through the windows from the house.

He pushed up onto one elbow. "We need Cammie. This thing needs to be closed. The demon horde might not be coming back, but there were a few on my tail. If they break through—"

"Don't worry." Donna jumped to her feet and went as close to the hellmouth as she dared. "I've got this."

She pulled out the paper Cammie had left on her nightstand and said a mental prayer that the Latin came out right. Then she lifted her voice and spoke the words. "*Ignes inferni cessant!*"

Groaning drifted up through the hellmouth as if the earth itself objected. The flames leaped higher and scraped at the earth around the hellmouth, burning it black. The ground started to shudder and move, and the fissures began to seal.

The groans turned into wails of protest and pain. The sound screeched across Donna's skin, raising goosebumps and setting her teeth on edge.

As the flames were cut off, Donna could see claw

marks deep in the hellmouth. Like something, or several somethings, had been trying to get out.

She backed away from it as the last crack closed. "There. It's done."

"Good."

She returned to Pierce. "We need to get you into the house. You don't look so great."

"I don't feel so great, but I'll be fine." He was laying down again. Eyes closed.

"You'd better be. Come on. Let's get you inside." She helped him to his feet. He leaned on her heavily, but she relished the weight of him. "I have to know. Why on earth did you jump into that thing?"

"Oh, that. Right." He reached behind him and pulled a glowing crystal blade from somewhere.

"Cammie's holy dagger?"

He nodded. "It is. But more importantly, it's your soul."

She stared up at him, shaking her head. "Why would you go back for that? I don't need it. I'm immortal."

"You can still be killed. This gives you one more chance to stay alive, and as queen you're going to need it."

"But Pierce, I thought you were *dead*."

He laughed. *Laughed*. "Sweetheart, I'm a reaper. Nothing can kill me. And souls are my currency now."

"Pierce. *Still*." As thrilled as she was that he'd returned, she wanted to smack him for putting her through such misery over something she considered inconsequential.

He held the dagger up and stopped walking. "Just give me a second." Then he pulled the glowing bit off the dagger with his fingertips and pressed it to her heart.

The glow melted into her body. And her heart started beating.

She sucked in a breath, almost choking on it. She reached for him, steadying herself. "I was just getting used to not breathing."

He smiled.

"But this doesn't mean what you did was okay. I've been a mess thinking you were dead. Don't ever do that again. Especially over something that wasn't even that important."

He frowned. "You think getting your soul back wasn't important? Because I disagree. Being queen means you're going to be in that many more crosshairs than you were before. You need every chance you can get to stay alive and outwit whatever comes at you next. What if you'd already lost your soul and the hellmouth needed to be opened? Someone would have died. For real." He shook his head. "I told you I'd do everything in my power to protect you, and I meant that. I still do. Nothing you say is going to change that."

"What on earth made you think you could take on hell and win?"

"I talked to Will about just how far the whole immortal thing went and how much dominion reapers really have over souls. That talk convinced me I could do it."

"So Will's to blame for all of this? Why didn't he say something?"

Pierce snorted. "It was all my idea. And he didn't say anything because I made him swear not to. In case things didn't go the way I planned and I couldn't get your soul back. I didn't want you counting on something I might not be able to deliver. I'd do it again, by the way."

She laughed softly. "You're so stubborn."

"You're one to talk." He grabbed her and pulled her into his arms, kissing her properly.

She sank into him, not quite believing he was really here. "I missed you so much," she whispered. "Don't ever leave me again."

"I won't," he whispered back.

She pressed herself against him, her head on his chest. He'd risked so much just to bring her soul back to her. There would never be another gift that compared. Or another man so brave and true. "I love you."

"I love you, too. I'm sorry I scared you."

"It doesn't matter now. You're home." She looked up at him. "By the way, Francine is doing great, Lionel is going to be the next New York governor, Bunni is slowly but surely improving, and Lillis and Yavi are dead. Short version of that long story, I killed them in their dreams."

"I'm so glad to hear about Francine and Bunni. Lionel's a great choice." Then his brow bent. "But I'm going to need the long version of that last one."

She smiled. "I'll tell you the whole thing, I promise. Oh, and Fitzhugh is dead."

He grinned. "I *really* want the full version of that."

She hooked her arm through his. "Come on. Fitzy's tale isn't quite as much to tell. I'll fill you in on the way back to the house, where I'm sure everyone is going to want to hear all about your adventures in the hellmouth."

"Sounds good. But maybe after I get a shower and something to eat? And a nap. I haven't slept since I took that leap."

She nodded. "Let's go straight up, then. There will be plenty of time for storytelling when you're ready."

And right now, she wanted him to herself for a while. Even if that meant just being with him while he slept.

# Chapter 40

The next several days passed in a whirlwind of planning, arriving guests, and massive amounts of organization to make the coronation happen as scheduled. Marcus and Charlie worked together like they'd been a team all their lives.

Because of the new guests, Donna couldn't be absent from meals. Not all of them, anyway, so as much as she would have preferred to dine alone in her apartment with just her crew of friends, that wasn't always the best choice.

She reminded herself that once the coronation was over, things would calm down. She hoped.

She made it a priority, however, to sit down with Queen Francesca, King Lucho and King Konstantin, who'd recently joined the Allied Vampire Nation, via video feed, so that they could finally select the new council that would handle disputes. The Primo Concilio was composed of twelve fully vetted citizens from the four uniting nations.

Gone were the days of the nameless, anonymous council passing judgement in shrouded secrecy. At least for those who belonged to the AVN.

Other rulers continued to join them, giving the new

nation even more power. All of the rulers, new and old, shared a video meeting to talk about the future. As a group, they felt like it was just a matter of time before the Immortus Concilio was no more.

Spirits were high.

Bunni continued to improve. And Kace stayed by her side.

Lionel arrived, much to Francine's delight.

Temo and Rico worked with the household security team to ensure the estate was as well protected as it could be.

The rest of the group took it easy when they could, something Donna wholeheartedly approved of. Soon, most of them would be headed back to New Jersey. Donna didn't want to think about her friends leaving her, although she knew it had to happen.

As the days ticked away, there remained more to do for the coronation, but Donna spent as much time as possible with Pierce, keeping him close and reveling in having him back. He had some recovery to do, so she pushed him to rest, spending every second of her rare down time with him.

Her list of things to do only seemed to grow.

Fortunately, picking out her coronation gown was something they could handle together.

"I don't need to sit," he insisted.

"Do it anyway," she countered.

He frowned at her. "I'm fine. I promise."

"Pierce, just do it. For me?"

With a sigh, he settled into the chair she'd dragged into the massive closet.

"Thank you." She smiled at his grumpiness. It was kind of adorable. "The coronation is going to be exhausting with so many people here to deal with, all the ceremony, and the big banquet and, oh, did you know each governor is supposed to pledge their fealty to me? Seems a little medieval, but I get the idea."

"They'd better. After what you've accomplished this week, they'd be idiots not to."

She laughed. "Well, any who don't make the pledge will be summarily dismissed and replaced with governors who will. Starting a new vampire nation is a team project. I need all of them onboard. A difference of opinion is fine. Disloyalty is another thing."

"I agree." He grinned mischievously. "Your Highness."

She rolled her eyes good-naturedly. "All right, on to the dresses. Maybe I should have two. One for the coronation, and one for the dinner that follows. The second one should be a little more comfortable and a little less over the top. I'll try on the ones we pulled and—"

"Seems like an age ago we did that." His gaze took on a faraway gleam.

"It does. So much has happened since then." She watched him as he seemed lost in thought. That had been happening ever since he'd returned. Even if he didn't want to talk about what he'd been through in the depths of that hellmouth, she understood it had been the most difficult thing he'd ever done.

And he'd done it for her. Hard not to feel moved by that. And guilty.

But he'd made the decision to do it. She hadn't asked, so she refused to allow herself to wallow. The only feelings she chose to acknowledge were gratitude for what he'd done and joy that he'd returned.

That didn't stop her from worrying about him, though. About the way the dark shadows around him grew darker and more menacing when he slipped away from her like he was doing now.

Could reapers have PTSD? She was starting to wonder.

"Pierce? Sweetheart?"

"Hmm?" He looked up at her. "What was that?"

"I'm going to try on the first dress now."

He nodded, smiling again. "Wonderful."

She took the first dress, a brilliant blue gown with a jacquard print and one shoulder finished in a ruffle detail, and slipped into it behind the privacy screen.

As she changed, it occurred to her that it might be beneficial for Pierce to talk to Dr. Ogden. There didn't seem to be anything wrong with Pierce physically, although she hadn't seen him in his reaper form since that first night, so she didn't know what shape his wings were in or how much healing they had left to do.

Clearly there was something bothering him. Maybe Dr. Ogden could help. Maybe it would just be useful for Pierce to talk to someone who had some distance from the whole thing. Someone who, as they said, didn't have skin in the game. And because Dr. Ogden was a respected physician, maybe Pierce would listen to him.

She stepped out in the blue dress. "Okay, I know what I think about this. But I want to hear your impression first."

"You look beautiful in it, which isn't surprising, but it doesn't seem royal enough. Not for the coronation, anyway. Maybe the dinner after. The coronation is a big deal. It's a once in a lifetime event, and the dress has to reflect that. Which reminds me, have you looked through the jewels yet? Because whatever dress you wear has to go with the jewels. And the crown."

"Do I get a say on the crown? I just figured it was kind of pre-selected."

"Marcus would know for sure, but I was thinking you could choose which crown will be used to officially make you queen."

She put her hands on her hips. "We should ask him now. I'd hate to pick a dress only to find out it clashes with the rest of the stuff I have to wear."

Pierce pulled out his phone. "I'll find out. We need him for the combination to that vault anyway."

"Thanks. This dress is a no for the coronation, right?"

"Right," Pierce answered as he typed.

"On to the next one." Which was a gold-sequined

wrap with long sleeves and a slim silhouette. Donna had her doubts about it, but until a dress was actually on it was hard to tell.

She looked at herself in the mirror and snickered, then she stepped out, arms open wide. "Look at me, I'm not just the queen of the vampires, I'm also the queen of disco."

Pierce broke into laugher. "Okay, that is definitely not the one. I mean, you look fabulous in it but only if you're headed out to Studio 54. Who picked that?"

She gave him a stern look. "Pretty sure you did."

"Then I'm firing myself as your fashion consultant." He got up. "I need to do some more digging through these racks."

"While you do that, I'll try on the next one." She picked up a dress and took it with her behind the screen while he rummaged. It was a strapless white silk, very structured, with a large angular bow at the waist and a small train.

She liked the way the dress looked on her, but add a veil and it would definitely work as a wedding gown. She decided to show it to him anyway. "I already know what you're going to say about this one."

He turned away from the dresses he was sorting through. His gaze swept her from head to toe and he smiled. "You would make a beautiful bride."

She gave him a smile accompanied by a head tilt. "You think I look beautiful in everything."

"Because you do. But bridalwear isn't right for a coronation."

"Hello?" Marcus's voice called out from the living room.

"In here," Pierce answered. "Closet, that is."

Marcus joined them. "I've come to open the vault." He smiled at Donna, who was still in the white gown. "Very pretty."

"But not the gown I'm wearing for the coronation. It's not right."

"I'm sure whatever you decide on will be spectacular. But Pierce was right in that it might help to have a look at the jewels you'll be accessorizing with."

"I can't wait," Donna said.

"Let me get the vault open." Marcus went through to the second room of the closet, spun the dial with the appropriate combination and opened the heavy vault door.

Donna sucked in a breath as she saw what was inside.

# CHAPTER 41

Row after row of diamonds. That was all Donna could see. Bright, sparkling diamonds.

There were other gems, too, all of the heavy hitters. Sapphires, rubies, emeralds, pearls, and an array of others in colors too numerous to count. Some were set in gold, some in platinum, some looked new and some looked ancient.

Marcus pulled out the first shelf. "These are more of the day-to-day pieces. Most of the matched sets and all of the crowns are in their own boxes."

She shook her head. "I don't know where to start. I assume you know what most of these crowns look like. Why don't you show them to me and explain them all. If they need explaining."

"Some of them do," Marcus said. "They all have stories of where they came from. Some were gifts. Some were passed down from the queen before Artemis. One, Artemis purchased on her own, but she claims it once belonged to an Egyptian rival. She outbid the British Museum to win that piece."

"Wow." Donna glanced at Pierce, who'd come over to have a look. "Sounds pretty interesting, don't you think?"

He nodded. "I do. And I think it's a great idea to hear their histories. You should wear a crown that you connect with."

"All right," Marcus said. "I'll just pick a box to get us started."

And so he did. The first crown was a traditional-looking tiara of diamonds and emeralds set in platinum. "This was a gift from the previous king of South America. The emeralds are Columbian. Artemis only wore it once, to the dinner honoring the king's visit."

"Very pretty," Donna said. "Could be an option if I wear green. Put it in the maybe pile."

The next crown was much simpler. Hammered gold set with rubies and garnets intertwined with serpents. "This is the crown Artemis outbid the British Museum for. It's said this was once worn by Hatshepsut, one of only two confirmed female pharaohs. This crown was a favorite of Artemis's. She wore it often."

Donna grinned. "That looks like Artemis. So much like Artemis that there's no way anyone else should ever wear it. Perhaps we should put it on display under her portrait in the great hall?"

Marcus's brows shot up. "Does that mean you're planning on keeping her portrait up?"

Donna nodded. "I was. Why? Do you think I shouldn't?"

"It's not that," Marcus said. "I just thought you'd replace it with your own. The painter is scheduled to start your portrait after your coronation photos are taken."

Donna blinked. "Really? Is that a royal protocol thing?"

Marcus smiled. "It's not royal protocol exactly. More like royal tradition."

"Oh." She thought it over, glancing at Pierce. "I guess I could move Artemis's portrait to—no, wait a minute. I don't really want an enormous painting of myself looking down at me every time I go into that room. I don't mind Artemis being there. After all, seeing her is a nice reminder of the path I traveled to get here."

Marcus frowned. "Does that mean you want me to cancel the painter?"

Pierce put his hand on her arm. "Don't cancel. Have your portrait done. Put it in the foyer. Then any guests who visit will be reminded of exactly which queen this estate belongs to."

She tipped her head. "You really think they'll need reminding?"

"I think it can't be a bad thing. Especially with all the visitors you're likely to get over the next year or so."

"All right." She held her hands up. "Let the painter come. As for Artemis's favorite crown... I say we either display it somewhere in the house, or it belongs in a museum. But I was thinking an Egyptian museum as opposed to a British or American one."

Marcus nodded. "We could certainly discuss loaning it to them. I don't know what protocols you may be aware of, but it's generally frowned upon to sell, give away, or destroy any piece of the royal jewels."

"I see. But loaning would be all right?"

"Absolutely."

"Then maybe we should reach out to them."

Marcus repacked the crown. "I'll put it on my list."

"Put it at the bottom," Donna said. "It's not a priority."

He smiled. "I would agree with you on that. There is one thing you might consider a priority, however. Artemis's ashes. I asked Harper to reserve a small amount so that Artemis's final wish might be fulfilled."

Donna blew out a breath. "To be interred in her family's crypt in the Paris catacombs. But now there's no family to do that, right?"

"Right," Marcus answered.

"Then I guess we'll have to take care of it. Remind me in a few days about that, all right? I'm not sure my brain can handle one more thing right now."

"I'll absolutely remind you. On to the next crown?"

"Yes, please."

He took out the next box and crown. This one featured pearls and diamonds. "This was a gift from another king. Forgive me, but Artemis has three pearl and diamond crowns and without reading the provenance sheet, I can't recall who gave her this one."

"No worries." Donna shook her head at the piece. "Very pretty, but looks rather sedate for a coronation."

"Agreed," Pierce said. "More like a crown for an afternoon tea."

Donna snorted. "I don't see a lot of afternoon teas in my future, but who knows. What's the next one, Marcus?"

"A gift from the Prime, many, many years ago. Another somewhat historical crown that is believed to have been owned by a Scottish princess." He took it out of its box.

The crown was a simple twist of gold covered in green enamel ivy leaves with small opal berries.

"Oh, that is very pretty. Maybe for the dinner? I suppose it's not fancy enough. But it's really delicate and beautiful."

Pierce nodded. "Depends on the dress."

"Put that aside," Donna said. "As a possibility."

"Very good."

Next, Marcus pulled out the largest box in the vault. "This actually just arrived for you. I put it up here a few days ago. I meant to tell you."

"For me? From whom?"

"From New York. From the Fae King. He asked me to keep it somewhere safe, so I tucked it into the vault. I apologize for not telling you sooner but as you're aware, we've been a little busy."

"We have. I can't believe Ishalan sent something. What is it? Open it," Donna said, pressing her hands together in her excitement. Ishalan hadn't said a thing.

With a nod, Marcus lifted the lid off the box. Inside was a large object in a black velvet bag with a ruby satin drawstring. A crisp ivory envelope sat on top with the name "Belladonna" swirled on it in silver ink.

Marcus picked it up as if to open it. He stopped. "This is your gift." He handed her the envelope. "You should really be the one to open it."

"All right." She took over from him, setting the envelope aside to immediately loosen the drawstring. "But first the crown."

Pierce chuckled.

"Oh, wow. Look at this." She lifted out a tall crown of intricately worked black metal set with tiny diamonds, black pearls, and blood-red rubies. Black velvet lined the inside where it would rest on the wearer's head. It was gorgeous and completely unique. "I've never seen anything like this."

"Neither have I," Pierce said. "Maybe you should read the note."

"Yes." She set the crown down on the velvet to pick up the envelope. She slipped her nail under the sealed flap, tearing through it to pull out the small card. It was crisp ivory, just like the envelope, but the card bore a royal-looking insignia.

She turned it around to show Marcus. "I guess this is Ishalan's royal crest?"

He nodded. "I believe it is."

She opened the note and read: "My dearest Belladonna, please accept this gift as a token of my congratulations on taking the throne. The Iron Crown has been in my people's possession for a long time. I wish I could tell you more of its history, but all I know are the legends that surround it. How it was made for the most beautiful vampire queen in the world. How it once graced the head of Astrid, the Viking Shield Maiden who could supposedly daywalk. How the rubies represent the drops of blood spilled in crafting it. How three hundred fae died in the battle where it was won.

"What I am certain of is that it is iron and I am tired of the way it makes my skin crawl when I am in the vault. Such a treasure belongs with someone who can appreciate it. I hope it finds you in good health. All the best. Long live the Queen.

"Yours, Ishalan."

She smiled as she looked up at Pierce and Marcus. "Can you believe that? Do you think any of it's true?"

"I do." Marcus shook his head slowly in wonder. "I've heard of the Iron Crown, but there is so much legend and superstition and rumor surrounding it that I never believed it was real. I chalked it up to another tall tale, like Astrid."

"Try it on," Pierce said. She gave him a glance. He nodded. "Go on. I'll help you."

He took the crown and lifted it. "Heavier than it looks, isn't it?" He carefully set it on her head, adjusting it slightly. "Does that feel all right? It's not going to slip off, is it?"

The weight of the crown was no joke, but she reached up and turned it minutely. "There." She looked at them. "What do you think?"

Marcus and Pierce both stared at her. Then Pierce's mouth curved in a smile. "I think you've found your crown."

She turned toward the closest mirror. She'd never seen anything so regal or unique. "I have. This is what I want to be coronated in."

With that decision, all that remained was to choose the dress. And the shoes and the rest of the jewelry, obviously, but the dress was their main focus.

She placed the crown in its box on the dresser island in the closet's main room. Marcus excused himself to return to coronation details. Pierce went back to searching the racks, and Donna pulled out her phone to text Ishalan.

*Thank you for the crown. There aren't words to describe how amazing it is and how thoughtful it was of you to send it. It's spectacular.*

She smiled as she hit Send.

"What do we have here," Pierce said under his breath.

She looked up to see he'd opened a tall, frosted glass-front cabinet tucked into the corner of the closet. It was filled with hanging garment bags. He took one out and unzipped it.

Before she could see what was inside, her phone chimed. She checked the screen. A reply from Ishalan.

*It pleases me to no end that you've found favor with it. And not just because I am happy to have it out of my stronghold once and for all.*

She laughed and started typing. *I'm not kidding about how much I like it. I'm wearing it to be coronated in. I wish you could attend, but I imagine the estate's iron perimeter would be a lot more uncomfortable than having that crown around.*

*Indeed. I shall watch the live-stream, as will all of my kingdom. Many of them find you fascinating. Rumors have been circulating that you and a few other rulers have decided to secede from the vampire nations. Is this true?*

*It is,* she answered. *And it's already happened. I'd be happy to fill you in on it in detail, but it's a lot for text. We need to have a call soon.*

*I agree. Until then, be well, Your Highness.*

*You, too, Your Highness. And give my love to Rixaline.*

*I will.*

When she tucked her phone away and looked up, she found Pierce had unzipped several of the bags and completely uncovered one of the dresses. At least she assumed that's what it was. There was so much fabric it was hard to tell exactly what she was looking at.

"What is that?"

He stood back from it. "I know it doesn't look like much on the hanger, but it's vintage Yves St. Laurent. It's unbelievable. Looks to be in pristine condition.

Strapless. Red silk dupioni. Yards and yards of the stuff. I suppose Marcus could tell us if Artemis ever wore this, but it doesn't show any signs of having been worn." He glanced at her, eyes bright. "I have a feeling this could be the one."

She wasn't convinced yet. "Really? The fabric is gorgeous, but it just looks…like a lot of dress."

"I agree, but a coronation dress should be a lot. It should make an impression on everyone who sees it. It should be just over the top enough to make people think that only royalty could pull it off. And don't forget you're going to be sitting in this dress, so it's got to look good while seated, too. I have no doubt this will look fantastic with all of that fabric arranged around you, cascading down over the dais and around the throne."

She narrowed her eyes. "I hadn't thought about the throne."

He looked at her. "You're a queen. There has to be a throne."

"I suppose so." One more thing to ask Marcus and Charlie about. She held out her hand. "I'll try it."

He handed the dress over, one hand on the hanger, the other arm loaded with fabric. "If not, there's a beaded black Halston in here that might work. I know we said no black, but might be worth trying it on. Apparently, this was Artemis's treasure trove of special vintage pieces. So far, they all look couture, too."

She was almost being swallowed up by the red dress and she hadn't even put it on. "Meaning?"

"Meaning they ought to be in a vault of their own. Or a museum."

"Interesting. About that black dress…" She could just see a bit of black sparkle peeking through the opening of one of the bags. "Don't you think a black dress with a black crown might be a little too on the nose for a vampire queen?"

"Maybe. It won't read as well on the live feed, either, so let's hope this one works."

"We'll know shortly." She went behind the screen, surprised that the dress didn't weigh more, which wasn't to say it was light, but the silk was floatier than she'd expected.

That was one plus.

Another was that she thought she might need a strapless bra but the dress was so well constructed that the bodice worked to give her all the support she needed. There was something to be said for ridiculously expensive couture. It fit like a glove. Even if this had been tailored for Artemis, it worked pretty well for Donna.

Maybe it could be taken in here and there, and it could probably be shorter, but with the right heels, that would be solved. She couldn't tell what she looked like in it. Right now, she just felt like she was trying to keep her head above a red silk sea.

She hoisted the bodice higher, made sure she wasn't

going to trip over the voluminous skirt by picking it up on both sides, then stepped out and dropped the fabric so it flowed out around her. "What do you think?"

Pierce's brows went up and his mouth came open. "Your Highness, you look spectacular. I would pledge my fealty to you a thousand times over."

She laughed and shook her head. "I need to see for myself."

She picked up as much of the skirt as she could and shuffled over to step up onto the platform in the center of the room. She gazed into the large three-paneled mirror. "Oh. This is quite a dress, isn't it? I feel pretty regal."

"Just wait," Pierce said. He picked up the crown and placed it on her head.

She stared at herself for a long moment, taking in the image before her. Hard to believe that was really her. Finally, she nodded. "You were right. This is the dress."

# Chapter 42

It was coronation day and Donna felt like a nervous bride. At least that was the closest comparison to what was going on inside of her now.

Being queen didn't feel anything like a marriage, though. Maybe it would have if she'd had a co-ruler to share the decision making, but being queen meant everything came down to her.

That was what made her the most nervous. That she'd screw up somehow. Make the wrong choice, or a bad decision. There was no deflecting anything that went poorly, either. She was the only one responsible.

Thankfully, she trusted the wonderful team around her. Even more so after what they'd all been through together this last week and a half. They'd stayed strong, backed her decisions, trusted her choices, and never wavered in their support. They'd even put their lives on the line for her.

She was blessed to have them. Just like she was blessed to be here for her amazing children, who'd be watching via the live-stream today.

She also knew she'd done a decent job as governor of New Jersey, even if she hadn't been in the position very long.

But now, as she stood outside the doors of the grand ballroom, which had been transformed into a throne room for the coronation ceremony, she was once again awash in doubt.

It was only human, she thought. Then she almost laughed. She wasn't sure she'd qualify as human if Pierce hadn't returned her soul. What a gift that man was.

Just thinking about him calmed her. He'd be waiting for her inside along with the rest of her friends and staff in the front rows. She was formally naming him as Queen's Consort this evening.

Not only would that offer him official protection as a member of her court, but it would tell the vampire world that he was more than just one of her staff. Of course, he didn't need the protection. He'd proven that.

Recognizing him as someone important to her would give him some status. It was all she could do for him in an official capacity.

She'd talked to Marcus about it, and while he said it was highly unusual for someone who wasn't a vampire to be named a royal consort, he'd thought it a cunning move.

She hadn't expected that response, but after he'd explained, it all made sense. As queen, she was quietly telling the vampire nations that the person closest to her was an indestructible reaper, a creature whose scythe was one of the few weapons that was always deadly to a vampire.

Marcus had taken it as her way of telling her enemies that she was as well protected as a vampire could be.

Once again, Pierce was keeping her safe.

She smiled and fluffed the enormous skirt of her dress. It had already been spread out behind her so it would flow along as she walked toward the throne.

She'd paired the gorgeous dress with simple black velvet stilettos that called out to the matte black iron of the crown about to be put on her head. Her jewelry was a suite of rubies and diamonds. At first glance, the necklace almost looked like drops of blood.

Rather appropriate, all things considered.

Her hair was sleek and straight, her makeup appropriately dramatic. She was as ready as she could be.

The *Queen's March* began to play.

She lifted her head. The doors would be opening soon. She'd be going down the center aisle alone, walking the long black carpet that divided the many guests who had come to watch her ascend to the throne today.

She swallowed, nerves ricocheting through her at warp speed. Forget marriage; she'd never done anything like this in her life. Never felt this kind of nervous anticipation. She put her hand to her bodice, where her crucifix was tucked inside for safe keeping, and said a prayer that she wouldn't fall or stumble or do anything to embarrass herself.

The doors opened and the music swelled.

She raised her chin, kept her eyes on the throne, and began to walk.

The coronation went by in what seemed like a flash. The crown was on her head, the Oath to Serve said, and the pronouncement by the emissary of, "Long live the Queen," was made so quickly she felt as if she'd barely entered the room.

She hadn't fallen down or done anything to embarrass herself, so for that, she was grateful.

Then it was time to address those in attendance and those watching. As Marcus had directed her earlier, she stood before the ornate throne as she gazed out over the audience. She made a mental note to ask him where on earth the throne had come from, because she was pretty sure she would have noticed a chair twice the size of a normal chair and covered in burgundy velvet and gilt just sitting around in one of the rooms.

"Ladies and gentlemen of the vampire nations, and those representing some of our supernatural allies, I thank you for joining me on this historic occasion. You honor me with your presence." She paused, grateful the few words she needed to say had been easy enough to memorize.

"I pledge to maintain my loyalty to this new nation, and to remain honest to those I serve. I vow that I will perform my duties to the best of my abilities with my utmost dedication until the day I am no longer on this throne."

So many solemn faces stared back at her. Except for most of those in the front rows, which held smiles.

"It is my wish going forward that we would be able to find peace with each other and with our fellow supernaturals. That we would prosper in a way that lifts us all. That we would value fairness above self-gain. These are values worth uniting over, and it is my solemn promise to my subjects and my peers that I will strive for those goals."

Lots of nodding heads.

Seemed like a good sign. She continued. "Joining me in that purpose are two new governors. I am pleased to announce that Lionel Prescott has been appointed the governorship of New York and Janice Guy has been appointed the governorship of New Jersey."

Donna had never met the woman until she'd come to Kansas a day ago for the coronation, but Charlie knew her and vouched for her. That was enough for Donna. A long call had confirmed that Charlie's suggestion was a good one. Donna felt confident that Janice would fill the position nicely.

Donna's gaze went again to her team in the front row. "I am thankful to have such a wonderful staff around me who also support these goals. It is to one of those staff that I am, this evening, granting the title of Queen's Consort."

She turned slightly to make eye contact with him. "Pierce Harrison. Please join me."

Pierce swallowed, emotion in his eyes as he stepped up onto the dais. He smiled at her, and she could tell he wanted to say something but not in front of this crowd.

She smiled back.

The emissary approached him and administered the Oath of Consort, which was basically Pierce promising to be ever faithful in his companionship.

With that done, Donna addressed the crowd again. "I wish you all well, an abundance of years, and thank you again for your kind affections."

She returned to her throne and the music swelled, announcing the end of the coronation ceremony.

The emissary walked to the front of the dais. "The pledging of fealties will begin shortly."

One of the perks of making Pierce Queen's Consort was that he could sit beside her during the rest of the events. Namely, the hours of pledges that were about to happen this evening and the next. And the next after that, if necessary. She'd hear them until there were no more left to hear.

A chair was moved onto the dais next to her throne. A smaller chair, obviously.

Tonight, there would be two hours of pledges, followed by her first official dinner as queen. A royal banquet.

Pierce came to sit beside her, bowing first as was required with so many eyes watching. "You did so well, and you look more beautiful than I can express."

She smiled and took his hand as he sat. "Thank you."

"Thank you for my title. I wasn't expecting that."

"I'm glad I could do it. I know some will see it as a political move, but I hope you know politics had nothing to do with my motives."

He nodded. "I know. But I'm happy to put a little fear into your enemies if I'm able."

She grinned. That was her Pierce.

One by one, the governors lined up and began to approach. Marcus introduced them all by name and state.

For two hours, she sat and listened to them promise to be faithful and true. Every single one of them presented her with a gift, which was apparently expected. Quite a few petitioned her for some kind of aid. She didn't mind that. Being able to help was what her position as sovereign was all about.

Charlie stayed nearby to record the requests and the gifts.

At one point, Pierce leaned over. "There's not going to be anything left to get you for Christmas."

She worked hard not to laugh. "Behave," she hissed at him. Inside, she was chuckling. He wasn't too far off. The gifts had so far included an apartment in the French Quarter from the governor of Louisiana, an opal the size of a hen's egg from the governor of Nevada, and an avocado ranch from the governor of California.

Donna was beginning to understand how Artemis had amassed so much wealth and property.

The two hours seemed like twenty and when they were finally seated for dinner, Donna's face had begun to ache from all the smiling.

Thankfully, her position as queen meant no one could approach her at the banquet just to chat. Seated at the elevated head table, with Pierce on one side of her and Queen Francesca on the other as her honored guest, Donna allowed herself to relax just a bit.

The crown was heavy on her head, however. And the truth was, she knew life was never going to be the same. Not the way it once had been. The evening's ceremony and the deference with which she was being treated were proof of that.

"You seem far away," Pierce said.

She sighed as she looked at him. "I suppose I was. Just thinking about how life is going to be now. And how much I'm already missing the way it was."

"What are you missing? Specifically, I mean."

She shrugged. "I don't know. I guess I was thinking about how we all used to order pizza and sit around watching movies. Do you ever think we'll get to do that again?"

His smile was instant and mysterious. "Sure. Probably next week."

Her eyes narrowed. "Next week? Why so soon? And why do you sound so certain?"

His mouth hitched up on one side. "Well, with

Christina and Joe Jr. being here for a visit, I just figured—"

She sucked in a breath and really hoped he'd just said what she thought he'd said. "What? My kids are coming?"

He nodded, grinning. "They are. The Millers, too. I hope you don't mind, but we figured as they're about to be your in-laws, might as well have them, too."

Her heart soared with happiness. "I don't mind at all, so long as I get some alone time with my kids."

"You're the queen. Whatever you want to happen will happen."

She took a deep breath, doing her best not to cry even though they'd be happy tears. "I can't believe you guys did this. I'm so happy. Thank you."

"It was Charlie's idea. She's been working on it. Fortunately, Joe Jr. was able to get leave."

She squeezed Pierce's hand. "I don't know what to say. Except thank you, again." She caught Charlie's gaze and smiled, putting her hand to her heart. "Thank you," she mouthed, not entirely sure Charlie would understand.

Charlie glanced at Pierce, then back at Donna and nodded. "You're welcome," she mouthed back.

Donna exhaled with a sense of new calm. Knowing she was going to see her kids did that to her. So did having the coronation behind her.

Soon most of these guests would be gone, the house would quiet down, and she could immerse herself in friends and family without thinking about being queen as much. There would be pizza and movies and laughter and love. She would make sure of that.

Maybe this new life wouldn't be that bad after all. Was that what Joe Jr. had meant by telling her to embrace the suck? To take what had been given to her and make the best of it? If so, she was dedicated to that from here on out. Good or bad, she would mine the joy from this life and this opportunity.

She lifted her glass of wine to take a sip as peace filled her. Maybe being queen would be sweeter than she'd imagined possible.

She was certainly going to do her best to find out.

Want to be up to date on new books, audiobooks, and other fun stuff from me? Sign-up for my newsletter on my website, www.kristenpainter.com. No spam, just news (sales, freebies, releases, you know all that jazz.)

If you loved the book and want to see the series grow, tell a friends about the book and take time to leave a review!

## OTHER BOOKS BY KRISTEN PAINTER

PARANORMAL WOMEN'S FICTION

**First Fangs Club Series:**

Sucks To Be Me

Suck It Up Buttercup

Sucker Punch

The Suck Stops Here

Embrace The Suck

COZY MYSTERY:

**Jayne Frost Series:**

Miss Frost Solves A Cold Case: A Nocturne Falls Mystery

Miss Frost Ices The Imp: A Nocturne Falls Mystery

Miss Frost Saves The Sandman: A Nocturne Falls Mystery

Miss Frost Cracks A Caper: A Nocturne Falls Mystery

When Birdie Babysat Spider: A Jayne Frost Short

Miss Frost Braves The Blizzard: A Nocturne Falls Mystery

Miss Frost Says I Do: A Nocturne Falls Mystery

Lost in Las Vegas: A Frost And Crowe Mystery

**HappilyEverlasting Series:**

Witchful Thinking

PARANORMAL ROMANCE

**Nocturne Falls Series:**

The Vampire's Mail Order Bride

The Werewolf Meets His Match

The Gargoyle Gets His Girl

The Professor Woos The Witch

The Witch's Halloween Hero – short story

The Werewolf's Christmas Wish – short story

The Vampire's Fake Fiancée

The Vampire's Valentine Surprise – short story

The Shifter Romances The Writer

The Vampire's True Love Trials – short story

The Vampire's Accidental Wife

The Reaper Rescues The Genie

The Detective Wins The Witch

The Vampire's Priceless Treasure

The Werewolf Dates The Deputy

The Siren Saves The Billionaire

**Shadowvale Series:**

The Trouble With Witches

The Vampire's Cursed Kiss

The Forgettable Miss French

Moody And The Beast

Her First Taste Of Fire

**Sin City Collectors Series**

Queen Of Hearts

Dead Man's Hand

Double or Nothing

**Standalone Paranormal Romance:**

Dark Kiss of the Reaper

Heart of Fire

Recipe for Magic

Miss Bramble and the Leviathan

All Fired Up

URBAN FANTASY

**The House of Comarré series**:

Forbidden Blood

Blood Rights

Flesh and Blood

Bad Blood

Out For Blood

Last Blood

**The Crescent City series:**

House of the Rising Sun

City of Eternal Night

Garden of Dreams and Desires

*Nothing is completed without an amazing team.*

*Many thanks to:*

*Cover design: Cover design and composite cover art by Janet Holmes using images from Shutterstock.com & Depositphotos.com.*
*Interior Formating: Gem Promotions*
*Editor: Raina James*
*Copyedits/proofs: Lisa Bateman*

## ABOUT THE AUTHOR

USA Today Best Selling Author Kristen Painter is a little obsessed with cats, books, chocolate, and shoes. It's a healthy mix. She loves to entertain her readers with interesting twists and unforgettable characters.

She currently writes the best-selling paranormal romance series, Nocturne Falls, and award-winning urban fantasy. The former college English teacher can often be found all over social media where she loves to interact with readers.

For more information go to www.kristenpainter.com

For More Paranormal Women's Fiction Visit:
www.paranormalwomensfiction.net

Made in the USA
Coppell, TX
18 April 2022

76764186R00213